WINDFALL

A HENRY LYSYK MYSTERY

BYRON TD SMITH

SHIMA
KUN
PRESS

First published 2021 by Shima Kun Press (Canada)

Web: shimakunpress.com

Cover by Jamie Keenan (www.keenandesign.com)

© Byron TD Smith 2021

Boeing 727 cutaway by Arthur Bowbeer © FlightGlobal. Used with permission. (Hardcover only)

BISAC **FICTION** / Mystery & Detective / Amateur Sleuth

ISBN 978-1-7753226-0-3 (paperback)

ISBN 978-1-7753226-1-0 (e-book)

ISBN 978-1-7753226-2-7 (hard cover)

ISBN 978-1-7753226-3-4 (paperback, large print)

For Tiffany, my sweetheart & partner in crime.

WINDFALL

CHAPTER ONE

I t was a simple plan. He had crossed the border into Canada late last night, eager to get what he'd come for.

Downtown Vancouver looked to him like just one more neighborhood of Seattle. To the north, south, and west, the city sloped down to the water. Despite the drizzling rain, morning sun slipped between the tall surrounding buildings, making its way down to the dirty street.

At his feet, a young woman slept in the shelter of the doorway. Her head rested on a blue hiking pack, her hair running down in long, knotted rivulets to the sidewalk. He stooped and stuck a dollar bill between the concrete and the makeshift pillow.

The only open door in either direction belonged to the convenience store across the street. The plastic table and chairs on the sidewalk next to the store were less than inviting. A chain weaved through their legs, ending at a gas meter.

In another hour the streets would fill with transients, and visitors who had wandered a couple of blocks too far from the tourist strip of Gastown.

He pulled on the door of the pawnshop before him, careful not to wake the girl. The deadbolt was still locked.

Stepping back, he looked again at where the overhead sign should have been. The long, bare fluorescent bulbs sat dull and gray, either burned out or without power. Only the poster-board in the window which read *We Buy Gold* in uneven, red permanent marker, confirmed he had the right place.

This time, he knocked hard enough on the glass between the metal bars that a layer of street dust shook from the filthy pane. He wiped his knuckles on his jeans and squinted inside.

Am I early?

His only means of telling the time were his laptop and the face of an old digital watch that he'd left taped to the dash-board of his car.

His eyes passed over what he could make of his reflection in the powdery window, his hair and clothes giving up that he had slept in the car. He was perfectly aware of this fact, as his fifty-six-year-old body reminded him. He farted, stretched, pressed his shirt over his gut with his hands, and grinned at himself, some-thing he ordinarily avoided doing since being teased in school. Other children had been eager to point out that when he smiled, his exaggerated round face widened like a jack-o'-lantern. Even unsmiling, his broad features and downturned eyes gave him the appearance of a miserable Cheshire cat. A Cheshire man.

But today was different. It was a good day.

The sound of scuffling came from the other side of the door, and it opened with a high-pitched scrape. Not waiting for an invitation, the man took one last look at the sleeping girl and shouldered his full frame inside.

He stood face to face with a pale man in his thirties or forties, too thin, and just about six feet tall.

"You're TreasureHunter1971?"

The Cheshire man nodded. His eyes were still adjusting to the light, which darkened towards the back of the store. "Is there anyone else here?"

"No," the younger man said as he turned on the lights and stuck out his hand. "I'm Julian."

"David. It's nice to finally meet you." He shook the small, bony hand and gave the Canadian his practiced smile. Julian was a stranger, and it should stay this way. So he had settled on the name David on the drive north the night before. It sounded biblical and trustworthy.

Julian re-locked the door and led them past the hanging guitars and the myriad retail cabinets of watches, rings, video game cartridges, knives, memorabilia, and other items sold or abandoned. "This is pretty amazing, eh? It has to be worth a fortune."

The back room was even more confused. Metal shelves reached the nine-foot ceiling, stuffed with small items, mundane and odd. At the end of the shop was a metal loading bay door; the Cheshire man reasoned this must exit to the alley where he'd parked his car.

Another smile.

The loading bay was cluttered with stacked furniture: dining room chairs, kitchen tables, old stereos, and record players as big as couches.

Julian waved a hand at a haphazard pile of boxes bearing dates. Loose papers spilled on the floor, covered in shoe prints. The old exterior sign leaned against the cardboard stack. Brittle-looking and faded from age and weather, it read *Fullarton Bros. Silver & Gold.*

"Don't worry about stepping on this crap. It's all getting chucked. My uncle could sweet talk anyone out of something he wanted, but he never got rid of anything himself." He waggled his eyebrows. "Maybe that's a good thing, eh?"

The Cheshire man barely registered the story. His eyes fixated on the large safe, equal in height to his six feet and with not one, but two combination dials.

"But I'll bet this is where you keep the best stuff, huh?" He reached out and touched the larger dial.

"Sure. Let's get down to business," Julian said. "This is crazy, right? If this is the real thing . . . What did you say it was worth?"

"To a collector? I don't know. Maybe a thousand bucks?"

"Awesome. I barely clear that in a week here. I can't believe he was sitting on it this entire time. He never told anyone until he told me, and that was just before he died."

"We agreed on a grand, right?" The older man shook the knapsack on his shoulder. "US Dollars."

Julian placed his hand on the side of the safe. "And you've got cash?"

The older man nodded. "Yeah. That pretty well cleans me out. That and a bit for gas to get home." He gave the dial a small twist. It clicked, and the hair on his arm stood on end.

Julian looked the Cheshire man in the eye for a long moment. He gave a quick nod, pulled back his hand, and dropped it into his pocket. His lanky body twisted as he struggled to pull out a bulky ring loaded with dozens of keys of various ages, shape, and size, sticking out in all directions.

"He was my mum's brother, and my dad was a bit of a deadbeat. Uncle Kev took me under his wing a few years ago and asked me if I wanted to learn the business. Still, I never figured I'd take over the shop. Help me with this."

Julian tapped the keyring against the side of a large, silver cash register, resting on a deep freezer he had been obscuring with his thin frame. He carried on talking as they lifted the heavy piece and lowered it to the ground. "He was pretty crafty, Kev was. Three years I worked here, and he kept this secret nearly the whole time. 'You play your best cards last,' he'd say."

Julian tried the keys on the freezer, one after the other.

"Sometimes people would have to give him salmon or halibut, even venison, to pay back their loans and get their stuff. Turns out that it used to happen often enough that he got himself a freezer. You see it less and less now."

He winked as he lifted the lid, clearly proud of his secret. "Best hiding spot in the house."

The freezer was almost empty. Julian leaned in, his feet nearly leaving the floor before he straightened back up, holding two blocks of wood, held together with twisted wire. After some fussing, Julian separated the blocks to reveal a plastic freezer bag.

The Cheshire man took the bag with trembling hands.

This is real. I'm doing it.

"Can I take it out to see?" he asked, opening the bag.

"Careful, Dave." Julian's boastful tone was now tinged with uncertainty. "No one's touched it in, like, forever."

From the bag, the man who had lied about his name being David slid out a single American twenty-dollar bill. Time stood still as he took it all in. He'd seen thousands of twenties in his life, but this one was special. It pulsed with energy; a thrum that passed through his hand and up his arm.

"It's real, right?" Julian said.

The older man reached into his jacket pocket and pulled out several folded sheets of paper, covered with numbers and letters in an impossibly small font. His eyes squinted, darting back and forth between the bill and the list of serial numbers. His fingers slid down page after page until, eventually, he found the range of numbers that matched.

I was meant to find this.

He felt the young man watching with the eyes of a gambler on his last dollar.

"Yes. It's real."

"I knew it." Julian pumped his fist in the air, followed with a twirl and some running on the spot.

"This is just incredible," the older man said. "It's unbeliev-able that your uncle even had it, let alone kept it in perfect condition like this. All the others that have surfaced are damaged somehow. Where did he get it?"

"No idea. If this one is mint, it should be worth more, right?"

The Cheshire man twitched at the question. "We have a deal."

"But you said this one's different. Better. Really rare. How much more do you think it's worth?"

"It's nothing to you. It's twenty dollars."

"It's a piece of history, man. A treasure map. You're gonna get rich? Break me off a piece."

"It's more than that," the older man said, melancholy in his throat.

Frowning, he looked again at the plastic bag lying next to the list of serial numbers on the freezer.

"What's this other card with it?"

He slid an index card from the bag and turned it over in his hand. One side was typed on, and the other had numbers written by hand.

"That's the old stock card," Julian said. "We've got to write down the name and address of everyone that leaves us stuff. For the police. He kept them together for— What's it called?" He scratched his head. "Providence?"

"You mean 'provenance'. As in a record of who owned it and where he got it from."

Julian trembled, and his voice rose. "Holy— That makes it worth even more, right? Like what? Ten grand?"

The man who had driven from Seattle, who had slept in his car, and who Julian knew as David stared at the small card.

Name and address? Am I that close?

He registered Julian's mouth moving, speaking, but there were no sounds. Perfect silence.

As though in slow motion, he held out the twenty-dollar

bill, letting it go just before Julian's thin fingers could close on it. The small banknote rolled in the air, down to the floor.

With a sharp inhale, Julian bent to pick it up and, in doing so, added his own force to the knee rising to meet his face.

He shot upright and fell back onto the ground, slamming his head against the concrete.

The Cheshire man grit his teeth and grunted as he lifted the stunned Julian up, tipping him headfirst into the freezer.

The young man started to regain his senses. He kicked out with his boot, twisted his body, and scrabbled with one hand at the larger man's belt.

Adding the weight of his torso, the Cheshire man slammed the freezer's lid on Julian's outstretched arm.

A scream of pain and fear echoed in the back room.

Julian's arm disappeared, and the older man briefly caught the light inside the icy tomb going out as the lid sealed shut.

The Cheshire man climbed atop the freezer. The shouting sounded distant, words indistinguishable. He felt the pounding from inside the freezer on the backs of his legs and looked down at the keys on the floor in dismay. They were too far to reach. He might have to sit here awhile.

Blood rushed in heavy, quick beats through his neck and arms.

With a trembling hand, he retrieved an orange plastic pill bottle from his jacket pocket. He shook two white pellets into his mouth and swallowed them down. He slid himself further onto the cooler, settling in. The keys, the bill, and the card lay on the floor.

It must be so cold to jump out of an airplane.

CHAPTER TWO

The Cheshire man set the pen down next to his half-eaten dinner of fries and looked up from the newspaper. Watching the house was tedious. The hardest part was not overstaying his welcome in the little café.

Amongst blocks of boxy, brick apartment buildings, the shorter two-story house with its symmetrical gables was a holdout from an era long preceding the city's densification. The chestnut tree in the front yard, its trunk as wide as a car, was older still. A blanket of fallen leaves and rich brown seeds extended onto the sidewalk and road.

The repeated sirens had unnerved him at first, even though he knew that Vancouver General Hospital was nearby, and they had to be ambulances. Still, who would want to live so close to that?

Through the window, he watched as a figure in a pea coat got out of a taxi, illuminated by the patchy glow of a streetlamp through the chestnut branches. Finally, someone was approaching the address across the street.

The silhouette of the man appeared young. At least it didn't move as an old man should. Carrying a bag in each hand, the figure climbed the few brief steps, and disappeared inside.

A light came on in the bottom left window. The Cheshire man scribbled quick, untidy notes to himself and returned to his meal and his vigil.

Warm, dry air escaped as Henry Lysyk shouldered open the door into the hallway of the old converted house on Richardson Street.

He set his overnight bag and laptop against the door jamb and tried a few keys in the lock before it opened.

Henry pushed his bags inside with his feet and called out. "Shima."

A thump came from the bedroom. The black cat that ambled around the corner rubbed its chin against a brown, lidded banker's box on the floor. Henry's old office fit lamentably easily into the single cardboard cube that had sat unpacked and otherwise untouched on the floor since Henry had moved in.

The cat stopped five feet from Henry before flopping over onto its side, revealing a patch of white on its chest. Henry spoke to the small beast as he shook the rain from his coat and pried his heels from his shoes with his toes.

"Sorry, buddy. But if I leave the windows open the rain gets in." The apartment still smelled of the unfamiliar Ikea furniture, which he'd purchased only five months earlier in a single frantic shopping trip. Practical furniture, cutlery, sheets, and rugs bearing faux-funky patterns occupied every room. Still, the bookshelf in the living room was empty.

Henry picked up the mail from behind the door. He flipped through the envelopes and tossed most of them, unopened, into the recycling as he followed Shima into the kitchen.

A note greeted him on the table. The cursive writing was the earnest script of his thirteen-year-old niece, Frieda. It explained that she had fed and groomed the cat while he was away. She had signed off on her report with a small *TM* next to her name.

Clearly protecting her brand from second-tier imposters.

He liked to believe that if he had children of his own, they would be just as interesting. Although, it was months now since they had spoken or seen each other in person. Still, Henry liked to throw a little responsibility and money Frieda's way, and Shima required little looking after.

He didn't have the energy to come up with an alternative cat-sitter now, even though she had never gotten the hang of the job. An ant trail from somewhere behind the fridge crossed the counter and ended in a tiny feast at the pile of dirty tins and plates in the sink.

The cat's food, on the other hand, was safe in its bowl on the floor, surrounded by an ingenious dinner plate moat of water. Maybe it was time to expand the job description beyond just keeping the cat alive.

He pulled the newspaper apart and chose the Sports section to roll up and begin batting at the column of ants.

When he had worked full time for the bank, a weekly newspaper was his favorite delineation between the office's long days and the short evenings and weekends of personal time. Now, there was an excess of the personal time, which a daily delivery of news helped to fill.

Recycling the speckled pages, he sorted through the remaining sections for the crossword.

Creases deepened on his forehead as he sifted through the paper, page by page, looking in vain for what should be there.

An explanation popped into his head.

Tomas.

Tomas Duran was Frieda's father. (*Are we still brothers-in-law if I'm separated from his wife's sister?*) Henry could picture the scene. Tomas drove Frieda over and, ignoring that it didn't belong to him, he took the crossword for himself.

Henry returned to his phone and hammered out a text with his thumbs.

Hi, F. Home safe. Thanks for looking after the boy. I'm glad your dad could help. H. Xo

Perfect. Just passive-aggressive enough.

The reply came with speed accessible only by generations born after the dawn of the internet.

Hi Hen. Poppa didn't come. I biked on my own. You forgot to leave money. F^{TM}

Apparently, not only was he a poor detective but a neglectful employer of child labor, too.

"Not Tomas," he informed the cat. It couldn't be that there was never a crossword; the entire Arts section was missing. The alternative explanation was too awful to voice; evocative of Sarah's gas-lighting games in the last days of their marriage.

Henry's hands were unsteady as he sipped at his tea and mumbled to himself. Shima listened and offered no insight, choosing instead to begin washing. A thick downy layer of hidden white fur flashed beneath the black coat as he groomed.

Shima, now eighteen, had been Henry's before the marriage. In the urgency of leaving, Henry had walked away from nearly everything. The marriage had lasted fifteen years, throughout thirteen of which Henry believed they were happy. There was a lot that could have been divided. Choosing expediency and sanity over negotiation, Henry had taken little more than the cat he'd started with.

If it weren't for the little cat, this entire scene of missing newsprint and generic, practical Swedish furnishings would be someone else's life.

Henry texted Alex, one of his few remaining contacts from his past life. A rare friend, and his lawyer.

Can you talk? Important!

Agonizing minutes passed.

On a date. Cool down. Lunch tomorrow.

Tomorrow seemed far away. Worse, lunch meant proper socializing, ordering, pleasantries, chit-chat. People.

2 minutes? Henry typed.

The answer came back.

Tomorrow noon. The usual.

Henry paced. "The usual" hadn't been "usual" for months. That long-gone pattern was a reminder of his days working at the bank's head office. He and Alex would meet every Monday for the buffet lunch at the Tandoori House. This would be doubly awkward since Natali's restaurant was one of the businesses that Henry was fired over.

His phone buzzed, and he tapped it against his forehead rather than looking at the screen.

Alex was acting as Henry's lawyer in his divorce, as well as helping with the fallout from Henry's termination from the bank. There would be no way to get through the meal without having to face the lingering agony of his past. When did it all go wrong?

His phone buzzed again.

I'll pick you up.

Alex was also one of the few people who knew where Henry was working now. And, he was persistent.
Buzz.

Tomorrow works? Hello?

Henry frowned at the message. It lacked Alex's usual confidence. Henry replied,

Yes. Looking forward to it!!!

If it took a lunch to speak with Alex, then so be it. But Henry wouldn't go down without a solid three sarcastic exclamation marks.

Henry ranted quietly to himself as he undressed and turned out the lights around the apartment. He'd have to pretend to be cheerful with people tomorrow. "Great. No complaints," he'd say when they ask how he's doing. "Things are looking up."

His words became bubbly, messy mumblings while he brushed his teeth at twice-normal speed.

He didn't see the final text arrive, with three exclamation marks of its own. If he had, Henry would have realized that he had sent his enthusiastic response to an entirely different thread.

Yay!!! F^{TM}

CHAPTER THREE

Henry's feet hit the floor, and his neck screamed with pain.

If I'm going to keep sleeping on the couch, I need a better pillow.

He drank his coffee at the kitchen table. Here were the tallest and widest windows in the apartment. They faced the road and, across the way, a street-level café on the corner of a set of brick apartments. The southern exposure received sunshine throughout the day. For this, the kitchen was warm and bright.

In the early evenings, when Henry returned home from work, the dining table always needed sweeping of fur. Shima's table-sleeping was a new habit and not one that Henry would have tolerated at home, but now, "We are all making sacrifices," he'd say.

He paused halfway through the carafe of coffee for a quick shower. He put on a dark suit, pressed white shirt, and a tie with diagonal stripes. Through careful wardrobe shopping, no conscious matching was required. Everything paired with everything, although it made for a lot of blue and dark gray in the closet.

Henry noticed the time on the stove; he was going to have to hurry to get to work on time, and the next rent payment was due in several days. He chewed his dry toast. The lease term of six months was ending. It would be month-to-month from now on. But how many months?

With one hand petting Shima, he opened a drawer and withdrew a thin cheque book. A piece of dry toast waggled from his mouth. "Until there's a plan, my friend, we're stuck here a little longer."

A small group of young girls walked past and waved. Henry knew this was for Shima. Still, he waved back.

Joggers hustled by as Henry worked through the last of the coffee and signed cheques. Four was more than enough. That would carry him through to the end of February.

More students walked past, headphones separating the world they saw from that which they chose to hear. And all manner of people dressed in business suits and conservative skirts strolled by, each with determined intention in their stride.

Everyone going somewhere they wanted to go, while Henry's life was merely spinning wheels on the spot.

On his way out, Henry fed the envelope of cheques through the mail slot in the rental company's door, across the hall from his own. There was a darker patch of blue on this door, where there had once been a metal number two. It was a better-than-convenient arrangement; one more person he didn't need to speak to. Except for the old woman upstairs, Henry had thus far managed to avoid the other tenants.

He looked at his watch and stepped up the pace.

He took his bicycle from its place in the hallway and hustled it to the road. Even though Mr. Munroe didn't really need Henry to be present in order to open the bookstore, when there is only one person left in the city willing to offer you work, you don't show up late.

CHAPTER FOUR

At ten minutes to twelve, Henry's stomach started to growl. He took another pile of books from next to the front desk and carried them to the narrow stacks of shelves. He and Mr. Munroe were settled into a routine.

Mr. Munroe, of indeterminate age but clearly still working in defiance of retirement, held court behind the desk, pricing and buying books as they were brought in. He sat a little more upright and held in his stomach, even straightening his salt-and-pepper beard, as he joked with and teased customers young and old.

Over his shoulder, Henry said, "This is the last stack. Unless something comes in over lunch, I don't think you'll need me this afternoon."

With a stiff wave of his arm, the bookstore owner said, "We'll find something to keep you busy."

It was obvious that business was slow. Nevertheless, Munroe had given Henry part-time work as an act of kindness, mercy even, when the stories in the newspaper had made him otherwise unemployable.

Sandwiched between Penguin Classics and Harlequin Romance, Henry heard the bell of the front door.

"Good morning, Sir. Do you carry any books on classical Mediterranean baseball?"

The familiar tapping of a wooden pencil on the edge of the desk indicated Mr. Munroe was contemplating the request.

"Homer!" Munroe said with a bellowing laugh. "Well done, Alex. Still haven't stumped me, but that was your best yet."

Henry slipped the last book into its place on the shelf and joined the pair at the counter.

Alex was dressed, as ever, in a fine, pressed suit. He wore his hair short and immaculate, as though it had been cut the day before. The lavender lines of his necktie matched the accents on the arms of his glasses.

Henry thought of the now-unnecessary wardrobe in his closet and tucked his shirt in where it had slipped out a little.

"Right on time," Alex said. "Oh! You reminded me of a joke. Ask me why I'm not good at comedy."

Henry asked, "Why are you not—"

"Timing!"

Alex and Munroe howled. Even Henry cracked a smile.

"May I take your venerable employee for lunch?" Alex said to Munroe.

"Only if you fill him with drink. The boy's so serious."

"I'm right here," Henry said.

"Well, don't rush back. Enjoy yourself."

Still laughing, Alex pushed open the door, and Henry followed onto Granville Street. They walked without thinking, their conversation uninterrupted by a need to discuss where they were going.

Henry explained about the missing crossword. "Is there any chance that you gave my address to Sarah's lawyer?"

"Zero," Alex said. He held his hands up in front of his shoulders. "I've been addressing all documents in care of my office. Honestly, I don't even know where you live. You haven't had me over." He feigned hurt. "Haven't you got enough on your plate? You want to pick more fights with your ex, too? You think she, or Stewart, took your newspaper just to troll you?"

Henry shrugged. "Crossword. You know Stewart as well as I do. You don't think he'd do something like that just to dig in the knife? For kicks?"

"Honestly, Hen? I don't. It's only a paper."

He rested his hand on Henry's shoulder as they walked. "You've got to let some stuff go. It's going to take time. But you are going to get your life back."

Henry gave Alex a skeptical sneer.

"Sure. Easy for me to say. I don't have a bank coming after me. But, speaking as your lawyer now, I have to tell you that you should get someone else, someone who specializes in this sort of thing, to settle this for you."

"No, I trust you."

"But I don't do this, Hen. I'm a trusts and estates guy. The bank has an army of lawyers with better suits than mine."

"You're the only one I trust. And you're just fishing for a compliment on that suit."

Alex shook his head and punched Henry in the arm. "You mean I'm the only one who will cut you a deal on fees."

Henry's walking pace slowed in contrast to the speed of the words that followed. "Once I find real work, I'll pay you in full. I can't take any more hours from Mr. Munroe. As it is, it's so slow in there that I'm beginning to dust the polish off the shelves. It's obviously a pity thing."

"It's okay, man. You've got to let people in. You saved his tail."

"All I did was let him know he should make a payment on his loan."

"Sure. But if it weren't for you, he wouldn't even have his bookstore. It would probably be another Starbucks."

Henry was well aware of what he had accomplished, and its cost. At the bank, he had held the dangerous-sounding role of

Senior Risk Manager. He tested internal controls, to ensure they would detect or prevent things like theft, fraud, or failing to comply with government regulations. It wasn't the loftiest accounting role, but Henry relished the puzzle-solving part of it, and was renowned for his creativity.

When the economy had showed signs of slowing six months ago, the bank hustled to identify delinquent business loans and flag them for immediate collection. The official explanation was that it was good corporate hygiene to be in the front of a line of creditors if the businesses go under, rather than at the back, sweeping up scraps and dregs.

Quite unintentionally, Henry stumbled across communications elucidating the true intentions of the strategy. Beneath the guise of responsibility, clearing out many of these small loans would conveniently improve loan-to-deposit metrics that would, in turn, grant massive bonuses to management, and heap congratulations on the board of directors for being so proactive. It was even magnanimously suggested that some businesses would be eligible for replacement loans—at higher interest rates, of course.

This time, Henry's employer did not appreciate his creativity and initiative as he called each of the businesses a day before their turn on the chopping block. If they made a payment, he told them, any payment at all, the bank couldn't close on the loan. In the bank's own fine-print, only defaulted loans, with absolute failures to pay, could be foreclosed on.

In their statement of claim, the bank cited twenty-three businesses Henry had saved from foreclosure. Publicly, they were labeling him as a fraudster, citing breaches of private data. Either way, he knew they were ignorantly well short of the real number.

"They all paid, Alex. Every last one of them."

"Of course. And how much did Munroe pay again?" Alex asked.

"Fifteen dollars."

"Yeah, if I was the bank, I might be ticked, too."

The pair laughed as Henry pulled open the door to Natali's restaurant.

Once inside, they weaved through the line of people waiting and took their places at a table marked *Reserved*. Alex, facing the back of the restaurant, waved at Natali in the kitchen. Henry turned in his seat and did the same. The elderly Indian woman with the white kerchief on her head beamed back and shouted, "Two minutes!"

Alex picked the conversation back up. "So, the trip to Toronto? What did they say?"

Henry's eyes dropped into his lap. "I don't even know why they took the time to meet with me." He fussed with his napkin. "I'm nation-wide news. Since they can't get their hands on the truth, the real story, it's all this speculation about fraud and theft, hacking even. Until this is settled, I'm tainted. At best, I'm a curiosity."

Alex leaned forward, his tie curling on the tabletop. "Forget them. I never liked the idea of you moving to Toronto anyhow. It's not going to be quick, my friend. The bank is pissed, and their opening position is that you defrauded them out of millions."

The number was no longer shocking. Henry had read the bank's statement of claim so many times that it was just one more thing.

"Bull. I didn't take a cent. Everyone made legitimate payments. It's all within corporate policy. At best, I deferred their recovery of some debt."

"However you put it, they're mad."

"That is abundantly clear. I can't even get my own money out to switch banks. My accounts are frozen." He looked up with wide eyes. "Maybe they have someone watching me."

"Don't go getting paranoid on me now."

"Is it unrealistic? Think about it. I get Stewart that job in IT, and what happens? He hops into the sack with my wife. Maybe he turned Judas at work too."

"You don't know it." Alex specified quickly. "About work."

"It's the only explanation. Anyhow, he's dead to me."

"And me." Alex held up his copper glass of water for a toast. "To bachelorhood."

Henry raised his own glass and took a long sip to suppress the angry rant building on the tip of his tongue. The awkward segue only reminded him further of Stewart's double betrayal.

"You're aware they've fired Stewart now, too?" Alex said.

"What?"

"They think that he had something to do with it. They think that he helped you try to cover it up somehow."

"That's garbage. Stewart's tech-smart, but he's a moral simpleton. His altruism caps out at paying five bucks a month at the office to wear jeans on Fridays. Those bastards have it backwards. He's exactly the kind of guy who would stay there forever and now he's so much collateral damage?"

"A second ago he was dead to you."

"That's different. This is just wrong. They're trying to make it all seem bigger than it was so the directors don't look so foolish." Henry pressed the side of a clenched fist into the table.

Alex leaned back in his chair and crossed his right leg over his left. Henry had seen him do this in client meetings. He was settling in for a lecture.

"Seriously," Alex said, tapping the table with his index finger. "I need you to rethink your response to these guys."

Henry shook his head, anticipating where Alex was going.

"If you went public with the names of all the business owners you helped, the papers might get the real story. They'd have to stop calling you a fraud, and the bank wouldn't be able to keep claiming that you were lining your own pockets anywhere. Easy peasy."

"Except where they go back on all those businesses, Alex. Maybe they'll call the loans anyhow or drop some other financing the business needs. What's the point in cutting someone a break if you're just going to toss them under the bus? No, if the bank needs that info, they're going to have to get there themselves."

"Those people will want to help."

"Then maybe someone will come forward on their own. But I'm not going to ask."

"I will. I think you'll find you have more allies in this than you think. Just give me the list." Alex held out his hand as though Henry carried such a thing on his person.

"And I'm not making you complicit."

"Stop being this guy, Hen."

"What guy?"

"The suffering martyr. It's all fine to take one for the team once in a while, but look at what it's cost you."

"If you're talking about Sarah, I think she and Stewart were out the door before things blew up with the bank."

"Well, my friend. You tell me, then. What's your plan?"

Henry pinched the bridge of his nose beneath his glasses until it hurt. "I don't know. I'm desperate. My only advantage is that, personally, I've got nothing left to lose."

Alex picked up on the change of subject.

"I'm sure it feels like that. That's why I'll never get married. I've seen too much. It's like trying to find an ambulance driver who rides a motorcycle. It won't happen because they've seen too many ruined lives. In your case, at least, the divorce is coming along nicely. The primary concern is that you kept things so simple that I'm not going to get much out of you in the way of fees."

Henry laughed despite himself. He appreciated Alex making light of the situation, in addition to all the time that Henry was sure Alex wasn't charging him for. Alex didn't specialize in divorces either, but Alex insisted that Henry use him anyhow. There wasn't going to be much to it. Henry realized that his marriage was more of an administrative exercise to unwind, rather than a contentious, drawn-out battle.

In fact, Henry was more than a little sad that he hadn't been able to complicate the marriage in those fifteen years. He was jealous of another Henry, in a parallel universe, burdened with red tape, enormous legal fees, discussions of children.

"I'm glad that, for you, it's easy. It's fine, though. I've got great nieces and nephews. It's like being a parent, but you get to give them back when the real work starts." Henry's canned response rolled off his tongue, and he knew that Alex had heard it more than a few times already.

"How are they?"

"Who?"

"The nieces and nephews."

In his hibernation, Henry hadn't seen anyone in months.

Alex crossed his legs again. This time, Natali saved Henry by bringing out their food; her only excursion from the kitchen during the lunch service. She set the stainless steel plates on the table. "There is no Mr. Stewart today?" she asked.

Henry just looked at the food, as Alex answered. "Stewart will not be joining us for the foreseeable future."

Regardless, Natali said, "Lunch is from me today. No pay. Enjoy."

Henry looked up, his mouth opening to protest, when Alex's hand touched his arm.

"Thank you, Natali," Alex said.

The old Indian woman smiled and pressed her palms together in front of her chest.

The two men returned the gesture.

When she'd gone, Alex said, "You have to take the good, too. Some people can appreciate what you did."

"Maybe. But it's going to take a lot of curry to get back to square one."

The fragrances rising from the sauces in the small copper bowls were divine. Earthy cumin and sweet anise beckoned for their attention. Alex and Henry helped themselves to generous portions of rice and curry.

Henry seized the opportunity to change the subject. "So how was your date last night?"

"Good," Alex said through a mouthful of naan. "Quiet."

"Quiet? From all the texts, I figured you were into your third bottle of wine or something."

Alex stopped chewing, confused.

"Quiet, as in someone made me dinner, and that was the extent of it. What do you mean by 'all the texts?' You're the one who doesn't respond."

They exchanged light accusations back and forth and took out their phones to prove each other wrong.

Alex held his screen out towards Henry at arm's length, but Henry didn't look up. He just stared at the string of texts with Frieda on his own phone.

The parental units are going away for the week. Can I stay with you and Shima? Mum can drop me off tomorrow after dinner & I won't get in the way.

Tomorrow works? Hello?

Yes. Looking forward to it!!!

Yay!!! F^{TM}

Alex took Henry's phone and guffawed with the *schadenfreude* of a time-tested friendship.

"Looks like you've got a house guest," he said, wiping a tear from his cheek with the back of his hand.

"Get real. She can't stay with me."

"Why not? I'll bet you're still sleeping on the couch anyhow."

"I should never have told you that." He took back his phone and re-read the texts. "I can't take care of her."

"You looked after her when she was younger. I thought kids got easier as they got older."

"That's not what I mean. I'm not ready for this."

"Ready for what?"

"I don't know. She's Sarah's niece."

"And she's been your niece forever, too, right? You were just saying how much you like being an uncle, and I don't think that stops just because you divorce her aunt."

"I guess. I think. Yeah. She still cat-sits. I haven't got a plan, though. I'm just busy."

"Busy doing what? Shelving books for Mr. Munroe? Solving the mystery of the missing crossword?" Alex leaned back and slid one leg over the other. "Maybe this is what you need. A break from the drama. A bit of, and I'm saying this because I love you, a bit of lightening up."

"I'm light," Henry said, frowning.

Alex stuffed more naan into his mouth, laughing.

CHAPTER FIVE

Henry brushed the sheets and blankets flat on the folding Ikea bed that, minutes ago, had been his couch. He looked at the banker's box, sitting against the wall in solitary protest. One more thing to deal with; the archaeology of his professional life.

He lifted the lid and peered inside. A mug, a framed photo of him and Sarah in Tofino from several years ago, his company cell phone, a framed CPA certificate. Everything had gone down so fast that the company simply locked him out remotely rather than ask for his phone back. All detritus of his professional past. All trash now, or recycling.

Henry looked at his watch, figuring he had enough time to make a dent in today's crossword; a preferred distraction. He replaced the lid of the box. The past could wait.

He placed a kettle on the blue flame of the gas stove and chose a tea bag.

Unfolding the Monday newspaper with a pen in one hand, Henry skimmed each article in the first section, in turn. It could have been the same as yesterday, for all the headlines: housing prices, disaster, economy . . . He gave the business section only a fraction more attention, relieved not to see his own name in print.

There was something meditative about alternating one's attention between the various articles and the kettle, slowly building to its crescendo. Henry didn't even mind when the paper tab of the tea bag slipped over the side of the cup and into the tea.

Generally, the Arts section was filled with colorful covers of books that he summoned the mental intention to read, but whose names he would never recall. The Arts section should contain all of this and the crossword...

Again?

Henry pulled out the Local section. Sports, Life, Travel, Fashion. And he started again. Business, Local, Sports, Life, Travel, Fashion.

He flipped through each section page by page, more and more quickly. The later sections were printed with increasingly poor quality, and Henry's index fingers and thumbs became darkened with ink, a barometer for his rising frustration.

He ran his hands through his hair, leaving it standing on end. A gray smudge on his forehead disappeared into the thinning hairline. He separated and unfolded each section of the newspaper. As he inspected each page and confirmed the absence of the sought-after puzzle, he dismissed it into the air with a toss of his hand.

He stood, relaxing his hand in defeat, and dropped the black felt-tip pen that he secretly reserved for the sole purpose of crosswords.

A doorbell rang somewhere. When the thin, echoey gong came again, Henry realized that someone was at his door.

"Are you kidding me?" he said to Shima, who looked thrilled with this turn of events; there were so many sheets of paper to lie on.

I didn't know I had a doorbell.

Henry raced around the room, scooping up the large sheets of newsprint, crumpling them into a single, furious ball, which he stuffed with unnecessary force into the blue, plastic recycling bin.

He glanced around and checked off his mental list aloud.

"Groceries, couch, sheets, bathroom, towels, Shima."

The cat, already seated next to the door, cooed upon hearing his name.

"Here we go, little man."

He took a deep breath and opened the door.

"Hi!" Rachel and Frieda stepped into the apartment. Frieda bent down to pet Shima, who appeared quite pleased, as though Henry had arranged the visit for him. Rachel and Henry greeted each other with a hug. Rachel's embrace lasted longer than Henry's, and she patted him on the back in a motherly sort of way.

"We've missed you," she said, before letting go. "Say hello, Frieda."

"Hi, Hen."

"Hello, Fred."

Frieda was wearing what appeared to be a hood and cape, which extended all the way down to the floor. It was olive drab wool and pilled as though it were old. Her shoulder-length chestnut hair had blue streaks scattered throughout, which weren't there the last time he saw her. In addition to the backpack that Rachel was holding, Frieda had brought a small leather satchel, strapped across her shoulder and chest. Her T-shirt read, *I WANT TO BELIEVE.*

Henry stuck his head out the door. Sure enough, there was a doorbell next to the jamb, painted the same ochre as the wall.

"Is everything okay?" Rachel asked.

"Yeah, great. I'm still figuring this place out," he said, closing the door.

"It's been a long time."

"It has. I'm finding new routines, though. Once things settle down, I'm sure we'll see more of each other." As soon as the words left his mouth, he thought of Toronto.

"I hope so. I'm sorry, but Tomas is in the car. I can't stay long."

"Is everything okay?" he asked.

"It's fine. We're off to a sort of couples' retreat. We're all getting older, you understand."

Henry kind of understood. Maybe. "Oh, sure."

Rachel looked around. She pointed at the banker's box on the floor. "Still unpacking?"

Henry sidled his body in between Rachel and the box. "Just office stuff."

She nodded, happy to leave the subject.

"This is a pretty small place. Are you sure you've got room for Frieda? We were going to put it off until the end of the week because Sarah's away, but since you were available, we thought . . ."

Henry followed her gaze to a pair of newspaper sheets on the kitchen floor. He strode over and picked them up, folding them neatly. The recycling was overflowing, so he placed them on the table as though they belonged there.

"No. We'll be fine. I have space. The couch folds out."

"Sure, but if you need a hand, Sarah said they might be back early on Wednesday."

Not on your life.

"Thanks, but I can take care of things. We'll be fine."

Rachel appeared less confident but willing to move on. "Well, get a hold of her if you need to. And it's nice that you're still roughly in the same neighborhood. How many units are in the building?"

"Four. No, five. The one across the hall sort of doesn't count. There is an elderly gentleman below me. Upstairs there are two suites. The one right above me is a young woman I've never met. I was told she works from home."

"Her name's Tess," Frieda said from the floor. Shima had climbed onto her back, so she lay flat for him to settle down. Covered in her olive green, Henry thought she looked like dense ground cover. "We met her on the way in. She seems super-nice and she has really short hair."

"Is that so?" Henry continued. "The other suite is Bernadette. She's in her sixties, a bit of an old hippie, and seems to help out with the running of the house like the garden in the back."

"So, who owns the building?" Rachel asked.

Henry wondered where this was going. Was he going to need a background check?

"It's some numbered company that has the suite across the hall as its office, but I've never seen anyone coming or going. I just slip rent cheques through the mail slot. Bernadette's the one who showed me the place. It's a bit strange, but it's pretty common to incorporate a company in order to get financing for—"

"Bo-ring!"

"Frieda, don't interrupt," Rachel said.

"No, it's fine," Henry said. "I promise that I won't bore you with accounting and business stuff while you're here. Alright?"

"Thank you," Frieda said, wincing as Shima sniffed deep into her ear.

He watched her try to sit as still as possible so as not to scare the old cat away, even though he knew it was a horrible feeling to have a cold, wet nose poking around in there. Shima had a curious interest in ears, and he often startled Henry awake this way.

Henry's face softened.

Rachel broke the silence. "We should get on the road. Frieda has eaten. She'll show you her study schedule. Do you have everything you need?"

"Yes," Frieda said, still unmoving.

After saying their goodbyes, Henry and Frieda watched from the kitchen window as Rachel's car pulled away.

Henry spoke first. "Want to play a game?"

Frieda shrugged as only a thirteen-year-old can. "If you want to."

"With or without?"

"With or without what?"

"Ice cream."

Frieda looked down her nose at him and put on a posh New England accent. "Skipping ice cream is for chumps."

Henry fixed the ice cream while Frieda set up the backgammon. She couldn't be trusted to scoop a reasonable serving.

In the past, at family Christmases, Easters, and even camping trips, Henry and Frieda played games continuously. Other adults would congregate in the kitchen to talk, the living room to watch television, or the dining room to drink. But without fail, somewhere in the house, Henry and Frieda would be set up with chess, checkers, mancala, or crib. They finally settled on backgammon as their game of choice. It provided just the right balance of chance, strategy, and opportunities to stick it to your opponent.

Rolling the dice, Henry asked, "So, what's with the cape? Are you a superhero?"

"It's a thief's cloak," she said with the same tone she would use to imply he'd never heard of blue jeans. "I've been playing Dungeons and Dragons with a couple of other kids from my home-school group." She fingered the circular brass brooch that pinned the cloak together over her right shoulder. "I got this from my friend for my birthday. She wrote the message in

Elvish herself because I'm an elf-thief. It's awesome, but my dad says it looks like the Pepsi logo."

Henry congratulated himself for not having asked about the Pepsi logo.

"Mum says you got fired for stealing from the bank."

"Does she?" Henry was only surprised at how unsurprised he was by the question. "If I stole something, shouldn't I be in prison?"

"I guess," she said, a spoon dangling from her mouth as she rolled the dice.

"Maybe I escaped."

Frieda's hand paused for a moment, before continuing to bounce her checker along the points of the board.

"I didn't steal anything. I bent some rules to help some people."

"But you got in trouble."

"Yes. It's fair to say that the bank and I disagree on the spirit of the rules."

Frieda hurried to swallow her mouthful of ice cream. "There are nine alignments in Dungeons and Dragons that dictate how you go about in the world. I play chaotic good with my elf-thief because it's about being a good person just because you want to be, not because someone told you to or because you are following the law."

Henry was well aware of D&D alignments and couldn't disagree if he wanted to. "That sounds pretty alright."

He shifted the subject back to her cloak. "And where would I find such a fine garment, if I wanted one?"

Frieda held the sides of the cloak wide open, showing off its size. "Online," she said with enthusiasm. "It's got hidden pockets, and it came with a set of lock picks."

Frieda produced a little leather pouch from inside the cloak. Henry picked it up and looked inside at what could be mistaken for evil dental instruments.

That's actually pretty cool, Henry thought, with more envy than he cared to admit.

"So, you're still picking locks?"

"Oh, sure." She waved a dismissive hand at him. "The set that you bought me was just for beginners, though. I've learned way more on YouTube. I can pick almost anything now, except those ones with the circular keys. That set's too expensive. You're on the bar, by the way," she said, returning their attention back to the game.

After a few quiet turns, Henry resigned himself to the inevitable and dreaded topic.

"Hey, Fred. Things have changed because Sarah and I aren't together anymore. I just want to say that if you have any questions, don't be afraid to ask. I'll do my best to answer them."

"Okay," she said. Then she added with a smirk, "You remember how to play this, don't you? It sure doesn't seem like it."

In spite of her trash-talking, the tides turned at the end, and he managed to stick a number of her pieces on the bar, sending them back to the start and beating her soundly.

They cleared their bowls. Henry made the unfolded sofa-bed while Frieda watched and brushed her teeth.

"Are you still my uncle?" she asked through a mouthful of foam.

Henry stopped cold. A lump began to form in his throat. He swallowed it back with as much grace as he could.

"Yes. I think so."

"I do, too," she said, and she popped her brush back between her teeth.

They said their goodnights as Henry withdrew to the bedroom. It seemed not so long ago that she would have asked him to read her a story. Her favorites had been Tintin adventures. "Go back to the peril," she would say, and he would re-read the dangerous bits over.

What does being an uncle even look like anymore?

Henry woke up once in the night, confused by the new surroundings. He felt around the strange bed for Shima, who was usually at his feet, if not sleeping right on his chest. He peeked out of the bedroom door at Frieda. Relaxed and asleep, her face rounded and became even more cherubic. Under her arm, the old cat looked up at Henry and gave a light coo. Henry returned to bed.

He tried not to dream of crosswords.

CHAPTER SIX

Frieda Duran played what she called 'Daredevil' whenever she woke in a new location. She lay still and alert and tried to take in as much information about her surroundings without opening her eyes.

She remembered that she was lying on Henry's sofa-bed. She felt Shima lying next to her, his paw outstretched onto her arm. Frieda heard the old cat yawn and deduced by the smell that he had already been fed. She heard light sounds of dishes being placed onto the table, by someone trying to be quiet. There was an unmistakable aroma of fresh coffee and she lifted her head.

"Good morning, Fred," Henry said from the kitchen.

Frieda got up and joined him in the kitchen. She wore a blue T-shirt with a Superman logo and red shorts with a yellow band. She picked up a clay mug from the table and sipped at the coffee, steam rising into her nose. Henry had let her drink coffee for a couple of years, in moderation. Although, in one of those contradictions that made sense only to adults, he would get upset if she used too much sugar, so she had learned to drink it black.

Henry was already dressed. His suit and shirt looked

baggier than the ones he used to wear. She had heard that old people shrink.

Poor Hen. Maybe it's starting early for him.

He checked his hair in his reflection on the kettle. "I'm heading off to work. Help yourself to toast and fruit. There's leftover pizza that you can have for lunch. I'll be home around five. After today, I've got the rest of the week off, and we can do some hanging out. Fair?"

She nodded, peering at him over the mug as she sipped.

Henry cleared the dishes, speeding up as adults do before they leave the house.

"Do you have your keys?" he asked. "I put the money I owe you on the fridge. Do you need more money? You have my number, right? Do you know what you're going to do today? Any questions?"

"Yes. No. Yes, schoolwork. No."

At this, Henry stopped puttering, looked at her, and laughed. This wasn't his out-of-control sort of laugh that sounded like hiccups and looked like he was stifling a sneeze. This was his single loud burst, as though he'd been surprised, which sometimes upset people at dinner but never Frieda. Having expelled his guffaw, he looked relaxed and happy. She remembered him always being that way when she was younger.

Henry continued to tidy, and Frieda played with Shima next to her on the chair. She dangled her earbuds over the little tuxedoed cat, and he tried to scoop them into his mouth.

"They smell like ear," she said to no one in particular.

"Please don't encourage him, Fred."

I miss the old Hen.

After Henry left, Frieda dressed and returned to the table to start her work. She had scheduled a Skype session with her French tutor, math, and creative writing for the day. She tried to sandwich the bad stuff in between the good.

Midway through her math, Frieda got stumped. Trying to

Google for help with the first problem, a geometric proof, had led to a Wiki rabbit hole, a series of TED talks, followed by YouTube, and now it was nearing lunch.

Frieda shunned the pizza, helping herself instead to an apple, a piece of cheese, and a box of crackers. With a loud, "Come, Shima!" she marched the short distance to the couch and laid it all out in a picnic. The old cat watched and purred while she ate. When she was done, he followed her to the door where she sat on the floor.

She laced her boots. "Hen's going to notice if I make more coffee, little man. I'll be right back." Frieda tucked her creative writing book into her satchel and beamed at her own play on words. *Write back. That's awesome.*

She had discovered the convenient little café across the road on one of her visits to feed Shima. There were booths next to the windows facing the street and small bar stools affixed to the floor the length of a long counter. They reminded her of mushrooms in video games that you scored points for jumping on. She took a seat at the bar.

A woman wearing a black apron around her waist brought a menu. Frieda observed the name tag on the woman's chest and said, "Just a coffee, please, Deborah. Dark and bitter, just like me."

Frieda was pleased with her quip. She heard someone say it once and everyone had laughed. When Deborah only raised an eyebrow in surprise, Frieda worried.

Was that racist?

She opened her notebook to the back, where she kept her lists and added a couple of entries.

18) origin of "dark and bitter just like me"
19) understand racism

She wrote and sipped for more than an hour. Deborah

didn't seem to be too offended because she called Frieda "Honey" and "Darling" and kept the coffee topped up. Frieda's list grew.

20) what is an appropriate tip for exceptional service???

Frieda left the café, work done for the day. At least, all the schoolwork that she was going to do. She was puzzling through details of her new story in her mind and didn't see the man in the hallway until the glass door was nearly closed behind her.

He straightened up quickly from a crouching position next to the door across from Henry's. At his full height, he towered over the small girl. By the snapping sound of the door's mail slot, Frieda figured that he must have been trying to see into the apartment. He knocked on the shadow of the number two with a slow beat of deliberate patience. Standing with his back to Henry's apartment, he turned to acknowledge Frieda. The lower half of his face widened into a smile, but his eyes remained serious, scanning her up and down.

The man's grin was so broad that Frieda could see the wet inside of his cheeks. His hair and clothes were a mess.

Upstairs are two women, and the old man downstairs is in his eighties, Frieda recalled. This guy's older than Hen and Dad, but not as old as Grandpa.

Frieda drew her shoulders back and slid one hand to her satchel, in case he was a purse thief. As she approached, she smelled his stale odor. She walked past Henry's door, stepping over a newspaper on the floor, to the stairs at the end of the hall without looking back. She imagined her ears pivoting to face the hallway behind her, attuned to each little sound.

At the top of the stairs, she broke into a sprint to the nearest door and knocked.

Is that my door?

Tess Honma straightened up on her stool.

A second, more insistent rapping lasted a little longer.

She dropped her brush into the glass of gray water on the corner of her drawing table. The water darkened a little further. She hopped off the yellow barstool and padded her way across the wide-open apartment, the hardwood warm from the sunlight beneath her bare feet.

Tess opened the door to see a young girl about to knock on Bernadette's door across the hall.

"May I help you?"

"Hi. Can I come in?" the young girl said, as she ducked under Tess's arm and slipped into the apartment. Once in, the girl added, "Thank you. I'm Frieda."

"Right. We met yesterday. You were with your mum, and you were visiting the guy downstairs."

"That's Henry. He was married to my mum's sister but not anymore. That's why he has to rent. May I have a glass of water, please?" Frieda stared at the open door.

Tess closed the door and noticed Frieda's shoulders relax. She fetched a glass, filling it from the kitchen faucet. By the time she turned around, the young girl had already settled down in the living room. The choices in the living room were few. Tess couldn't recall ever having had a guest to her apartment in the several years she had lived here, so there was little need for more than the necessities: a small kitchen table and chairs, a couch from which to watch television, bookshelves, art on the walls, and her makeshift art studio.

She handed her curious young guest the water.

"Thank you," Frieda said, her mouth already on the glass, taking a long drink. She sat on the couch and looked for somewhere to set the glass down, deciding on the floor.

Tess studied the girl. Frieda had that clash of styles that spoke of the early days of youth's individuation. Rather than being limited by stereotypes and categories—punk, goth, prep, jock, geek—the young girl in front of her sampled from all the buckets, trying things on without the burdens of matching and clashing. Blue streaked hair; a hippie leather satchel; a writing pad swollen and stuffed with additional loose pages; a T-shirt bearing what could only be a recipe for poutine: *Fries. Curds. Gravy.*

Curious and amused, she took a spot next to Frieda on the couch. "So, are you making the rounds and introducing yourself to everyone in the building today? Or am I special? Bernadette across the hall is very nice, and Mr. Benham, below your uncle, is always looking for people to talk to."

"I'm, uh, I'm staying with Hen and Shima for a bit. He's at work right now, and I'm supposed to be studying, but I felt like some company. You seemed nice, and I thought I would say hello. So, I guess I am sort of making the rounds. But I wasn't planning on meeting everyone."

"I didn't know Henry lived with anyone."

"He doesn't. Shima's a cat. He's real old. Like, older than me."

"That is old. Well, it's nice to meet you more formally, Frieda. You can call me Tess. That's what my friends call me."

"Hi, Tess," Frieda said, smiling and picking up her glass.

As the girl drank deeply, her eyes ran over Tess's hair, face, shirt. It was an innocent inspection, suggesting the curiosity was mutual. Frieda's eyes stopped at the tattoo on Tess's forearm.

"Is that real?"

Tess looked down at the black-ink stylized man in a suit, his head the dot at the bottom of a question-mark that floated above him. "It is. I got it when I was twenty."

"How old are you now?" Frieda asked with the directness that only youth or seniority can muster.

"Thirty-eight."

The young girl worked the numbers in her head.

"I'm thirteen. So, I wasn't born then."

Tess laughed. "No. You wouldn't have been. What sort of studying were you doing?"

"Writing. I'm a writer. I was doing math earlier, but I'm a writer. I'm homeschooled, so I get to choose my curriculum and develop my strengths. It's better because then I don't have to study information that I will only ever use to pass a test."

"But it gets lonely sometimes?"

"Sometimes. There are a bunch of us homeschoolers that get together for field trips and things, but I probably won't see them this week."

Frieda rose from the couch. She walked to the bookshelves, each overflowing: the first with paperbacks and hundreds of random magazines, the second with graphic novels and comic books. She reached out and ran her hand over the spines of the comics.

"Are all these yours?"

Tess straightened up and grinned at the surprise in the girl's voice.

"Yup. All mine. If you like comics, and there are any you'd like to borrow while you're staying with Henry, you're more than welcome to take them downstairs."

Frieda looked back over her shoulder at Tess with wide eyes.

"I do. I will. Thank you."

"In fact, if you're a writer, then you are probably a big reader, too. I would recommend this one." Tess walked to the bookshelf, her hand knowing instantly where to find the thick hardcover. "It's called *The League of Extraordinary Gentlemen*. If you're a fan of classic stories, Edgar Allan Poe, Dracula, the Invisible Man, then this is for you." She handed the book to the girl.

Frieda looked at the cover. A motley team of people was

gathered together, looking resolved and stern: a woman, an old man, a monster, a tall Sikh fellow, and the Invisible Man. She pointed to an image on the corner of the book. "That's your tattoo."

"Right. This book changed my life. It's where I learned that some stories are so great that people love them for decades, centuries, even."

Frieda looked at the book as though it had suddenly become a holy tome. "I'll take really good care of it," she said, putting it upright in her satchel so that it stuck halfway out. "If I tell you something, will you promise not to laugh?"

"Of course."

Frieda recounted going to the café alone, returning, and seeing the man in the hallway downstairs. "He was super awkward, like he wasn't supposed to be there. Like he was casing the place. And I had this thought that was kind of, 'Frieda, don't open Hen's door in front of this creepy guy.' But I couldn't just turn around and leave, so I pretended that I lived upstairs here."

"That's okay." Tess looked at the clock in the kitchen. It had already been a productive morning. "We can hang out here for as long as you want and go down together later."

"And then, when you come down, you can meet Shima," Frieda offered.

"That sounds great. I love cats." The girl's company was refreshing. "Say, since you like comics ..."

"What?"

"Let me show you something you might think is cool."

She had never shown anyone her art studio set-up before. In all the world, this was the place most sacred to her. She hesitated and looked again at the girl who had interrupted her day. As she turned to walk to the front of the apartment, she gave a nod to Frieda in the direction of her studio.

CHAPTER SEVEN

The phone in Henry's pocket gave a jolt and buzzed as he let it ring silently.

"I'm sorry. What was that?" he said to the portly, middle-aged man whose handlebar moustache received all the grooming and attention that was denied his oily hair.

"An omnibus. It's a gift for a friend, and it has to be an omnibus."

The phone gave another irritating shake.

Per Mr. Munroe's policy, Henry did not simply point in the direction of the science fiction section. He signaled for the customer to follow and, in long, quick strides he led him to the stack of copies of *The Hitchhiker's Guide to the Galaxy*.

The store phone which had not, in Henry's recollection, ever announced its presence before, rang and was cut short on its second bell. Mr. Munroe was in the back office and must have picked it up.

The mustachioed man eventually appeared at the end of the aisle and caught up, whereupon he delivered a lengthy and detailed explanation on the virtues of having an omnibus of all five volumes of Douglas Adams' classic saga.

"You don't mean a box set?" Henry asked.

The man rolled his eyes. "If you had read the books, instead of just watching the movie, you'd understand. It's not five stories; it's a single, epic tale of the vast potential of the human spirit. And it deserves recognition as such."

"Oh, I've read them. I only mention it because it's cheaper to buy them separately."

Henry handed him the thick, single tome.

"Why?"

Henry shrugged. "I guess because we have so many?"

The customer's conviction vanished, and Henry waved as the man left carrying five books under his arm.

Henry shot his hand into his pocket. One missed call, no voicemail, and a text.

Shima is out. Tess is helping me look. She said to call you. – F^{TM}

He read it a second time and spun around to face the chair where Mr. Munroe could ordinarily be found. Behind the chair, the door to the back office opened, revealing a small room barely big enough for the desk that had been squeezed in there, let alone the piles of books on the floor and the desk itself.

Mr. Munroe, still sitting down and holding the doorknob, said, "You've had a couple of calls."

"A couple?"

"I'm sorry. The first was an hour ago, but you were with a customer and I got busy."

Henry waited. "Yes?"

"Ah, the first call was from a Kat Hunter. And just now a call from a Tess Hom... Homma? They both said that you were to call Ms. Hunter."

Henry excused himself and grabbed his jacket from the coat hooks behind the counter.

"No problem," the old man said from his cave. "I'll see you next week."

Henry called Frieda's mobile as he hurried from the store.

Cat hunter. Cute, but not funny. Shima's never been outside.

There was no answer. He re-read the text, jaywalked across the street to his bicycle, and raced to Richardson Street.

Henry let his bicycle drop against the apartment door opposite his own. Stepping on his newspaper, he burst into his suite.

"Frieda?"

No girl.

"Shima?"

No cat.

He looked back at his texts. Another had arrived.

Upstairs with Tess – F^{TM}

Henry ran up the stairs and knocked on the door of Unit 3, immediately above his own. There was no answer, so he knocked again, louder and longer.

"Frieda?"

"*Oui, monsieur*?" said a voice behind him.

He turned to see Frieda's face, mostly cheeks and framed by her brown-and-blue hair, peering out from the door behind him.

"Fred." Henry walked straight into the strange apartment and gave her a hug. "Are you okay? Where's Shima?"

"We found him. He was with Bernadette."

"Why was your phone off? Wait, why was Shima with Bernadette?"

"Oh, my phone is at Tess's. She and I were drawing in her apartment and I wanted to show her Shima, but when we got downstairs, he was gone. Bernadette thinks he might have gotten into the walls. How cool is that? Like a secret passage for cats."

Feeling lost, Henry looked around. The apartment was similar in size to his own, but it retained all its original walls. Instead of being wide open, it was still broken up into several small rooms. He stood in the living room. The entrance to his left opened onto a kitchen stocked with avocado-green appliances from his childhood.

The walls were vintage plaster and covered by only the odd small painted canvas and framed photos. The floors were hardwood and covered with Persian rugs of various dimensions. The room was in the front of the house and bright for the light pouring in through windows like those in Henry's kitchen. The furniture was uniformly mid-century design, lean and teak. Wool and afghan blankets had been placed strategically around the living room: on the arm of a chair, the back of the couch, and beneath the coffee table. Henry coveted the vintage furniture that spoke to him of style and permanence.

Henry recognized Bernadette, of similar vintage to the furniture, as the woman who had shown him the apartment. She had bright, relaxed eyes, and unblemished pale skin that avoided wrinkles due to her naturally plump, but not fat, body type.

Seated next to her was another, younger woman. She was pretty, fit, and looked back at him with amusement. Her hair was, indeed, cut short and so jet black as to assert some Asian heritage. She was dressed casually in a T-shirt and rolled up jeans. Her dirty bare feet surprised Henry and felt revealing, although he couldn't pinpoint why. Both women held cups of steaming tea. Next to the teapot on the coffee table was a plate with a stack of white-bread sandwiches, cut into triangles.

Shima lay between the two women on the couch, with Bernadette's free hand resting on his back.

"Hello, Henry," Bernadette said. "Frieda here has been keeping us quite entertained. She's one of the good ones."

"I'm very glad to hear that. It's nice to see you." He looked again at the artsy young woman, sitting cross-legged. "And you must be Tess?"

"And you must be Henry. Nice to meet you."

Henry waved uncomfortably at both women as he stood, still confused.

"Fred, how about you tell me more about your day?"

"After our tea," she said, her tone excited. She helped herself to a half-eaten sandwich from the coffee table and spoke with a bite in her mouth. "I went out to find a good space to write. Sometimes a new environment helps get the creative juices flowing. When I came back, there was a smelly dude in the hallway downstairs. I think he was creeping on the apartment across from yours. I didn't want to open your door with him right there, so I came upstairs and Tess let me in."

"Thank you," Henry said to Tess.

"It's no problem. I was stuck on something anyhow. Plus, Frieda's pretty cool."

Frieda's face reddened. She carried on.

"Tess is a comic book artist, like for real. She draws *Enigma Team 6*, and *Time Doctors*. She has her own studio where she makes real comics, and it's right upstairs from you and you didn't even know. I told her that I write, and she said we might get to work together someday."

He felt his heart slowing down and his body relaxing as he listened to Frieda's enthusiasm. A chill reminded him that he had broken a sweat, riding as fast as he could.

"That would be quite a break."

Tess returned Henry's smile, and he realized his collar was damp. He pulled at his sweaty shirt so that it wasn't sticking to his stomach.

"I know, right?" Frieda said. "So, we hung out there until we were sure that the creepy guy would be gone. She gave me a tattoo." Frieda pulled back her sleeve to reveal an ink drawing on her arm of a medical caduceus and pocket watch. "I'm never washing this off."

She paused for a breath, then continued. "Tess came with me downstairs so I could show her Shima, but he was gone."

Bernadette cut in. "The little prowler just walked right out of my closet as though it were the most natural thing in the world. He scared the hell out of me. Let me show you."

Tess helped her get up and, as they followed Bernadette to the bedroom, Henry saw that she held her side and walked more slowly than when they had first met.

"Is everything alright?"

"Just a little wear and tear is all," Bernadette said, dismissing his concern with a wave. "It comes and goes. There are gaps going into the walls where there used to be French doors. I think he got in there. I believe your bedroom closet has the same thing."

In the short hall to the bedroom, two framed photographs stood out from all the painted art. One was a color picture of a much younger Bernadette standing next to a man at the edge of a canyon. Her mouth was open in laughter; joy visibly unfazed by the tendrils of long, dark hair blowing around a headscarf and into her face. The second, smaller image was a black-and-white photo of a younger woman, twentysomething, sitting in a wooden garden chair with two small children in her lap.

Henry hurried to catch up to the group in the bedroom. Each side of the wall into which the closet was cut had a three-inch gap from floor to ceiling.

"The old doors would have slid in there when they opened," Bernadette said. "They were probably taken out when the place was divided into suites. Long gone before I moved in."

"Mine is the same," Henry said. "I thought the openings

would be too small for him to fit through. I guess I was wrong."
He looked down at the old cat who appeared very content with
himself.

Little bugger.

"I spent half the morning looking for my bloody ear plugs,"
Bernadette said. "I can't sleep a wink without them, and I sometimes steal a nap in the afternoon. This little monster, though,
he wandered around my home until he found them. He just
picked one up and carried it right to me."

Absconding, more likely.

Henry glanced at Frieda who was already looking back at
him with wide eyes. She pointed at her ear. Henry shook his
head. *Do not mention ear wax.*

"I figured he was yours. Anyhow, before I could get to my
nap, I heard these two young ladies outside, shouting, and I
went to see what was going on."

"We were looking for Shima," Tess said. "And now, here we
are."

"Well, thank you both for your help with holding my life
together," Henry said with a small bow. "We should probably
get out of your hair and figure out what we're doing with the
rest of the day."

"Why don't we all have dinner?" Frieda said.

"Great idea," Henry said. Why not? They would decline
anyhow. "But we aren't making anything special. It's only
spaghetti."

He noticed that Tess wasn't wearing any makeup. She was
an effortless sort of pretty.

"I'll bring wine," Bernadette said. "But first I have to follow
up with the building manager. I'm surprised there was
someone showing up to the office downstairs. I can't imagine
what they wanted."

"That sounds great," Tess said. "Give me a bit of time to take care of a couple things and then I'll come down and join you. Can I bring anything?"

"Just you," Frieda said.

Henry carried Shima down the stairs in silence, trying to figure out how it was that he suddenly had dinner guests.

CHAPTER EIGHT

The Cheshire man inspected each of the coloured, Canadian bills before laying them on the table.

Monopoly money. Why can't they just use real dollars?

The server had cut off his refills, so he would have to pack up soon and leave the café. He looked at the bag next to him in the booth. The clothes from the second-hand store still had a musty smell. It was only supposed to be a day trip, but now he was spending someone else's cash on a change of clothes.

The battery on his laptop was going to die soon anyhow.

He pulled the manila folder from his bag; his case file. Taped to the inside left cover were the twenty-dollar bill, still inside the sandwich bag, and the pawnshop card. The front of the card had cryptic notes written in blue and black ballpoint.

WFT
1584 Richardson St., Vancouver, BC
Duffel (1) Jackson (9,380)
November 29, 1971 RENEW October 31, 1972 RENEW
October 31, 1973 RENEW October 31, 1974 RENEW October
31, 1975 CLOSE January 31, 1976

The back of the card was even less helpful: just a list of numbers, counting down from fifty to one.

From yesterday's search through the recycling bin of 1584 Richardson Street he had compiled a list of the current tenants, none of whom were Duffel or Jackson.

He had thought of reaching out to the owner of the building and found the title available online. Again, more money he didn't have. This time it was a credit card.

Soon, though, there wouldn't be any more financial worries.

The title report said that the apartments were purchased in December 1971 by a numbered company: 121702 BC Ltd. The company's address was listed as Unit 2 of the building. If the company was the building's manager, maybe it had a list of past tenants. Maybe the trail would become hot again.

But no one answered the door. There was no listed phone number for the company. Nobody went in or out, and he couldn't wait indefinitely.

His laptop made a pinging noise. He closed the manila folder, pushed the colorful cash aside, and opened the laptop. He was still logged in to the site and had received an instant message from another user.

@swimmingwithfishes *I think I found what you're looking for. I can't tell when the last day register was updated, tho. Are you sending payment by e-transfer?*

@treasurehunter1971 *E-transfer. How much did it cost?*

@swimmingwithfishes *$100. But that's in Canada$, so I don't know what that is in US$. $5? LOL*

@treasurehunter1971 *LOL I'll send it today.*

@swimmingwithfishes *Cool. Sending docs now.*
ATTACHMENT – NoticeChangeDirectors.pdf 170KB

@swimmingwithfishes *Are you going to tell me what
you're working on?*

@treasurehunter1971 *Things are still sensitive. Pretty soon,
you'll know. Huge news.*

He downloaded the attachment and opened it to find scans
of old legal documents, incorporation details, formal notifica-
tions of a change in the directors of 121702 BC Ltd. Until now,
getting details about the company had proved difficult for
himself and the people he knew online.

Shareholders, he was told, would be nearly impossible to
find; not so for directors. So, he wouldn't find out who the
actual owners were, but at least he'd have the names of people
in charge.

There had to be people who could find these sorts of things
out, but they were probably expensive, and he was already
stretched thin. He had only brought enough cash for the bill,
his credit card had to be maxed, or close to it, and there had
only been a couple hundred dollars of cash in the pawnshop.

So, he'd make do with the directors.

The legal register included only three entries.

President J. Johnston 29/11/1971
Resigned J. Johnston 23/12/1974
President R. Benham 23/12/1974

Each time he saw the Canadian day-month-year format, it
was one more reminder that he wanted to get home. Johnston
was a new name. Benham, however, was not.

His case file contained copies of all his most important

documents. He flipped past a map of Oregon and Washington states, marked with scattered red lines; a black-and-white photograph of a man in a suit with a woman and child; his list of serial numbers for US twenty-dollar bills; artist renderings of a man wearing sunglasses; newspaper articles, reproduced from the internet. He withdrew the list of tenants he had compiled for 1584 Richardson Street.

Unit 1 Henry Lysyk
Unit 2 121702 BC Ltd.
Unit 3 Tess Honma (& daughter?)
Unit 4 Bernadette Pruner
Unit 5 Ronald Benham

The old man downstairs. Benham. He was a director, or he had been. Either way, he could help get in contact with the company.

The Cheshire man scrolled back through the pdf. His screen dimmed, as warning of the failing battery. He stopped on the incorporation information and read it over twice before the screen blinked off and began powering down.

The incorporating entity that created 121702 BC Ltd. was someone, or something, called "WFT".

He slid the pawnshop card from its plastic sleeve. There was the breadcrumb, in tidy handwriting laid down nearly fifty years ago: *WFT*

The card shook in his hand. He would search the internet for the meaning of the letters later and it would be impossible to learn. The internet was cluttered with trite garbage. The number of results would be ridiculous.

Those details paled in comparison to what this meant. Everything was connected.

I've found you, 'President' Ronald Benham. How fitting.

He flipped back and forth between his list and the register of directors on his computer screen.

You changed your name, but you left a trail for me. No one else could put it together, but I did. You were too smart for them. So smart that they gave up. They quit. Now that they're gone, I've found you.

He had been so focused on the numbered company's apartment. Not a complete waste of time, but misleading. So far, Benham only appeared through the windows, never outside. The old man was the right age.

Clever. Because it's you.

The Cheshire man beamed widely at the server standing next to him. She repeated her question.

"Did you want to start with a new coffee?" She gave the urn a little waggle in the air.

"No, thanks," he said, still grinning. "I'm just heading out."

He slid himself and his pack from the booth. With a quick look back over his shoulder, he satisfied himself that he'd left nothing behind.

Outside, the street was quiet. The air clean. He filled his chest with breath, trying to calm the tremble of anticipation in his hands.

The streetlight flicked on, a beacon to the house and the end of his search. He stepped from the sidewalk onto the street. He could feel the grin on his face, wider than ever.

An unexpected second light came on over the basement stairs as the front door opened. A figure silhouetted by the light of the main hallway clung to the railing as it descended the stairs. The old lady upstairs was leaving.

His steps shortened and his path began to curve, away from the house.

She disappeared behind a hedge below the main floor's windows.

This wouldn't do.

He bit his cheek hard. He stuffed his hands into his pockets to keep them still as he alit on the sidewalk, passing around the glow of the streetlamp, carrying on, leaving the house behind him. Leaving the basement. Leaving the old man.

The trail was nearly fifty years old. He was so close. But it couldn't be rushed. It had to be right.

Patience.

Tomorrow.

CHAPTER NINE

These people don't know me, Henry thought. *They have no expectations. This will be fine.*

Henry had bought six of everything when he furnished the apartment: glasses, knives, forks, plates. He and Sarah used to enjoy hosting dinner parties. Now, though, it felt more like parading people through his defeat.

Downstairs, Tess arrived first. She and Henry sat at the table with glasses of the wine she had brought.

Frieda, meanwhile, had fashioned an apron for herself out of a dishtowel tucked into her jeans, and bustled about the kitchen. Henry watched her put on a show of randomly opening cupboards in order to orient herself to the locations of things, and she helped more than he had ever seen with making the dinner.

"Fred, since you're in charge of the sauce, tell me what you think. Is it missing anything?"

Frieda tried it. "No more wine, but it needs basil." She returned to the drawer of spices.

"Sounds good," Henry said. "Don't turn your back on it for too long. It's a gas stove, so it cooks differently than the one you've got at home."

Henry looked back to see Tess reaching into her glass with her middle finger, just touching the wine.

"Something in there?" Henry asked, leaning to rise.

"No," Tess said, rubbing her middle finger off against her thumb. "Just playing."

"So, do a lot of people call you Fred?" Tess asked.

"Just Hen," Frieda said over her shoulder.

"Because it's short for Frieda."

"No, that's silly."

Henry watched the domestic scene: the attractive woman watching the young girl sort through spices, having a quiet conversation, as a nice meal is prepared. Shima stood on his back paws to see inside the drawer as well.

"When I was a kid," Frieda explained, "I had a book of explorers that I used to make Hen read to me. Frederick Cook was my favorite, even though people say he didn't really make it to the North Pole or climb Mount McKinley. I thought it would be cool to go to the North Pole."

"So, he calls you Fred."

"Yeah, but I changed my mind when I got older. Now I want to climb Kilimanjaro. Some people think it's in Kenya, but it's really in Tanzania. From the top you can see the curve of the earth. Hen said he'd take me."

"That sounds amazing," Tess said, clearly entertained.

Henry looked at Frieda, stirring the sauce. Traveling together was something they had talked about doing with Sarah, as a trio. Kilimanjaro was not something that had been discussed in earnest, let alone mentioned, in a couple of years.

"You still want to go to Kilimanjaro?"

"More than ever."

"With me?"

"Well, we talked about it," Frieda said, with an uncharacteristically shy tone. "It would be neat to have an old promise like that come true. You'd need to get in better shape, though. The altitude is supposed to be really tough."

Henry wanted to give her a hug but hesitated to do anything that might embarrass her.

"I think thirteen may be a bit young for Africa, but maybe sixteen or seventeen would work. We should start planning and talking to your folks." He patted his stomach loudly. "That'll give me plenty of time to get into shape."

Frieda gave a whoop and splashed the wooden spoon into the sauce. She wrapped her arms around Henry's chest and tried to lift him from his seat.

He tussled her hair in return and said, "I think we're almost ready. Can you run up and see if Bernadette needs a hand?"

"Yessir, Mr. Lysyk," Frieda said, coming to attention and giving a sharp salute. She marched out the door, taking care not to let out the old cat who had become her shadow.

Henry offered Tess more wine. She slid her glass forward on the table.

"Is everything alright with Bernadette?" he asked as he poured. "She looked like she was in pain earlier. I even noticed you helping her from the couch."

"I know. I mean, I don't know. I've seen it, too, but she's never told me what's going on. Bernadette's always had tons of energy; she runs circles around me in the garden. It seems to have gotten worse in the last couple of months, though. I'm afraid to say anything because I figure if she wanted me to know, she'd tell me. You surprised me by coming right out and asking."

Frieda came back in.

"That was quick," Tess said.

"I found her in the hallway."

"Enough," Bernadette said, laughing. "Found me in the hallway, my butt. I'm still a ways off from getting lost in my own home. I was already coming down."

It was only when Frieda directed everyone to their seats that Henry noticed she had made little name placards for each of the place settings. She seated herself next to Bernadette and placed him and Tess together.

After Bernadette had left, they taught Tess how to play crib. To her credit, Tess was only skunked once. At ten-thirty, Frieda moved her belongings to Henry's bedroom. He would sleep on the couch tonight so that he and Tess could continue talking, while Frieda went to bed.

"She's an awesome kid," Tess said.

Henry reached across the table and finished the bottle of wine into their glasses.

"She is. I'm pretty lucky. I have more nieces and nephews, too, but they live on the island."

"Do you see them often?"

"I don't. It's far. I'm busy, etcetera, etcetera. To tell the truth, I don't even see that much of Frieda these days."

"Because you're busy."

"Because it's awkward. I always wanted kids, but at some point Sarah, my ex, decided she didn't. Eventually, I rationalized that it would be enough to be an uncle." Henry took a deep breath. "Can I share something with you?"

"Please."

"I've had this recurring dream. I'm in a park with tall, dry grass, maybe Stanley Park. I can see something moving the blades in front of me and it's Shima. I'm following him because I'm worried that he's going to go on the road. I try to corral him. And I realize, when I see him sniffing around, that this is it for him. This is all he has. I have to keep him safe, but I also have to let him take everything in. It's like I'm the custodian of his experience in this lifetime."

Henry took a long, slow sip. "I feel like I'm meant to care for someone. I want to be a part of Frieda's life, but Frieda is Sarah's side of the family, and I have no idea how this works after a divorce."

"My bet is that kids don't care about that sort of stuff. Fred adores you."

Henry ran his hand through his hair, his palm conveniently wiping the corner of his eye.

"How about you? Children? Boyfriend? Cat? Are you from Vancouver?"

"No, just the opposite. I grew up in the Yukon. Never wanted kids or cats. I treasure my independence too much."

"You sound like a friend of mine." It was only yesterday that he and Alex met for lunch. Only a day ago he had no idea that he would have so many people in his personal space.

Tess swirled the wine in the glass so that it rose high on the sides, almost to the lip. She got up from her seat and walked over to the living room as she spoke.

"Maybe that's selfish, but the way I see it is I'm the only person who needs to be responsible for me. I don't depend on anyone else to take care of anything or expect anyone to make me happy."

"So, the opposite of selfish. You've never had a relationship?"

"Not never. I wanted to get into comics, and it meant traveling, going to conventions and showing my art to people in the business. It was too hard on my relationship then, and I made a choice. I chose me. I can follow any path, talk to whomever I want, succeed or fail without being accountable to anyone." Although they rang true, her words had the same, rehearsed cadence as Henry's when he spoke about children, nieces, and nephews.

"I wish you had spoken to me fifteen years ago," Henry said.

"If I'd known that was an option, things might have been different."

"But then you wouldn't be here right now."

"Unemployed, unemployable, and divorced," Henry said, grinning into his glass.

"I think there's more to you than that." Tess stopped in front of the pale wooden bookshelf. It was such in name only, being conspicuously absent of books. Only a stack of a dozen LPs adorned one of the four shelves.

"A lot of space here." She flipped through the records. "Nothing but Bowie, and an expectation that you'll gather some reading material?"

"I took only what I needed, I left everything else."

"Which included Bowie?" She held up the black-and-white cover of the *Heroes* album. David Bowie's unfocused eyes stared away from the both of them, into space.

"In university, I started trying to get all of his stuff on vinyl. After... Well, Sarah hated him."

It sounded small when the words were given voice; so much smaller than the act of removing them had been. "She'd only chuck them anyhow."

Tess studied him from across the room, squinting, and pursing lips.

"What?" Henry asked.

"What makes you special?"

Not a question Henry was expecting. "What do you mean?"

"I mean, this apartment was vacant for months before you moved in, even though the city's in a housing crunch. You couldn't have been the first person to apply for it, but here you are."

"Here I am." Henry's words were less of an answer than a question of his own.

"Unemployed, unemployable, and divorced. Bernadette saw something in you, I guess, if she put in a good word."

"I can't imagine." Henry offered a weak shrug.

"What say you put on some music?" Tess said, gesturing at the handful of records leaning on Henry's one bookshelf.

Henry laughed. "I didn't get the record player."

She nodded appreciatively and straightened out the albums on the shelf. "You've got a nice laugh when you get out of your head. What do you do for fun?"

Henry regretted saying the first thing that came to mind, even as it left his mouth. "Crosswords?"

"Old school." It was her turn to laugh. "I haven't done one for years and years. I guess they're meditative?"

"They are," he said, hopping up from his chair to retrieve today's paper from the living room. "A puzzle's a pretty great way to sort of shake off the day."

Henry unfolded the paper as he spoke. Business, Style, Travel, Focus. "Are you kidding me?" He flipped through the sections again. "There's no Arts section. There's no crossword."

"It's in a different section?" Tess said.

"It's not," Henry said, too quickly.

He went through the paper one page at a time. "This is the second day in a row that someone has taken my crossword."

"Taken?" Tess asked, her voice not quite hiding a snicker. "As in someone deliberately stole it? Maybe the paper skipped a day. Maybe Mr. Crossword is sick, and he can't make his deadlines."

Henry gave a weak smile of agreement. *Was it Fred? That seems like an unfunny thing to do. Not like her.*

"Maybe it was Bernadette," Henry said.

"Busted. She's definitely your thief. She tried to steal your cat earlier. Is anything else missing?" Tess made a show of looking around the room with wild, wide eyes.

"I'm not crazy," he said.

"You know a crazy person would say that, right?"

"It's a long story. There were some . . . issues when I

divorced. My ex and her boyfriend aren't supposed to know where I live. And I wouldn't be surprised if the bank that I worked for was watching me."

"That's a pretty dramatic story. Do you hear yourself? One hundred percent crazy."

Henry could see the levity in the young woman's face as she wound him up. Surrendering to the logic before him, Henry clinked the bowl of his wineglass against hers in a toast.

"It's ridiculous," he said. "There's some reasonable explanation, I'm sure."

They sat at the table and talked a while longer, while the wine ran down. Tess spoke about traveling, about the business of comic books, and what it was like to be a woman in her industry. Henry also spoke of past travels, avoiding the topic of work, past or present. Were it not for the missing puzzle, Henry would have been hanging on her every word.

As they said goodnight at the door, Henry peered out and scanned back and forth in the hallway.

"One more thing," Tess said, placing her hand flat on Henry's chest. "Your dream about walking through the park. You know *you're* the cat, right?"

And, with that, she disappeared up the stairs.

CHAPTER TEN

B ernadette threw one of her pillows from the bed. The clock reminded her in glowing red numbers that sunrise was only a few hours away.

She was growing used to sleeping with the physical pain in her abdomen. It was her mind, tonight, that fought sleep. She lay in the dark with her eyes wide open, playing over Frieda's story about the man downstairs.

Was it a mistake? What did he want? Who was he?

No one had ever come looking to speak with somebody from the company, so far as she knew. She always took care of finding new tenants for Richardson Street, fielding questions about repairs and maintenance, and even collecting and returning deposits. Even though she'd had help from time to time, now it was just her.

Before dinner, she had gone down to visit Ron in Unit 5, which was partly below ground, adding still more stairs to the trip.

It started as it always did. The old voice inside the apartment shouted, "Come in!" and she obeyed.

Is this never locked?

"In here, Bernie," came a voice from deeper in the apartment.

A small, old man sat in a reclining chair, in the living room. Ronald Benham's hair was nearly gone, except for wisps over his ears. His eyebrows were forests of white, gray, and black that had grown out of control, hairs curling back on themselves. The old man's face sported a day's growth of coarse white hair. He wore a button-down shirt that was clean, but no longer perfectly white, and brown pants. A small tube ran across his upper lip and over his ears, providing him with oxygen from a small cylinder next to the chair.

"Do you need more T3s?" he asked.

"No, thanks. I'm not here for painkillers. Although, I'm finding they aren't doing the trick like they used to. What's the next level up from there? I'm scared to ask."

"I don't know. I think there are T4s, but I'll have to get a different prescription for that. None of this stuff is over the counter. If you just went to the doctor yourself, you'd be able to get it, right? We wouldn't have to mess around with all this online prescription nonsense. What about the old good stuff? It's made a comeback."

"What are you talking about?"

"Grass. Mary Jane. My doctor said that it comes in forms that you don't have to smoke now. You can get it in oils and even candies. It's Hallowe'en for geezers."

Bernadette laughed and shook her head. She took a seat on the couch next to Ron's big chair.

He continued. "Seriously, it was just fun when we smoked it in the garden, but now they're calling it some kind of miracle drug for all kinds of things. Arthritis, headaches, pain. I was thinking of getting a prescription."

"For fun."

"Of course," he said, looking at her from the corner of his eye.

"You do love your candies," Bernadette said. "And, those were good days, sure. I'm just looking to take the edge off the pain. I'll think about it, though. It could be fun."

"Do you even know what's wrong?"

Bernadette leaned back into the cushions of the couch. As she stretched, a small fire awoke in her side.

"I do." She struggled to find words that wouldn't make it all sound so dramatic. "I just found out. A woman from church has a daughter who's an intern at Vancouver General. I was able to get some blood tests, privately." She turned herself to face Ron. "It's the c-word."

"Aw, sweet Joseph and Mary, Bernie. Why don't you bite the bullet and go to the doctor? You live a handful of blocks from Vancouver General, and they're one of the best research and treatment centers in the world."

Bernadette smiled and shook her head. "Ron, we've been friends long enough that you know what my answer to that is going to be. As the great Robert Frost once said, 'The best way out is always through.'"

"He wasn't referring to refusing medical treatment." Ron leaned forward to get up. "Can I make you a coffee?"

"No, it's alright, I can't stay long. I'm having dinner with Tess and the new young man, Henry, upstairs. But I can put water on for you."

"Would you, please?" Ron sunk back into his deep chair. "How is it that you come to have dinner with the new guy?"

"His cat got into the walls and showed up in my apartment. He has his niece staying with him and, oh Ron, this little girl, Frieda, she is just the funniest thing you've ever seen. She's so articulate and well-mannered, with an imagination like you wouldn't believe."

"Is that the plan, then? This is going to be a house full of artists when we die?" Ron began to cough, gently at first, and then with increasing violence.

Bernadette walked back into the living room and sat on the couch next to Ron's chair. She reached across the side table and rubbed his back until his coughing fit was done. His body shook as he struggled for a deep inhale.

Bernadette looked away. "There's something different about Henry, though." She pursed her lips. "He checks a lot of the right boxes, but he's not exactly what I expected. He comes across a bit high strung. Nosy, even."

In between short, scratchy breaths Ron said, "Don't go crazy second-guessing, Bernie. You've always made the right choices."

Bernadette put her hand on his and they sat just like that, in silence, until they were interrupted by the kettle. Bernadette returned to the kitchen. She had made coffee and dinner in Ron's apartment countless times over the years; she couldn't recall, but it must have been her that had organized his kitchen in the first place. He had just become a bachelor when they moved in decades ago. He was in his forties and she in her twenties. Fast friends, they looked out for each other, and looked after each other, when needed.

She handed him the coffee. "Milk, no sugar."

"Thank you. Now, will you tell me why you're here? It wasn't for drugs, and I'm pretty sure it wasn't for another of my lectures on doctors and hospitals."

Bernadette took a deep breath and began. "There was a man here today." She described Frieda's seeing the man in the hallway.

"The part that I don't like," she said, "is that she thinks he was peeping through the mail slot. He's not just someone knocking on the door of a business or a friend. Normal people don't do that."

Ron shrugged and blew on his coffee. "I guess they do, if they're curious."

"But curious about what? The only thing that's changed is

Henry moving in, Ron." She felt her eyes welling and tried not to blink. "Do you think he's brought this with him?"

Ron smiled. "Oh, Bernie. There's no point in getting worked up. It's just someone with poor manners. God knows the world is letting people get away with murder these days. Maybe someone wanting to ask about vacancies?"

"I doubt it. There's no sign or anything saying that's the company's address."

"That company has been good to us over all these years, Bernie. It's built a roof over our heads and put food on the table. The lawyers have everything sewn up so tight that no one will ever be able to undo it."

She kissed him on the cheek before she left. He was her oldest and dearest friend in the world. His advice had always been right in the past. She tried to imagine what her life would have been like if they hadn't met, and it was too crazy to contemplate.

Maybe it's just Henry's little cat, with its black-and-white suit, bringing back all these old fears.

1971: THE PASSENGER

The passenger looked around at the others seated in the terminal. In his dark suit and overcoat, there was nothing to suggest that he was different from any other man there; the uniform of the middle class trying to maintain its dignity as everything in the world fell apart. Or maybe they simply couldn't see what was happening.

There were fewer than forty people sitting in the hard-plastic chairs, waiting for the boarding call. A Boeing 727 should seat somewhere around a hundred and fifty. Thanksgiving used to be the most travelled time of the year. Now, lots of young men were in Vietnam. Some had crossed the border into Canada to get away from the draft. Those who stayed behind were getting laid off left, right and center; maybe they had gone north for Canadian jobs, too.

A young blond woman, perhaps in her early twenties, wearing a dark airline uniform and a pillbox hat spoke over the PA.

"Passengers for Northwest flight 305 from Portland to Seattle should now prepare for boarding."

He looked down at the copy of the Oregon Statesman in his

hand. A small box at the top of the front page gave the forecast. "Variable cloudiness with scattered showers. High near 50. Low tonight near 35."

Cold. It's going to be cold. I didn't need to pay a dime to learn that.

He lit a cigarette with the dying embers of the one before and breathed deeply. He also didn't need to be the first one on.

The rest of the headlines were just the same miserable news as the last year.

Colleges Told to Cut Program, May Have to Fire 70 Profs.

Dow Jones Drops Below 800 Mark.

Bloody Nixon, though. He was untouchable, wasn't he?

Defense Funds Approved: Nixon Wins Votes in Senate.

Congratulations. Build more planes. But you killed the SST here, didn't you? Between that and the poor sales of the Fat Albert, Boeing had put fifty thousand people out of work in twelve months. That was a good name for the 747 program alright. Fat. That was where they should've trimmed. Not like the 727. There'd never be a better airliner.

He tipped his tinted glasses up to look at the plane outside on the tarmac. They had wheeled the boarding stairs up to the door in front of the wing. Women held their coats over their hair as they walked through the drizzle, belts blowing behind them. Men wearing suits just like his own hunched their shoulders as close to the rims of their hats as possible. Two stewardesses with tiny, useless umbrellas stood at the bottom of the staircase and went through the motions of helping people over the first step.

His foot felt for his meagre luggage beneath his seat: a paper bag and a briefcase. In all the sixteen years he carried that leather case to and from work, it had never felt so heavy.

With a last deep puff, he stood and pressed the remainder of the cigarette into the gray sand of the ashtray. He knocked ashes off his tie with the corner of the newspaper before tossing it onto his seat.

It's all the past anyhow.

Yesterday's news.

If this all went well, everything would be different. Tomorrow, he'd wake up a new man.

CHAPTER TWELVE

Tess slugged back the first glass of water. She refilled, and took it with her into the bedroom, peeling off her sweaty clothes. She had made good time, as far as she could tell: forty blocks in nine songs. She wasn't going to win a marathon, but it was still a fine start to the day.

She transferred her music to a speaker. *Lovely Day* by Bill Withers filled the room, and she danced out of her bedroom as the chorus kicked in. Some mornings the song was different, but never the routine that followed. By seven-thirty, she was showered, fed, dressed and in her studio reading through the writer's comments from the day before.

She co-created the *Time Doctors* comic with Luba Mirova four years ago, after meeting at the San Diego ComicCon. They had been seated next to each other at a table, to sign autographs. They hit it off and, although they were rarely again in the same room together, each found this to be the smoothest working relationship they had ever had. Scripts, outlines, layouts, and dialogue were all exchanged digitally. When necessary, the two met via video chat as naturally as though they shared a desk.

Tess sipped her coffee, sitting cross-legged in her window overlooking Richardson Street, taking in Luba's notes. Their process was efficient, and she read with that wonderful relaxation that comes from being ahead of schedule.

She sat like this for an hour, before getting up to make another pot of coffee. She flipped open her laptop and reached out to Luba. The thin, blond woman's face, with her angular glasses and Slavic features came up on the screen.

"You've nailed it again," Tess said, by way of a greeting.

"I hope not. I've got a couple more changes." Luba had never lost her thick Russian accent. "I tried to reach you last night. Did you lose power or something?"

"I was out."

"Out?"

"Out."

"You don't go out."

"I go out."

"You go out for shopping, yes. But you don't go out like ordinary people when they say they go out."

"I'll have you know that I had dinner with friends."

Luba twirled her arms in feigned shock and pretended to fall out of her chair. "Good for you. I want details."

Tess saw her own face blushing in the small inset image of herself.

"It's not a big deal," she said. "It was my new neighbor." Tess ran Luba through the previous day: the knock on her door, the search for the missing cat, dinner, the "stolen" crosswords.

"I have to admit, as far as days go, it was a good change of pace. I think I needed that. Henry's got his quirks, but there's some depth there."

Luba passed judgement with the clinical love of a close friend. "He seems like a paranoid, but the little girl sounds funny. Maybe she is not normal. Still, it is nice to hear that you went out. And I am worried about these holes in your walls."

"You're killing me," Tess said, laughing. Her phone rattled on her light table, announcing a new text. She read the message aloud.

Dear Tess - I'm taking Hen for lunch across the street. Then we're going to Granville Island and maybe Stanley Park. Would you like to join us?

And then a follow-up text came in.

(I'm Frieda from downstairs)

"Yes," Luba said. "This girl is good people. You should go."

Tess looked at the phone. "No, it's okay. We're in the middle of working."

"No," said Luba, her hand shooing away the camera. "You go. We will finish tomorrow. I like hearing that you are going out." Luba blew a kiss at the screen and hung up.

Tess walked into her bedroom, phone in hand. She tapped on the screen with her fingernail. What made her so curious about Henry? Was it because he had shared a lot of personal details? She, on the other hand, had a history of canceling meetings with writers and publishing companies at conventions, simply because she couldn't muster the courage that day to share her portfolio.

It occurred to Tess that, even though she had lived across the street for four years, she had never been in the café. Comic books paid the rent, but they didn't afford a good deal more in Vancouver. Any money left over at the end of the month got rolled into her nest egg. Not that she would ever be able to own her own home in this city, but rents were skyrocketing everywhere, and someday she might have to move.

She looked again at Frieda's message.

Today, Tess decided, would be a rare, indulgent, exception.

She replied,

Love to! And I have a surprise for you...

Tess trotted back to her laptop and added a watermark to the new script, diagonally across the page.

Top Secret – VIP Only.

She sent it to her printer and grabbed the sheets on her way out the door.

Henry heard the doorbell and turned from feeding the cat. Frieda was already running at the sound. She opened the door.

"Tess!"

"Hiya. Thanks for the invitation."

Invitation? Fred!

"I told you I would bring you something," Tess said, and she pulled some rolled up papers from her back pocket.

"What is it?" Frieda asked. "Blue blistering barnacles! It's the next issue of *Time Doctors.*"

"It's actually the next-next-next issue. You just can't share it with anyone until it comes out, okay?"

Frieda bowed deeply. "I promise."

Henry joined the conversation, putting a cardigan on over his T-shirt. "I'm guessing that you heard we're going for lunch across the street. Is it decent?"

"Never been," Tess said, shrugging. "I have something for you, too." She handed him his newspaper, winking. "I'll bet we beat the thief to the crossword."

Henry tried to sound more relaxed than he'd been the night before. Hopefully, eschewing the suit and tie would help with appearances. "It's a good thing. Otherwise, I was going to have to get the police involved."

"You asked her about the crossword?" Frieda asked.

"Yesterday's. That makes three that have gone missing."

"See. I told you it wasn't Poppa."

They walked down the hallway. "Maybe we should have cameras installed?" Tess said.

Henry got in on the fun. "I bet it was that creepy dude from yesterday. Mister Creepy." He waved his hands and made a haunting sound.

"Not funny, Hen," Frieda said, her lip curled in a sweet little sneer.

Henry followed Tess down the row of booths to the very end. It crossed his mind to sit next to her, but he took the bench across instead, his back to the door. He shuffled over to make room for Frieda and watched the young girl slip in next to Tess.

In the brief hours that he'd had to plan Frieda's visit, this wasn't how he had pictured things. He'd imagined himself and Frieda bonding over some activity or outing.

Maybe this is better.

The trio spoke incessantly during the meal. Tess talked about drawing, Henry cautioned Frieda only once about drinking too much coffee, and Frieda brought out her notebook with a long list of the most random questions.

"Oh my god, you're a riot," Tess said through tears as she used her phone to search the Internet for 'dark and bitter'. She convulsed with laughter and couldn't explain what she'd found. So she just laid her phone on the table for them to read.

Frieda wrote into her notebook: *Dark, bitter, and too hot for you.*

Henry tried to straighten his face while he paid at the counter. The server's mouth opened and closed as though she wanted to ask about the group but thought better of it.

When he returned to the table, Frieda and Tess were huddled together on their side of the booth and staring at him with wide eyes.

"Don't turn around," Frieda said. She bent forward over the table and spoke in a whisper. "Mr. Creepy is behind you." Her eyes darted over Henry's shoulder, to the booths behind him. "It's him."

Henry made to turn and look, but Tess placed both palms flat on the table.

"Stay calm now," she said, her face still and serious. "He keeps writing something. He definitely has a pen. He's thinking. Yes—" The corners of her mouth started to twitch. "It's definitely a crossword."

Tess and Frieda snickered.

Henry's head spun. From where he stood, he could see that the man had spread things out all over his table. There was a laptop, and a thick, worn manila folder. A plate of food sat on the far side of the table from the man, untouched. The man sat bent in his seat, with a posture of exhaustion. His face and hands looked huge, disproportionate to the neck and arms they belonged to. In one large paw he held a pen, tapping lightly on the crossword laid out on the table before him.

Henry covered the distance in quick strides. He heard Tess's voice behind him, indistinguishable.

"You wouldn't have the rest of that paper, would you?" he asked the man sitting in the booth.

Without looking up, the large hands started scooping the miscellany from the table and stuffing it into a shoulder bag.

"I'm sorry," Henry said. "I've just been having a bit of trouble with my own paper delivery."

The man stood up, holding his stuffed bag wide open. He stood inches over Henry, looking down. Henry recalled the meatiness of the man's hands as the stranger met his eyes.

"Move," the man said. His wide mouth cracked only slightly, turning down at the corners.

"I'm just asking because you've been poking around the building across the street."

The man stepped forward and away from the booth with his full weight. Henry was saved from being knocked down only by a pull at his elbow, in the direction of the entrance. Tess's firm grip insisted he follow, with no room for negotiation. Frieda was already rushing out the front door.

As he hopped sideways along with Tess, he watched the giant of a man disappear into the restroom.

Outside, Frieda was red-faced and breathing heavily.

"What was that?" Tess asked.

"What?" Henry said. "I only asked if he had the rest of the paper." The oddness of his own actions started to sink in a little. "The café doesn't sell papers and that guy only had crosswords. Three." He made a W with his fingers, as though this provided some greater evidence of a crime.

"Not everyone's out to get you," Tess countered, her hand lowering his.

Henry looked at the two of them. Frieda watched the door of the café behind him. Her eyes were wide and alert, like a small herbivore at an African watering hole.

"You're right," he said. "I didn't mean to make a big deal there. I wasn't trying to cause a scene. I'm sorry."

Tess let go of his hand, and her face relaxed. Frieda remained wound like a spring.

"Hey," he said, putting his arm around Frieda's shoulders. "Let's get on with our day. We're never going to see that guy again anyhow."

"Your uncle's a kook," Tess added, her tone lighter than before.

He steered Frieda in the direction of the road and Granville

Island. Still, before turning the corner at the end of the block, he couldn't help taking one look back at the café.

Three crosswords.

Three.

CHAPTER THIRTEEN

The Cheshire man finished counting aloud to six hundred before unscrewing his fists from his eyes.

His hands still shook as he tried to blink away the bright spots. He had already been surveilling the house for a couple of days. He recognized the three people who left the café; it was the guy from downstairs, the girl from upstairs, and the girl's kid. Now they knew that he was watching.

It won't matter soon.

He was so close to getting what he'd come for. A calm came over him at the thought of going home.

He started cleaning himself up. He dried his hair and washed his armpits with paper towels. His shirt smelled, but it had to be better than the older one in the car, so he put it back on. He looked at himself in profile in the mirror and sucked in his stomach. He leaned in close, almost touching the mirror with his nose, and grinned as widely as he could.

He scraped his yellow teeth with his fingernail.

Oh, Mama. I'm doing it. I found Daddy and I'm bringing him home. They aren't looking for him anymore and we can be a family again.

He reached one more time into his backpack, and took out the pill bottle, full again with the small, familiar white pellets.

Cheap Canadian drugs. That's one good thing about being here. But we don't have to worry anymore. Daddy is going to take care of everything.

He shook two into his hand, tipped his head back and swallowed them down.

Back in the café, his breakfast still sat on the table, cold, waiting for him. Those people were gone, though.

The Cheshire man crossed the street and descended the steps to Unit 5. He knocked several times before he heard the voice inside.

"For Christ's sake, come in!"

He entered the suite slowly, wanting to savor every moment of what was to come.

CHAPTER FOURTEEN

Granville Island was a bustle of activity. Tourists flooded the market, with its random shops and artisans. People filled the sidewalks up and down Granville Street, beneath the bridge. Others came and went on water taxis across False Creek. Musicians played in every open-air space not reserved for parking. And, scattered throughout, industrial companies carried out the city's commitment to a "working river", loading and unloading barges of concrete and equipment.

From where Henry stood with Frieda and Tess, he could see the rotating barrels of the mixing trucks painted like corncobs, strawberries, and pea pods.

"Who paints these?" Frieda asked.

"Students from the art college," Tess said. "Each semester, a group of students will repaint everything. It's a huge endeavor."

"Did you go to school here?"

"I didn't go to art college," Tess said. "In fact, I have a business degree from UBC. I thought about becoming an accountant." She turned her eyes toward Henry. "But, in the end, playing with other people's money, trying to help the rich stay rich, wasn't for me. I took some private art lessons, but mostly I just drew. A lot. Then, I had to start showing my stuff and asking for work. That was the hardest part."

Frieda squinted as though exerting effort to digest this information.

"I like to think that I helped people do more than get rich and stay rich," Henry said. "When I was with the bank."

"Would you read some of my writing?" Frieda asked Tess. "I think you might be able to use some ideas for your books."

"I would love to," Tess said, smiling. She put her arm on the young girl's shoulder.

Henry replaced his thoughts of jobs and careers with the scene before him. In another universe, this might be his family. A wife, a daughter, a day at Granville Island. But it wasn't. It never would be. He had tried and failed. As sweet as the scene may appear, it was painfully different from how he had thought his life would turn out.

He looked at Frieda, in her T-shirt with a three-eyed gorilla and with her leather bag full of god-knows-what, and he simply loved her. This would have to be enough.

Tess said something, breaking the silence. Henry wondered whether she had sensed his increasing heaviness and was grateful to have been snapped back to the present.

"Hi," he said.

"Your phone is ringing," she repeated, pointing at his pocket.

"Oh." Henry looked at the caller ID. It was Sarah.

Ignore.

"Is everything okay?" Tess asked.

Henry realized he was scowling and exaggerated raising his eyebrows in order to iron the creases from his brow.

"Everything's cool." His phone buzzed to let him know there was a voicemail.

Henry waved the annoying device and shrugged his shoulders in apology. "Let me just listen to this." He turned his back and walked several steps away.

The connection was weak, the message scratchy, the voice too familiar.

"Henry. It's Sarah. We are . . . sooner than expected. Stewart . . . with the bank. So we . . . pick up Frieda, or you can drop her off. I'd like . . . you don't have to run into . . . I'll call . . . back around five-ish."

Henry wished he carried his earphones. The phone was hot against his cheek and his palms were moist.

Wiping his hands on his pants, he turned back to Frieda and Tess. Frieda was crouched down, trying to coax a seagull from under a picnic bench to her empty hand.

"You're good to stay with me all week?" he asked her.

Without taking her eyes off the bird, she gave him a thumbs up.

He typed several replies before settling on the wording.

We're having a great time. Fred's with me all week. Sorry to hear your holiday was cut short.

Perfect. Send.

Frieda had found a bun from god-knows-where and was tearing off pieces to throw at the seagull.

"That was your aunt. Where's Tess?" he asked.

Sarah and Stewart are getting back at five. Henry looked at his phone. It was three-thirty.

"She went to the washroom. Do you like her?"

"Sarah?"

"Tess." Frieda looked confused.

"Tess? Yeah, she's great."

"No. I mean do you 'like her' like her?"

"You are charming." He gave her a soft punch in the arm. "She's nice, but I don't really 'know her' know her enough to 'like her' like her. Do you follow?" Henry had already wondered whether he liked Tess after saying goodnight yesterday.

If timing is everything, I've got nothing.

"Well, I think you like each other. She likes art. You like art. She studied business. You're a business guy. Both of you are sort of not-grown-up and like to have fun. Except for just now, I think she brings out the old Hen."

"She seems fun. I just need to sort some things out, though. Life doesn't move that quickly."

"Maybe you're just not doing life right."

Before Henry could recover from the sucker-punch of thirteen-year-old Zen wisdom, Tess was back.

"Shall we keep going?" she said.

"I hate to cut things short," Henry said, "but we need to get back. I forgot there was something I was supposed to do. It won't take me long."

Frieda made a disgusting choking sound. "Right now?"

Henry's shoulders slumped. "I'm really sorry. I have to get somewhere before it closes."

"Well, can't Tess and I stay here?"

Henry looked at Tess. A smile broke out on the young woman's face and she brushed her short bangs with her fingers.

"That would be grand," she said.

Henry brushed aside thoughts of what Rachel might say and slipped Frieda some cash. They agreed to meet back at the house, and he started up the hill.

He had an hour and a half. It would take him nearly a half hour to walk back to the house. Frieda's cloak hung next to the door when they left.

He should just make it.

Tess held the sharp, steel scissors against her chest and surveyed the scene in her living-room. Her light table and supplies were covered with a sheet, and young Frieda sat perched atop Tess's yellow barstool, with a towel across her shoulders.

"To catch the blood," Tess had explained, snipping scissors in the air for emphasis. Brown and blue hair peppered the floor, the towel and the sheets.

"Can I see it?"

"Almost."

"What do you think of Henry?" The lack of segue suggested the young girl had been hanging onto the question for some time.

"We only just met. Why do you ask?"

"Well, my dad says that Hen will never find work in this town again. So I was thinking that, maybe, if he was dating somebody he might not move away. Maybe."

"I think what your dad said is just an expression."

"Maybe. But wouldn't it be better if he stayed? He's not always so serious, and he's into a lot of games and music and stuff."

Tess stifled a laugh at the young hard sell. "I'm sure I'll get to know him better. First impressions are nutty, eh? I mean, he thinks someone is stealing his crosswords."

She fluffed Frieda's bangs with her fingers and stepped back to survey her work.

"Are you ready to see it?" she asked.

"Yes. Yes. Yes."

Tess took the towel off the girl's shoulders and followed her into the bathroom. Frieda let out a sharp scream of excitement. They both spoke at once.

"It's awesome."

"You look brilliant."

"Thank you so much."

"Your mom's going to love it."

"I look like you," Frieda said.

"A little, yeah."

Like a page from *Time Doctors*, Tess saw a younger version of herself looking back from the mirror.

A knock on the door interrupted the small party, crammed into the tiny bathroom.

"Come in!" Tess called out. Then, to Frieda, "Back on the stool. I see some bits we've got to clean up."

As they walked back to the front window, Henry entered the studio-cum-salon and said, "Look who I found."

He stopped short and blinked several times.

"I've been cutting my own hair for years," Tess said.

"Well, you've done a fine job," Bernadette said behind Henry. She carried Shima in her arms; the cat purred and cooed when he saw Frieda.

"I heard a scream, even with my poor hearing, so I came out to see what was going on. I saw Henry at your door and thought I would make it a complete set. This little monster here must have jumped two feet straight up at the noise."

Henry looked lost, like it was his first day on earth. "It's a big change, but it suits you."

"I texted my parental units and got an okay from Tomas," Frieda said, referring to her father by name. "He hated the blue anyhow."

"We got you something." She ran past him to the door next to which lay her satchel and a brown paper bag. She retrieved the latter and handed it to him.

"For me?" Henry turned it over to read the stamp from Zulu records on one side of the flat package, before sliding out an LP. *Blackstar*? "Are you kidding me?"

Tess could tell from the look on his face they'd made the right choice. A quick search online had revealed that David Bowie's last album, released only days before his death in 2016, was considered a seminal work in his catalog.

"Do you like it?" Frieda asked.

"It's perfect. Thank you." he gave her a peck on the top of her head, and she hopped back up onto the stool.

Shima hopped down to the floor and rolled around on his back in the cut hair, his white belly and chin straight up. Henry set the record on the kitchen table, scooped up the little cat and brushed him off onto the sheet.

As she snipped at straggling hairs, Tess watched Henry wander into her living room, scratching his curiosity itch and petting the cat draped over one arm. He lingered at Tess's bookshelf, and he paused appreciatively in front of one of her paintings before drifting to a hanging scroll bearing two large Japanese characters in scripted black ink.

"Honma," she said.

"Your dad's family crest?"

"Not a crest. Just the name. And it's my mum's family."

He turned to face her, a question etched on his face.

Tess had seen this look her entire life. People wrestling with questions that touched on ethnicity, family. Words become loaded with uncertainty, like delicately placing weight on a newly frozen lake. Wanting to know, not wanting to offend. Despite best intentions, most people left to their own devices cracked the ice beneath their feet.

"I just assumed..."

"Most people do. How was your errand?" she asked.

"My what? Oh, good. Perfect."

"Were you filing a police report?" Tess asked, laughing. Frieda snickered, too, in on the tease.

"I don't get the joke," Bernadette said.

"Henry has turned into Eliot Ness," Tess replied. "Let him tell you about his criminal conspiracy."

Frieda snorted.

Henry came to stand next to Bernadette in the kitchen. "Do you do crosswords?" he asked, in a suspicious tone.

Tears formed at the corners of Tess's eyes. She and Frieda contributed their own color commentary as Henry told Bernadette about his missing papers.

"Maybe the house is haunted," Tess said.

Frieda smiled. "Shima's figured out how to hold a pen."

Henry's tone bore a hint of defensiveness, although he tried to laugh along. "Whatever. It's a real person, though. Someone's taking them."

Tess patted him on his shoulder, in sympathy.

"A thief?" Bernadette asked. She looked over at Tess, who shrugged.

"It has to be," Henry said.

"I don't do crosswords, I'm afraid. Do we even have a paperboy anymore? And aren't there far more valuable things?"

Frieda climbed off the stool. "I agree with Hen that it's Mr. Creepy from the other day." She doubled over and shook the remaining loose hair onto the sheet.

"Well, someone's messing with me." He ran a hand through his hair.

"It's going to be an odd list of suspects, eh?" Tess said, folding the sheets carefully. "I'm sure you aren't going to break the case tonight. So, would anyone like a gin and tonic? I was also thinking of ordering pizza. And..." She added dramatic emphasis. "I have a record player."

"That would be lovely," Bernadette said. "I'll get started. Fresh limes?"

Tess nodded. "In the fridge."

"We should get Shima fed," Henry said, picking the record up with his free hand and pointing at the door with his chin.

"It's alright, Hen," Frieda said. "I'll take care of Shima. I have to send off an assignment anyhow, and I can have leftovers. You stay up here as long as you want."

"It's settled," Tess said, clapping her hands together. "Adults night upstairs."

Frieda gave Tess one more great hug, threw the old cat unceremoniously over her own shoulder, and headed out the door.

Tess espied the unsubtle wink that the young girl threw at her uncle on her way out the door. She also caught his blush in reply.

CHAPTER FIFTEEN

Frieda had no school assignments to submit.

Why don't adults just stay happy? Hen goes from super-happy to super-sad in a nanosecond. But he's like old Hen when he's with Tess.

As she pondered the fickleness of the age-impaired, Shima wove himself between her feet and trilled his own contentment.

"That's right," she said to the old cat. "Yes. Turkey? Okay. No, it's just you and me tonight."

The plan was to spend this evening writing. A story circled around in her head: an ordinary girl who draws comic books and helps real superheroes solve crimes. Already, she was practicing her powers of observation. For one, she'd noticed that Henry had finally put away his cardboard box of office stuff.

As she placed Shima's dish on the floor beneath the kitchen window, she glanced out. Someone was walking away from the house. The figure turned to look inside their shoulder bag, their profile recognizable.

She dropped to the kitchen floor, out of sight from the window.

"Why is Mr. Creepy back?" she said aloud.

He must have come from the stairs leading into the old man's apartment in the basement. She lifted her head to peek out. He was still close enough for her to see he was covered in sweat.

Hen was right. He is the crossword thief.

Frieda hesitated for an instant. She could prove it. But it was going to be dark soon.

She vaulted to her feet, sending Shima scurrying into the bedroom (and into the walls and upstairs again). She grabbed her satchel and felt it for keys. The lock-picks in her cloak clinked as she threw it over her shoulders and raced for the door.

Frieda leapt down the steps of the building and sprinted to the sidewalk where she looked in all directions. She spotted Mr. Creepy next to the café. He dragged his feet as he walked, moving away from the apartment building. Frieda checked the pin on her cloak, pulled her hood low over her eyes and ran to the corner.

She watched from a crouch as the figure continued to the end of the block. There, he turned left and out of sight. She dashed to the corner, as close to the buildings as she could, and came to a dead stop at the end. She peered with one eye around the building, spotting him stepping off the sidewalk and getting into a dirty, off-white car.

Frieda didn't know the makes of cars, but this one looked like the sort that children draw. What she could see was that the license plate was unusual. An extra number. A different color.

Then, it struck her.

He's leaving.

She could stay where she was and take down the license plate as he drove past.

Or...

She stood up and looked around. What was she going to do? Steal a car? She was only thirteen. She made two mental notes:

1) learn to drive

2) learn to hot-wire a car

Frieda turned and ran back toward Henry's building as fast as she could. She rounded the corner at a full sprint, cutting across the road, having barely glanced ahead for traffic. Her hood fell back off her head and her cloak fluttered its encouragement behind her.

Go. Go. Go.

The hospital was only a block from Henry's apartment. There would have to be cabs there. It was also the way to get to the big roads, Granville and Broadway.

For sure, he'll have to pass by.

Frieda ran into the parking lot of Vancouver General Hospital toward a line of waiting cabs. She aimed herself at the lead taxi. The driver stood outside his door, facing the hospital, talking on his phone. She brushed past him, opened a door and climbed in the back seat without a word. She just looked at the cab driver through the open window, breathing heavily, until she saw the dirty square car pass them. She shouted, "Get in! Get in!"

Snapping out of his initial surprise, the driver climbed in and started the engine. He got out a pad and pen.

"Where are we headed this evening?"

He raised his eyebrows out of curiosity and amusement as he smiled at her in the rear-view mirror.

"We need to follow that car."

She had been as right as she had been swift. Mr. Creepy's car was rolling towards the hospital.

He paused. "I need an address."

"The address of wherever that car is going is the address that we are going to."

"You're serious?" His large eyebrows were still curious, but less amused.

"Deadly."

Frieda looked in her satchel and counted. With the money her parents had given her, and the money Henry had paid for cat-sitting, the money from today, less her coffee, less Henry's record, she had . . .

Oh, math, I hate you.

"I have sixty-eight dollars. That means that we can drive for . . . thirty-four dollars before you have to bring me back here. Go! Follow!" She jabbed and pointed in the direction Mr. Creepy had driven.

The driver pulled out from the parking lot, turned left and soon pulled up right behind the square car as the light turned green. The two cars left together.

"He can't realize that we're following him."

"Oh, of course," the driver said. "Otherwise, what would be the fun?"

Frieda thought about hiding under her hood but decided that she would be less recognizable with her new haircut. Then, she realized why the license plates were unusual.

The car was from Washington State.

I hope I have enough money for this.

CHAPTER SIXTEEN

A s her cab crossed the bridge into downtown Vancouver, Frieda made a mental note. They were passing over Granville Island, where she had spent much of the day with Tess.

Worst-case scenario, if I can get to Granville Street, I can make it back on foot.

She checked her phone and saw that she had seventy percent battery left. Frieda had never been downtown alone. False Creek separated downtown from much of the lower mainland. She lived in Kitsilano, a more rural neighborhood of Vancouver, with none of the tall buildings of downtown, and just a short bus ride from Henry's.

In fact, Frieda had only been downtown for shopping with Sarah, field trips to the art gallery and Science World, Whitecaps soccer games with her dad, and the one time that Henry had taken her to the big comic convention.

From the bridge, Frieda could already see the dome of BC Place Stadium getting larger as they crossed the Fraser River into downtown.

Granville Street looked so different on this side of the bridge. In Henry's neighborhood, Granville was mostly fancy clothing stores, art galleries, cafés and a theatre. These blocks had theatres, too, but it was a different crowd, a louder crowd. Even in the early evening like this, through the windows of the cab, she could hear shouts, laughter, music from bars and pubs, and buskers strewn here and there.

Her mum always said that you should remember the number of the taxi you ride in, in case you realize that you've left something. So she looked over the seat into the front and asked, "What cab number is this?"

"This is two hundred and fifty."

Her comment must have invited conversation.

"Who is it we're following?" the driver asked.

This seemed like one of those times where it was alright to lie, like when you're home alone and someone calls asking for your mum or dad. In that case, you were allowed to say that your parents were home, but unavailable.

"It's one of my dad's friends. I just need to see where that car is going. Do you know what kind of car that is?"

"That is some kind of Chrysler. A K-car, I think. Very popular car back in the day."

The car in front turned off Granville and the cab driver put his signal on to follow. "You're doing a great job," Frieda said. "What's your name?"

"My name is Naim. What is your name?" he asked, looking into the mirror to see over his shoulder.

"My name is Fred."

That's the best alias I can come up with?

"I'm named after my dad."

Gah!

Naim raised one curious eyebrow. "And may I ask why Fred is following Mr. K-car?"

Frieda stammered. Paused. Stammered again. What was she going to say? This weird guy keeps stealing my uncle's newspapers and I have to prove it so that he can find love and happiness? Pretty sure that would make her the creepy one.

She thought too long and her moment to convincingly lie passed.

"I don't want to say," she confessed. "I just need to see where he is going and then I can go back."

"Okay. Should I wait for you?"

She scanned the street as they turned right onto West Hastings. "I'm not sure yet. Can I decide when we get there?"

Frieda looked at the meter. It rolled over to twenty-one dollars. This was getting to be an expensive adventure. It had seemed like a good idea, but she was beginning to question her judgment.

West Hastings turned into East Hastings. The people on the sidewalk hustling in suits and jogging in clean, tight clothing turned into people sitting on the cement curbs, standing around shopping carts, or lying down. Outside of the dilapidated Lampert hotel, a dozen people leaned against the building.

Frieda's chest clenched as the K-car turned right and then left, backing into an alley. The cab slowed, rolled past, and pulled over.

"He's parked in there." Naim motioned with his thumb to the alley.

"If I pay you more, will you stay for a few minutes?"

"You don't need to pay me any more than the meter. I'll stick around." Looking through the back window at where they were, he asked, "Are you sure that you need to get out?"

Frieda closed her eyes and checked in with herself. She wasn't afraid. She felt sad for the people on the street, but not threatened. Her hand came up, and she rubbed the brass brooch that held her cloak. "I'll be fine," she said, handing Naim some cash. She got out, being sure to look back at the seat in case she'd left anything.

"Please stay. I won't be long," she said, pulling up her hood.

Naim gave her a comforting nod.

Mr. Creepy had already exited the alley and was heading back down to East Hastings. Frieda stayed on her side of the street and kept pace with him. He turned the corner. Watching for traffic, she bolted across the street. Frieda peered with one eye around the side of the building onto East Hastings and saw him disappear into a shop two doors down. She stepped around the corner for a better perspective. A bright green sign above the door read *Welcome Pharmacy*.

A small voice said, "Could you spare any change?"

Next to Frieda, sitting in front of a shop with barred windows, a young woman looked up at her, holding a paper coffee cup. A tall and dirty blue backpack rested against the building. Frieda thought the woman looked young, and fit, and as ordinary as herself. Only the tired expression and sun-hardened skin were different.

A sign in the window read *We Buy Gold* in large red-on-yellow letters.

This seems like the last neighborhood where people would be carrying gold.

She dug into her pocket and dropped her coins into the coffee-less cup.

The young woman whispered, "*Merci*," her eyes unwavering from Frieda.

Something about the blue backpack nagged at Frieda's mind.

Mr. Creepy was carrying a bag when he left the house.

She pictured him walking out of the alley in her mind and realized that he didn't have it with him right now. She turned with a flourish of her cloak and ran back up the hill to the alley. She had never picked the lock of a car before, but she thought she might be able to. She caught Naim watching her as she ducked into the alley and gave him one index finger in the air.

One minute.

I hope.

Her excitement deflated when she saw that the driver's side door of the car was unlocked. No lock-picking was required.

She crossed to the far side of the car and looked again in either direction for any other people in the alley.

Frieda opened the door, careful not to hit the neighboring brick building. The shoulder bag lay on the front seat. Her mind was dizzy with adrenalin. She dove in and began unzipping.

The bag was a mess of paper, like she imagined the contents of a boy's school locker. Feeling inside, she recognized a laptop, a flashlight, a picture frame, and pens. She stirred through the paper and saw a page from a newspaper: a crossword. This she stuffed into her own satchel and rummaged through the bag for more pages. She found only photos, and a folder with neat, tidy sheets.

Frieda opened the folder and Henry's name jumped out from a list of names on the first page.

The air changed instantly around her, like the first smell of ozone from a coming storm. Her stomach cramped and she needed to pee.

Frieda grabbed the sheet with the names and a handful more loose pages from the folder. She lost moments separating a twenty-dollar bill and putting it back. As quickly as she could, she zipped the pack up, backed out of the car, and closed the door.

A figure on foot turned into the alley an instant after the dome light of the car flickered off. Frieda ducked below the driver's side window, her eyes straining to adjust to the darkness and see through the windows. The shadow walked to the vehicle.

She slid low to the ground and flattened herself up against

the door. Deep, measured breaths didn't slow the pounding of blood in her arms and legs.

The sounds of the passenger door unlocking and opening were followed by the sudden brightness of the dome light. The rustling in the car lasted only a few seconds and the light and door were closed again. Footsteps crunched on the bits of gravel that had somehow found their way onto the paved alley street. Frieda shifted her weight onto her left foot, preparing to launch herself into a sprint to the waiting cab.

With her back to the car, her head swung left and right as her eyes readjusted to the darkness.

She held her breath and wondered if she could make it to a count of sixty.

At four, the footsteps started anew. Over the trunk, she caught the first glimpse of the massive man circling around to the driver's side.

Could she outrun him? If he was fat, maybe. But he was big, so maybe not.

Frieda sprung to her feet and grabbed the driver's door handle, pulling it open as hard as she could. The metal door scraped against the brick building and stuck fast. Light spilled out of the car, between her and Mr. Creepy, before she twirled away to the alley's exit.

She heard the man shouting behind her and ran as fast as she could to the cab, getting in on the street side.

"Start the car!"

Naim was pulling away before she had fully closed the door behind her. Frieda hammered it locked with her fist and looked back for the first time. No one followed. But the startled look on Mr. Creepy's face when their eyes met was burned into her mind.

Naim appeared relieved to see her again. "Are we ready for home?"

"Yes, please, Naim," she said between breaths. "Thank you for waiting."

Feelings of success tempered her adrenalin. By the time she got back, she would only have been gone forty-five minutes.

And under budget.

Still, her hands shook as she flattened the page with the names onto the seat next to her. It was a handwritten list of the apartments in Henry's building. Two were circled. *Unit 2 – 121702 BC Ltd.* and *Unit 5 – Ronald Benham.*

Naim made small talk on the way back to Richardson Street, but Frieda's mind was too distracted to engage with anything other than a dull yes or no, and to provide the address to the café across from Henry's.

She watched Naim drive away before crossing the street to the apartment building. The roads were empty, but sirens shrieked in the distance. Shima greeted Frieda inside Henry's suite, flopping down in front of her for strokes along his chest.

She flipped back her hood, her wool cloak falling to the floor in a heap behind. Her hand shot to her shoulder.

Where's my brooch?

Oh, God, please let it be in Naim's cab.

CHAPTER SEVENTEEN

Henry heard the sirens before the others. The first one hadn't given him pause. The house was only blocks from Vancouver General and the sound of ambulances was a common background noise. He noticed that these were much louder, though, and there were several.

"Hang on a sec," he said to Bernadette and Tess, before rising from the couch and walking to the window.

A fire engine and an ambulance were parked in front of the house. There was no activity on the small lawn between the building and the sidewalk, but the lone fireman standing next to his engine was looking in Henry's direction.

"They're here."

"What do you mean?" Tess asked.

"I think they've gone downstairs."

Bernadette stood up, kicking over a glass tumbler of ice. "Ron!" She rushed out the door and down the stairs.

Henry and Tess followed. Henry stopped to look in on Frieda who, apparently, could sleep through anything. He closed the bedroom door behind him before catching up with the others.

Outside, the front yard was a muted chaos. Red and white

lights strobed against the front of the house and into the looming branches of the old chestnut tree. The loud, low rumble from the idling fire engine seemed to absorb as much sound as it produced. Activity centered on Ron's suite, half below ground and hidden from the street by a holly bush.

Henry stopped at the top of the steps and peered down through the open front door.

Paramedics lifted an old man wearing an oxygen mask onto a gurney. Bernadette was already next to the patient, holding one of his thin hands.

Two firemen in bulky jackets and pants emerged from the basement suite and guided Henry and Tess out of the way as the paramedics maneuvered the gurney to the door. One held a clear plastic bag aloft and spoke to Ron, asking questions. As the group crossed the lawn, the idle responder on the sidewalk was spurred to action. He hustled to the back of the ambulance and opened the door.

Bernadette collapsed into Tess as the procession with Ron passed them. "Someone attacked Ron," she said between shallow, quick breaths. Her face was red and wet with tears, her eyes wild with panic. "I have to go with him." She rolled out of Tess's arms and started after Ron and the paramedics.

Stunned, Henry turned to the nearest firefighter. "Are you taking him to VGH?" He pointed at Bernadette. "Can she ride in the ambulance? She doesn't have a car and neither do I."

"Are you family?"

"I'm a neighbor. We're all neighbors. I don't know if he has family."

"Yeah." The firefighter was far too calm for Henry's liking. "Well, I can't imagine why they wouldn't go to Vancouver General. He needs immediate attention. He's dehydrated and he may have suffered a series of strokes. Jesse!" The firefighter shouted over Henry's shoulder and motioned towards Bernadette. "Okay if she rides along?"

"S'fine!" yelled back the paramedic at the foot of the gurney who was already speaking to Bernadette.

Henry peered into the apartment but could see little from the doorway.

The firefighter interrupted his curiosity. "Did one of you call 911?"

Henry blinked and shook his head. "No. We were all upstairs. All except Mr. Benham."

He looked over his shoulder at the ambulance. Tess and Bernadette were there. More sirens grew close.

"Well, someone called."

"It wasn't Mr. Benham?"

With a sympathetic wince, the firefighter said, "I don't think that he could have placed the call."

Henry ran over to Tess, standing next to the ambulance. Before he could get a word out, Bernadette asked, "Can you stay here, in case we need something?"

"Of course," Tess said. "Call me for anything."

Bernadette nodded, sobbing, and pulled herself the rest of the way into the ambulance.

Henry and Tess stood with arms touching as the ambulance pulled away, revealing two police cruisers.

A voice from behind. "What happened?"

Henry turned to see Frieda at the front door of the house, barefooted in her cloak. He walked up the steps to her, shaking his head.

"It's Mr. Benham."

"Was he attacked?"

Frieda's face paled, and Henry chastised himself for scaring her. "No. Nothing like that. Maybe he had a heart attack or stroke. It could have been an accident."

"Where did Bernadette go?" Frieda asked.

"The hospital with Mr. Benham," Henry said. "I think they're like family."

A police cruiser had arrived, and Tess was speaking with one of the uniformed officers. A fireman led the other officer into the basement below.

As Tess was gesturing upwards towards her own suite, Henry caught her eye. He motioned at Frieda and pointed inside the building. She gave a thumbs up.

"Come on," Henry said, steering the young girl into the house by her shoulders. "Bernadette and Tess are going to keep us updated on Mr. Benham. The best thing we can do is get back to bed. We'll find out more in the morning."

"Do the police want to talk to us?"

"No, Fred. We don't know anything."

CHAPTER EIGHTEEN

Tess was sitting with one of the police officers at the bottom of the steps when Henry came back outside. It was hard to see stars past the bright streetlight, but the cool air suggested it was a cloudless night.

The two of them could have been sisters. Tess was the relaxed, artsy one who cut her hair short. Constable Tipton, as she introduced herself, was the serious one, with her red hair pulled back in a stern ponytail that could only have been braided by someone obsessed with perfection. Otherwise, they sounded and looked alike. Both sat with perfect upright posture, Tipton's aided in part by whatever bulky vest she wore beneath her uniform.

"Have we heard if he's going to be okay?"

"Bernadette texted to say they are running tests, whatever that means. They need to figure out what it was. He may have had multiple heart attacks."

Henry looked back and forth between the two women. "So, why are the police still here?"

"My partner is downstairs right now," Tipton said. "We are following up on the call to 911."

"From whom?"

"Exactly. We don't know, but Tess was telling me that you were all upstairs this evening, is that right?"

"Yeah. I mean, Frieda was downstairs, but she wouldn't know anything. She's just a kid."

"The call came from a payphone downtown. This much we can tell. And you were out all afternoon as well? Tess tells me she and your niece got back around five."

"I wasn't much later than that," Henry said.

Tess squinted hard at Henry.

The Constable must not have noticed Henry squirming under Tess's inspection, as she rose from the steps.

"Well, I should head to the hospital and catch up with your friend. Bernadette, is it? I'll let you folks try to get some sleep."

"Could you please give this to her?" Tess asked, handing over a reusable shopping bag with clothes poking out. "They're his toiletries and a change of clothes."

She shook their hands in turn and gave them cards.

"No problem. If you think of anything, just call me."

Tess was the first to speak as Tipton disappeared out of earshot into the basement.

"You came home."

Henry looked back at the stare again.

"What do you mean?"

"Your 'errand'. What was it? You came home."

"How do you know I came home? I had to take care of something personal."

"All suddenly like that? Your bike was gone when we got back. It wasn't locked up next to the stairs, so you must have come back for it after you left us at Granville Island."

"Okay, so I took my bike. I don't have a car. What of it?"

"What of it? You just told a police officer that you were not here."

Henry shook his head. "I just don't want to have to explain where I was. It's private."

"Tell me."

"It's private."

Long, silent seconds passed as they looked at each other.

"Tess, please. It has to do with my work, why I got fired. I just don't need more people digging in that. And I don't want to put you in an awkward position."

"Would I approve?"

"What?"

"Would I approve?"

"What kind of question is that?"

"You're asking me to trust you. You say that it's better for me if I don't know. I'm asking whether—based on what you know about me—I would approve or disapprove of whatever you were up to today."

Henry looked Tess in the eyes, and said, "You'd approve."

"I'd better, Henry. I'm a good judge of character and I'll take a chance on you. But tell me or not, I didn't say anything to that police officer. So I'm a part of your story now, too."

CHAPTER NINETEEN

Ordinarily, Bernadette Pruner enjoyed mornings the most. There was a slowness to them that suited her. She could hear the house waking up. Tess's alarm went off at six on weekdays. The song changed frequently, and Tess had an eclectic musical taste which belied her age, all of which suited Bernadette just fine. Henry sang in the shower and talked to his cat. She couldn't understand what he was saying, but some mornings it was a heated debate.

Even though she couldn't hear Ron's suite at the best of times, there was still a palpable silence in the house this morning after last night's activities.

She looked at the clock in her kitchen as she filled a mug with coffee. There would be shift change in the Intensive Care Unit at nine, and they had explained that Ron would be having some tests after that. There was no visiting until noon.

She used to take the entire pot of coffee out to the garden in the back of the house. Since the pain had started in the early spring, it was enough to manage just a mug and the stairs.

Three Adirondack-style chairs waited faithfully for her company, rain or shine. Weather-worn and missing paint, they hadn't moved since she and Ron built them years ago. This morning, she sat in hers and surveyed the yard. The last of the fall vegetables were coming in, and the first windfall apples gathered beneath the gnarly old tree next to the fence in the back of the property.

She looked up at 1584 Richardson through the steam rising from her mug as she sipped. This old house had long ago become as much a friend as a home. In the window, little Frieda was looking down at her. They smiled and waved at each other, and Bernadette motioned for her to come outside. The young girl dropped out of sight, only to reappear around the corner seconds later, wearing a white martial arts outfit, with a green belt.

"Good morning, Frieda. Do you have a karate class this morning?"

"I used to take judo, but I stopped," Frieda answered, as though that was a complete explanation for her fashion choice. "Did you grow all of this?"

"Yes, I did. Well, I had some help. Ron helped me build the raised beds years ago, and they were getting old. So last year Tess and I replaced them. It was quite a bit of work taking them apart, moving all the dirt, and building new ones."

"Is Mr. Benham going to be okay?"

Bernadette admired the plain-speak of children. "It's a lot for someone his age, so he's going to stay in the hospital for a bit and he may need a procedure. But I'm sure he'll be fine."

"Are you going to visit him?"

"I'm going before lunch."

"Can I come?"

Bernadette looked closely at Frieda. The young girl appeared sincere and concerned. "Of course you can. If Henry brings you. Did you meet Mr. Benham?"

"No, but I saw all the ambulances and firetrucks and police last night, and I just want him to be okay."

"Well, I'm sure he'd love visitors if he's feeling up to it."

Frieda seemed happy with this response, and she wandered closer to the garden.

Bernadette watched the young girl inspecting the prehistoric-looking thick leaves and stalks of kale and Brussels sprouts. Still, it was clear Frieda's mind was elsewhere.

"I learned how to lash poles together when I was your age. I was a campfire girl."

"I'm a Scout," Frieda said, without looking back. "Is that kind of the same?"

"I'll bet it's close. I'm sure we had Scouts. Are you a gardener?"

"No. We live near a park, but my parents don't have a garden. Our backyard is just a stone patio for barbeques." Frieda hopped on one foot on the flat step stones that carved a path between the beds. "Can I water for you?"

Bernadette shook her head. The days had been drizzly recently. Watering took care of itself in the fall. She motioned towards the apple tree. "You can give me a hand collecting those apples before the birds and racoons get them."

Frieda rolled up her thick, reinforced cotton sleeves and punched her right fist into her left palm. "Let's do it."

Bernadette found a pair of empty steel buckets and they began picking the crisp-looking bounty from the ground.

"Are they bad?" Frieda asked, inspecting a rosy apple for blemishes.

"No. Pink ladies ripen late. These may even be a bit early. Watch for holes, though."

"Don't you want the ones in the tree?" Frieda asked, eyeing the trunk and branches for climbing.

"They'll fall when they're ready. But if you see any really pink ones and you think you can reach them without killing yourself, you go ahead and knock them down."

Frieda shot up the tree and weaved through the tangle of

unmanicured branches, inspecting and tossing the occasional apple to the ground.

"There are tons," she said. "Are you going to make pies?"

"Cider," she said. Last year's batch had been her best yet, but it never lasted long. "If you want to make a pie for Thanksgiving, we can send you home with a bucket."

A fall chill blew through the yard, and Bernadette shivered, feeling jolted back to reality. She returned to her chair, watching Frieda climb and the odd apple plunk onto the lawn. How could this be such a perfect morning, while Ron lay in some hospital bed? A wave of guilt passed through her. Bernadette looked back again at the house.

It would break my heart to have to leave.

This time, Henry was in the window, and he raised his coffee mug in a toast.

When she was done, Frieda carried over two buckets of apples and took the second Adirondack, wiping her brow with exaggerated exhaustion.

"I built these, too," Bernadette said, tapping the arms of her chair.

"Wow," Frieda said, looking at the rest beneath her left arm. "You're really handy. How did you learn to do all of this?"

"When you don't grow up with much, you have to learn to do things yourself."

"You just figured this out?"

"This was one of those things that Ron taught me."

"Did you grow up together?"

"Oh, no," Bernadette said, pausing. "I met Ron just around the time that I moved here."

"Where did you move from?"

"I grew up in Portland."

"*Cool.*"

Bernadette shook her head and smiled. "Back then, it wasn't the hipster mecca you see on TV now. Portland was rough around the edges with rusty industrial trains and lots of people just trying to make ends meet. My mother was a hard worker. She held down two jobs just to raise my sister and me."

"Were your parents divorced?" Frieda winced at her own question.

"No. My dad was in the military, but he died in an automobile accident on the base when I was only three. That's when we moved to the city and started over."

Her Canadian life was similar, Bernadette thought. She had reinvented herself here, too.

The difference is that now I've learned to want for very little.

She loved this house, and Ron was right. She had chosen well.

"I totally want to see Portland," Frieda said. "It's on my list. You've probably been tons of places."

"Honestly? Growing up, I never looked very far ahead. I wasn't even aware there was a Vancouver outside Washington State. Now, I couldn't imagine living anywhere else.

"Ron and I drove to Calgary once, to go to the Stampede. The rodeo itself was fine. But it was the driving through the mountains and carrying on to the badlands that was magnificent."

"I want to see Drumheller, too."

"You'd love it. The landscape is like another world. And there are so many fossils."

Frieda's head bobbed in agreement. "Do you guys still go on holiday together?"

Bernadette looked at her hands. Her knuckles had begun swelling in the last year, and they creaked a little when she flexed her fingers.

"No, Ron's health makes it tricky to travel. He doesn't own a car anymore, and I don't have a license."

"You can't drive?" Frieda was aghast.

Bernadette laughed. "I used to drive. I just never got my

driver's license in Canada. Besides, everything I need's right here. In fact, until recently, I bicycled everywhere. I can walk for groceries. The bus downtown is quick. And if there's something big we need, one of Ron's daughters will drive us around."

"Have his daughters been told he's in the hospital?"

"They have. And if you come visit today, you may meet Bonnie."

Bernadette looked at Frieda and said, "You've got to take care of yourself, your home, and the people you love, no matter what."

Frieda looked back, and Bernadette turned away.

You're getting heavy, Bernie.

"This is your home, right?" Frieda asked.

"Of course."

The young girl picked at the arm of the chair. She turned to look at Bernadette before she spoke again. "But you're renting, right? I mean, you don't own this house. A company does."

Bernadette inhaled sharply at the reference to the holding company.

"You're very clever, Frieda." She leaned over the arm of her chair to get closer. "It doesn't matter who owns any of this. We are all just borrowing things while we're alive. This house was built before I was born and someone else called it home then. I've done so many repairs to this old house that this will be the part of me that lives on after I'm gone. Hopefully, people will call it home for a very long time."

She watched Frieda study the house, deep in thought.

A smile broke across the young face. "If Hen's still living here, you should totally haunt him, okay? That'd be funny."

"Agreed," Bernadette said, chuckling until the ache beneath her ribs told her that she was done sitting for now. She got up and walked through the garden.

I should give that medical marijuana a chance.

She laughed at the memory of sitting in the garden with

Ron, laughing and getting high. In these same chairs, decades and several coats of paint ago, they'd smoked their fair share. It sometimes made her paranoid, though. She worried about what might await her, were she to return to the States.

All of this would be left behind. This life, this city, Ron, this house.

In the silence, Bernadette watched Frieda withdraw into her own head. The young girl transformed from jovial to thoughtful and then to worried.

"Is there something on your mind?"

"I lost something," Frieda said, rubbing her right shoulder. "The brooch that held my cloak on."

"Do you remember how you lost it?"

"I think so. But I called the place where I thought I left it, and they said it's not there."

"I'll tell you what." Bernadette tapped Frieda's knee. "I have a brooch or two. Nothing fancy. You can borrow one while you're staying with Henry, or until you get yours back. How does that sound?"

Frieda squinted at Bernadette, who was backlit by the morning sun. She seemed to perk back up a little. "For real?"

"Yup. Let's go find one for you right now."

Upstairs, in Bernadette's bedroom, she unlocked a drawer of an old roll-top desk. "Don't be fooled by the lock and key. None of this jewelry is worth anything."

Bernadette found three trinkets for Frieda to choose from. Two were pin brooches, and the third was a medieval-looking Celtic brooch with a ring and a long, thick pin.

Bernadette couldn't miss Frieda's eyes locking on the Celtic brooch. "You like that one, don't you?" She handed the piece to Frieda.

"It's beautiful."

Frieda turned the tarnished steel costume jewelry over in

her hand. It was unadorned by any glittery jewels, and unengraved.

"It's very special. Let me show you."

Bernadette led them back down the short hall, adorned with paintings and a pair of photos in generic black metal frames, one black and white, one color.

"Can you see?" she asked, pointing at the faded, color image.

Frieda stood on her toes and squinted at the woman in the photograph.

"I bought that brooch on our trip to Calgary. The sun was so bright that I used it to keep a scarf over my head."

Bernadette looked at her past self. She had been petite in those days. Her long, chestnut hair stuck out beneath the rose-colored, makeshift head cover. It wasn't elegant, but the young Bernadette was too happy to care. She and a handsome middle-aged man stood at the top of a canyon, his arm over her shoulder. She grinned at the camera. His head tipped forward in laughter. The colors in the photo had faded over the forty-odd years, but she could still tap into those old feelings. Ron had conceived of it as a trip to help her relax, and she felt her shoulders sag even now.

"I see it," Frieda said, pointing at the brooch in the photo, small but clear. "You were very pretty."

"Thank you."

"You should keep this, though." The young girl held the brooch out to Bernadette. "It's special."

"It is. But I want you to have it."

Frieda threw her arms around Bernadette. The sharp pain in Bernadette's side ran all the way up her neck, and she thought for a second that she might pass out.

Bernadette separated herself and straightened her blouse.

As she saw the old brooch in the small young hand, she was struck by the accumulation of all that she'd given up this morning. Not simply the brooch, but pieces of her past. So much about herself. Thoughts of Ron, lying on his floor, feelings of guilt, questions about the company. It was all so overwhelming that she was letting her guard down.

"Now, go downstairs. I'll see you at the hospital."

"Okay," Frieda said, suddenly serious. "But can you come with me first? I have something to show you, too."

CHAPTER TWENTY

H enry poured fresh coffee into Tess's mug, asking, "Then who did?"

Tess sat cross-legged on a chair at the table, backlit by the sun. She shrugged. "I don't know. I was upstairs with you. But someone called 911."

"Do you think it was Frieda?"

"I didn't say that." She blew steam off her coffee. "The only other person that could be in the picture is someone who was there. But why would you call 911 and then take off?"

"What if they hurt him, accidentally or something? Did it look like someone had gone through his apartment when you were down there? Someone looking for something. Valuables?"

"Not that I could tell. But have you seen in there? He was just a guy living on a pension. It's as tidy as you'd expect. And what would he have worth stealing?"

Henry shrugged and took the seat opposite Tess.

"What concerns me is whether they found what they were looking for. If this is a case of someone stealing random stuff for drug money, then we should talk about getting a lock on the main front door."

"I agree. But when do we bring this up with Bernadette?"

As if in answer, Shima meowed and jumped off the couch. Frieda entered, Bernadette in tow. Without a word, Frieda hurried into the bedroom and closed the door, Shima slipping in behind her.

"Is everything okay?" Henry asked.

Bernadette joined them at the table, waving off an offered mug. "Everything's going to be fine," she said, looking at the bedroom door.

"Have you heard any news?"

Bernadette's voice was dull, less cadent than usual. "Ron should be alright. He was sleeping when I left last night. They're keeping him to undergo some tests, and he might need surgery for a pacemaker."

Tess's face wore a pained expression. "He damaged his heart?"

"No. They've been eyeing him up for the pacemaker for a while. Whatever this was, it must have been the last straw."

"Did he say what happened?" Henry asked.

"He wasn't in any condition to speak last night. It was just a heart attack or something, Henry. Nothing more."

A loud click from the old bedroom door announced Frieda reemerging. She'd changed into a T-shirt and jeans, and she carried her satchel in her arms.

"It's my fault." Her voice cracked, holding back tears.

Bernadette spoke first. "Oh, sweetie, it's no one's fault. It's just the inevitable awful part of getting old."

"No," Frieda said through swallows and breaths. "I saw Mr. Creepy come out of Mr. Benham's apartment after I went downstairs yesterday. It was him."

Henry's throat tightened. The others were stunned silent.

"Fred," he said in as calm a voice as he could muster. "You saw the man from the café, the man from the hallway, leaving Mr. Benham's suite last night?"

"Yes."

"Okay. Look, you aren't responsible for this at all. We can tell the police what you saw and, if this guy did something to Mr. Benham, it'll help catch him. There's no way that you could have known something was wrong, right?"

"Did you call the police?" Tess asked.

Frieda looked at her, confused. "No." She reached into her satchel and pulled out some folded papers. "But I found these." Her words and breath still came through in little convulsions. She pressed the pages flat onto the table.

Henry picked them up.

"What are they?" Tess asked.

He flipped through each. "A list of our names and our suite numbers. Some pages of a printout of an internet chat from some site called Net-Tectives, some old index card with our address on it and a list of I don't know what, and . . ." The last piece required no explanation. It was a different paper than the first two and, unfolded further, it was clearly a copy of the Globe crossword from last Saturday.

"Where'd you find these?" Henry said.

Frieda looked at Shima as she spoke. "He dropped them on the lawn when he left."

"You saw him drop them?" Tess asked.

"Yeah. I was going to tell you about the crossword because it proved you're not crazy, but I didn't get the chance."

"Jesus," muttered Henry.

"Did he see you go outside and pick this up? What if he'd come back?" Henry's voice cracked with worry. "I shouldn't have left you alone."

Frieda fidgeted with a metal brooch. It wasn't the Pepsi logo. She was taking too long to answer.

"Where did you get that?"

"Bernadette." Tears left trails over her round cheeks. "I don't want to get in trouble. I just wanted Tess to believe you."

Henry scooped her into his arms and squeezed. "No one's getting in trouble."

"And it wasn't Sarah who took them."

Henry felt a visceral punch and winced. She picked up on more than he realized. She always had.

He looked down at Frieda and saw that she was waiting.

"And it wasn't Sarah," he said.

Frieda wrapped her arms around Henry and hugged him back.

He tried to soften his voice, "Fred, we should give the police a call. We can tell them what you saw. It might be helpful, alright?"

Bernadette reached into the small pile on the table and took some of the papers. "I need to hang on to these," she said, folding everything together.

Henry frowned as the paper disappeared into her purse. "What do you need those for? The police are going to want them."

"We don't know that this... man had anything to do with what happened. Ron will be awake this morning and he'll set everything straight. Maybe something happened and maybe it didn't. There's no point in getting the authorities all wound up for nothing. They'll just send people off on a wild goose chase because of a bunch of papers and use up tax dollars. They're not important. As you said, it's just a list."

"Then why hide it?"

Bernadette spoke to Frieda. "If anyone asks you if there are more pages, don't lie. You say, 'yes'. And you say that I have this. But if no one asks, you don't have to say a thing."

Henry scowled and fought unsuccessfully to find the right words.

"Then we should go talk to Ron," Tess said.

"I'm sorry." Bernadette stuffed the list into her pocket and, rising from the table, dismissed the group with a wave.

She spoke to no one in particular as she opened the door. "I know Ron, and he wouldn't want the police to have this."

CHAPTER TWENTY-ONE

Henry made a fanning motion with Constable Tipton's card as he paced in the living room. On the other end of the phone, the officer had spoken with Frieda, and had listened patiently to Henry while he explained the papers, the confrontation at the coffee shop, and his crosswords.

He hung up and knocked on the bedroom door.

"Come in."

Frieda lay on the floor, leaning on her elbows in front of her laptop. Shima was stretched out over her arms, pinning her hands to the keyboard.

"Someone's going to go to the hospital to speak with Mr. Benham today," Henry said. "If the police are there, we can give them the papers."

"Did you mention Bernadette taking stuff?"

"No."

"How come?"

The reason sounded weaker aloud. "I guess I thought it could be mentioned later. But if I said something now, I wouldn't be able to take it back."

Fortunately, this appeared to make perfect sense, as she grunted her approval.

"Tess wants us," she said.

"Sure. We can tell her when we're going to the hospital."

"No." Frieda slid one arm out from under the cat. "She's been blowing up my phone for the last twenty minutes. Check yours."

He looked at the stream of texts.

We need to talk.
Are you done?
You need to see this.
Come up as soon as you're done.
OMFG Get off the phone.
HENRY GET UP HERE

Tess cleared her table of everything except her laptop and a sketchpad, several pages of which were covered in an increasingly maniacal scrawl of notes. She moved with urgency, her heart racing. Dishes clattered as she let them fall from her hands into the sink.

She flipped once more through the webpages open on her screen to ensure they were in the desired sequence. She ran to the printer and pulled off a map of Washington and Oregon, marked up with colored lines.

The knock on the door signaled that her time was up. A quick look through the peephole confirmed it was Henry and Frieda. The chain and deadbolt clattered as she let them in, and again as she locked the door behind them.

"Are we your prisoners?" Henry asked.

"You first. How'd it go with the police?"

"They're sending someone to the hospital. If we don't see them there, we should drop the papers off at the station."

"Did they say anything about what happened?"

"What do you mean?"

"About last night. What did they say?"

"Just that someone called it in anonymously. It didn't look like anyone had broken in. And Bernadette insisted that Mr. Benham had an accident."

"Of course he did," Tess said. She held up her empty palms, paused, raised an eyebrow, and closed her hands into fists. "Or did he?"

"What are you talking about?"

She spun on her heel and strode to her laptop on the table. "I think the explanation is in the pages that Fred found. I think our Mr. Benham is hiding a secret."

"Sure," conceded Henry. "Bernadette's being sketchy enough. But the pages that she left us with are just a bunch of emails."

"Not exactly."

"I think they are."

"They aren't."

Henry blinked and bit his lip. "So, what are they?"

Tess held her chin up and turned the screen of her laptop to face her two-person audience on the other side of the table.

"It's a private discussion in an online forum," Tess said, "between two members of something called Net-Tectives.com." She brought up the website. The background of the home page was dotted with fingerprints and shoe impressions.

"People come here to solve crimes. Amateur detectives. According to this, Net-Tectives members have successfully participated in the solving of over one hundred cold case files. They're intense about it."

She watched Henry and Frieda's eyes lock on the screen as she scrolled down through a list of hundreds of cases and names, mostly women.

Henry opened his mouth to ask a question, but Tess headed him off.

"Hang on." She flattened the pages of the conversation out on the table. "Our two users, *treasurehunter1971* and *juliancaesar*, are discussing a case they're working on."

"I didn't read it closely," Henry said. "I was more interested in what Bernadette took."

"Most of it is generic," she said. "But read this bit here."

@treasurehunter1971 *How is that possible?*

@juliancaesar *That's a secret. ;) Whats it worth?*

@treasurehunter1971 *Who knows? Thousands maybe.*

@juliancaesar *OMFG*

@treasurehunter1971 *Send pics.*

@juliancaesar *I'm not sending a pic online. Once something is on the internet, anyone can see it. Next thing you know FBI is kicking down my door.*

@treasurehunter1971 *I need proof. If it is real, I'm willing to pay.*

@treasurehunter1971 *Cash money.*

@juliancaesar *ATTACHMENT – IMG_1022.jpg 1.3MB*

@juliancaesar *does that work?*

@treasurehunter1971 *You have my interest for sure. Let's meet.*

@juliancaesar *I'm in Vancouver.*

@treasurehunter1971 *No sweat. I'm in Seattle.*

@juliancaesar *Canada :(*

@treasurehunter1971 *Oh.*

@juliancaesar *U there?*

@treasurehunter1971 *Checking a map. Far.*

@treasurehunter1971 *How do I know you're not scamming?*

@juliancaesar *You'll see the real deal in person.*

@treasurehunter1971 *I can drive up Saturday.*

@juliancaesar *PM me when you get to Van. We can figure out a time and I'll let you know where. It's easy to find.*

@treasurehunter1971 *See you then.*

@juliancaesar *Cheers.*

The discussion ended a third of the way down the last page. Tess was getting the reactions she hoped for. Both Frieda and Henry were rapt. Although, Henry looked doubtful.

"The FBI? Seriously?" he asked.

"Fair question. But if someone's name is 'Treasure Hunter', you'd expect whatever they're talking about to be valuable. And it sounds like someone was coming to get it on Saturday. I think one of these guys is Frieda's Mr. Creepy."

"I know which," Frieda said. "Mr. Creepy is the one from Seattle."

"Why do you say that?" Henry asked, still reading.

"His car has Washington State license plates."

Both Tess and Henry turned to look at her. "You never mentioned a car before," Tess said.

Frieda's eyes darted between the two adults. "I forgot until just now. When he left Mr. Benham's he got into a K-car parked by the café. It had Washington plates."

"A K-car?" Henry asked, frowning as though scanning her story with X-ray vision.

"I think it was a K-car," Frieda said. "One of those boxy ones like kids draw. It was yellowish white. I wrote the license plate down in my notebook."

"Did you?" Henry was no longer surprised by any of this. Of course she wrote it down. Why not? That's the most normal thing in the world.

"Anything else?" Tess asked.

Frieda bit her bottom lip and squinted in a grand display of deep thought. "No. That's it."

Henry and Tess watched Frieda in silence until the young girl started pulling her cloak closer over her shoulders.

"If there's anything else," Henry said, "let's talk about it."

"No. For real, that's it. We can call Sonja and I'll tell her about the car. I just forgot."

"Sonja?" Tess looked at Henry.

"Constable Tipton."

"Ah." Tess turned their attention back to the laptop. "Well, I have more as well." She walked them through how she signed up for free membership, to access and search all the various forums.

"Can you search for members?" Frieda asked.

"Smart girl. Yeah, we can." Tess tapped her mouse. "The one guy '*TreasureHunter1971*' has only been a member for a few weeks, his bio's blank except for 'Keller'. I guess that's his name?"

"Sounds like killer," Frieda said.

"I worked with a Keller," Henry said. "She was nice."

Tess continued reading. "He has no public posts. I even googled '*treasurehunter1971*', hoping that he might have used the same handle on some other sites. No such luck."

"So, now what?" Henry asked.

Tess leaned way across the table and pushed the laptop closer to the others. One hand pointed at the screen as she changed pages again with the other.

"*Treasurehunter1971* has only ever posted in one forum."

A list of posts confirmed that in his brief twenty-seven-day career as a Net-Tective member he'd only ever posted in a single forum: *Crimes/Cold Cases/WA - DB Cooper Hijacking Mystery November 24, 1971 Part 3.*

She leaned back, triumphant, as the page changed again.

"What are we looking at?"

"Just read."

Henry obeyed and reached for the mouse across the table.

Tess watched as the expressions on their faces changed, from curious to puzzled, and again to disbelief.

After several minutes, she rose. "Can I make you some tea?"

Henry shook his head. Frieda nodded. Neither could peel themselves away from the screen. Henry was scrolling further.

"Look at the next tab," she suggested, leaving them to catch up.

This was her *coup de grâce*. It contained images of maps, links to the FBI website, photos, and 884 posts. Parts 1 and 2 of the thread had thousands of posts each and she hadn't even scratched the surface.

Yet.

As she set the mugs on the table, Tess broke the silence.

"So?"

Henry looked up.

"Well, it's captivating, isn't it? In 1971, a man going by the name of DB Cooper boards a plane with a bomb and escapes with hundreds of thousands of dollars by parachuting out a stairwell under the tail, never to be seen or heard from again."

"Is this true?" Frieda asked.

Words burst from Tess, unable to restrain herself any longer. "A hundred percent. He's an American legend. The FBI searched for decades and finally stopped looking in 2016."

"And you think this is connected to what the guy from Seattle is looking for? Why he came here?" Henry asked.

"It makes sense, right? I mean, we can say he's looking for something. Secondly, this guy is from Seattle, and Cooper disappeared somewhere between Seattle and Portland."

"And," she continued, "the guy's name is '*treasurehunter1971.*'" She underlined the year in the air with her finger.

"Which is when parachute dude stole the money," Frieda said.

Tess fixated on Henry. "Are you going to say it? Or are you waiting for me to say it?"

His lips pursed, and he squinted at her, blinking.

Oh, he's thinking it.

"How old . . ." she started.

". . . is Benham?" Henry nodded as he spoke.

"What?" Frieda hopped up to her knees on her chair. "Mr. Benham is hijacker-money-man?"

"I'll bet," Tess said.

Henry held up a hand. "Wait, wait. Maybe the guy that Frieda saw only thinks Mr. Benham is Cooper." Henry scrolled to a hand-drawn wanted poster from 1971. On the left, a man in a business suit looked back through narrow eyes. On the right, prominent dark glasses masked much of the face which bore the same widows peak of hair and sliver of a mouth.

"Okay, if DB Cooper was thirtyish then, he would be in his

late seventies or early eighties now. It's the right age, but that means nothing on its own."

"Look. There's more." Tess took control of the laptop and started clicking. "I haven't read everything yet."

She turned the screen back. "*Voila.*"

It was a list of names and ranks on the Canadian National Air Force Archives site. The page banner explained that these were graduates from Summerside Airforce Base in Prince Edward Island. She highlighted one small name in the sea of letters: *Pte. Ronald Benham (1960).*

"That's got to be him."

Henry shook his head. "Maybe. But all you have is that he was in the military."

"The Air Force," Frieda said, and she shuffled around the table to sit next to Tess. "Like a parachuter."

Henry looked back at them, unmoving.

Frieda tried again. "Mr. Benham is DB Cooper."

"Are you proposing we take this to the police?" Henry wondered aloud.

"Take what?" Tess asked. "The license number? Sure. The Cooper stuff? I say no. They'd call us nuts. There's nothing that we have that they don't have. Let them do their own digging."

Henry was coming round. She'd touched upon a nerve of curiosity.

"And," Tess added, turning the screw where she knew it would have its greatest impact, "Bernadette must know. There's some explanation as to why she took that paper."

Henry scrunched his nose. "Now, that is a mystery I would like solved. But I don't think it's as grand as DB Cooper."

He blinked rapidly as he stared out the window.

The little café was busy, and Tess could see a young family in the booth where they had sat only twenty-four hours ago.

"Indulge me." Tess stood and held up a green, diamond-shaped keyring with a single key attached. "When I was in Mr.

Benham's apartment last night, I saw lots of old photos in his hallway."

She had already printed out the artist's sketch of DB Cooper from 1971 and held this up, too.

Tess waved the key like bait.

Henry shrugged and stood. "Sure. Let's see this."

1971: THE CASE

The passenger understood that the short-haired stewardess had to get up to relay his messages to the cockpit. He didn't like it when she left him, though. This one was sweet. Polite. The other stewardesses were also aware of what was going on, that was clear. He wanted to shout at them to stop looking at him, but so far this was still just between him and the crew.

She'd read the note. He'd shown her what was in the briefcase, and she believed him. Things were running on their own power now; stopping was off the table. The question was what would be waiting for him when they landed?

The plane had been circling Seattle for a little over two hours at this point. The pilot's announcements about mechanical issues and having to burn off fuel were getting repetitive. They had told him all the money was ready. It was the rest they were waiting for. He didn't want to land until it was all there: touch down, civilians off, then go. Or was the plane going to be surrounded by National Guard?

The chatter of all the other passengers on the plane had died into a bored silence after the first hour. Occasionally, someone would get up and walk past him at the back of the plane to use the washrooms. No one appeared to find it odd that the young stewardess would sometimes be there next to him, nor that he was still wearing his tinted glasses. No one looked twice at the briefcase on his lap, open only wide enough for his hand to rest inside.

Had he asked for too much?

A stiff icicle shot up his spine in an unfamiliar moment of panic. Had he asked for too little? *No. I did the math. This is all it's going to take. We're not criminals.*

The sudden crackle from the overhead announcement speakers was like a thunderclap in the quiet cabin. At the far end of the plane, one of the stewardesses left the cockpit, locked eyes with the passenger and nodded. The pilot's voice came on.

"Ladies and gentlemen, thank you for your patience. We've been informed by Sea-Tac that everything has been taken care of. Please fasten your seatbelts and prepare for landing."

CHAPTER TWENTY-THREE

The furnishings were all older and in worse shape than Henry had pictured in his mind. It didn't help that the paramedic had left footprints on the living room carpet.

From the entrance, Henry could see into the kitchen and living room. The kitchen lay straight ahead and a hall to the left would lead to the rest of the suite. The star in the living room was a well-worn green leather chair. An air tank and hose lay next to it on the ground. The chair was still reclined, and Henry thought he could almost see the imprint of the man who would have, should have, occupied it.

There were few dishes or furniture. In the hall, there weren't even many photos. Henry noted that the chemical smell of new furnishings had been replaced, perhaps decades ago, by the slightly stale air of a man alone.

He wondered whether Benham had any children.

"The photos are in the bedroom," Tess said, heading down the hall, Frieda in tow.

Standing over the chair, Henry read a man's daily routine from a side table. A pair of remote controls held together with an elastic band, eyeglasses, a JF Penn novel, a tipped mug with stains of coffee, and a small medicinal-looking spray bottle. Henry picked up the spray, Apo-Nitroglycerin, which sounded important. It was capped, so Henry reasoned that it shouldn't get dirty in his pocket. It may be good to bring to the hospital.

He nearly stepped on an orange pill bottle. It still held one small, white pill, but the lid was missing. So he got down onto his hands and knees to look under the chair. With a magazine from the floor, he swept out crumbs, tissues, and the missing lid. He sealed the bottle and kept it with the inhaler.

"We should clean up," he said to no one in particular.

Tess's reply was indistinguishable.

Henry continued exploring around the far side of the living room and into the kitchen. He tucked his hands into the back pockets of his jeans, unsure of why it felt important to disturb nothing. The discomfort that accompanies intrusion rose in his stomach. If he had gotten sick or cried, he wouldn't be surprised.

He found Tess and Frieda in the bedroom, removing a frame from the wall.

"What did you say?" he asked.

"I thought *you* said something."

"I said I thought we should clean up."

"Ah. Good idea, but let's check with Bernadette first."

A double bed with a large headboard made of dark wood occupied most of the carpeted floor. The open closet was crammed with boxes bearing felt marker labels such as *WINTER CLOTHES*, *BOOKS*, *RECORDS*, and *HOLIDAY*. Henry wondered whether Mr. Benham put up a Christmas tree.

On the bedside table were two more framed pictures. One was missing a photo; the glass of the other was so dusty that Henry had to remove it from the frame in order to see. The tint of the faded colors reminded Henry of his own childhood family photos. This family looked particularly idyllic, with a mother and a father about his age. They sat on a rock with three teenage girls, one of whom appeared to have been an unwilling subject.

Henry surveyed the bedroom, unsure of what he was looking for, until Frieda's voice broke the silence.

"This one," she said. She and Tess sat on the bed with a photo frame in Frieda's lap. The largest of eight photos in the frame was half the size of a sheet of paper.

Tess slipped the photo out of the back of the frame and brought it close to her face. Henry half expected her to sniff at it. She snapped an image with her phone before handing it to Henry.

It was a black-and-white image of three men in uniform, arm in arm. Each grinned with the drunkenness of that cocktail of youth and adventure. An ornate mansion filled the background with symmetrical towers and curving staircases. Beneath the men, a strip of paper was glued to the front of the photo, with a typed description: *Ronald B. Bryan D. Kevin F. at Schloss Favorite, Germany, October 1959.*

Henry took the photograph and squinted. He lifted his own glasses onto his head and looked again.

All three men wore the same uniform. Simple clothes, pressed, buttoned tight, with RCAF wings on their breast. Bryan's eyes told the story that it was he who had delivered the most recent punchline.

Condensation formed from Benham's breath as he laughed at the camera; the only hint of autumn. His pale skin shone like the clear sky in the background, in contrast to the dark uniform, as spartan of medals as his face was of experience. A wedge cap with two shiny buttons hid any evidence of Cooper's telltale widow's peak.

Henry flipped back and forth between the drawing and the photo. "It's not even close," he said.

"It is."

"It's not."

"You have to imagine an artist working from descriptions."

"If the witnesses were short-sighted."

"Try picturing him without the hat."

The most expensive thing Henry had seen in the suite was the recliner, and it might have been twenty years old. Two hundred thousand dollars in 1971 should translate into millions today.

"Does this look like the home of a millionaire to you?" Henry asked.

"Well, like you said, maybe he realized the money was marked and so he couldn't spend it."

"So he moves to Vancouver and rents a basement apartment for fifty years?" Henry stood and handed the photograph back to Frieda. "No. The Cooper who hijacked the plane was methodical. Calculating. Think about it. Why did he ask for four parachutes?"

"In case he needed to take hostages?"

"I don't think so. Nothing we read says he was trying to hurt anyone. But if the police thought he was going to take hostages, they for sure wouldn't sabotage the parachutes, right?"

Henry closed the closet door. Somehow, it felt more respectful.

Tess parried. "Someone who thought of those details would already have figured out how to launder the money."

"Or not," Frieda said. "Maybe the money's still here and that's what Keller was looking for."

"It couldn't be," Henry said.

"If he's not after the money, then what?" Frieda asked.

Henry tapped the image of the young air force officer in the chest.

"Let's ask Benham."

Keller coasted the car to the corner in front of the coffee shop. The police vehicles were no longer parked across the street in front of the house. There was movement downstairs, though. Someone was home.

He scowled.

He was on the right track. Or it could be a trap. The girl had dropped an old brass Northwest Orient Airlines pin in the alley for him to find. He recognized the logo: a wave inside of a circle. He had burned into his memory all the images of the hijacked plane.

Still, the message was uncertain.

Are they telling me I'm on the right track? Are they warning me to stay away?

There was no going back now. His father was lighting the way, and the signs were coming faster and faster as he neared the truth.

This was just a minor delay. The house would make itself available again soon. It would make its secrets known, and he would get what he had come for. This was now as unstoppable as time itself.

He turned the corner onto Richardson Street, toward Granville, away from the house.

CHAPTER TWENTY-FOUR

Vancouver General Hospital was a sprawl of buildings. Wide lawns and narrow roads cut between towers confused one's perspective. It was hard to say how many city blocks the entire complex covered. Henry barely spoke as they approached the first series of squat pavilions. He dipped in and out of Tess and Frieda's steady stream of excitement.

"But he didn't blow up the plane?" Frieda asked.

"No, it was a threat. Nobody even knows if he had a real bomb."

"But he showed it to the flight attendant."

"He did, but it's not like she was a bomb expert, right? Would you recognize a real bomb if you saw one?"

Frieda's jaw slackened, elongating her round features. "I might." She changed tactics. "What if he blew up in his parachute?"

Even Henry had to laugh. He held the door open for the pair as they entered the Centennial Building, per Bernadette's directions.

Tess's research while Henry had been on the phone with the police was apparently extensive.

"The thing is," she said, "people believe he made it down

because years and years later, someone found some of the ransom money washed up on a riverbank. They could tell it was DB Cooper's because of the serial numbers on the bills. And it was an eight-year-old kid who found the cash."

"What?" Frieda's palms shot to the side of her head, fingers spread wide. "That kid must be rich."

"It was only a couple thousand bucks, which means Cooper still got away with about two hundred thousand dollars. US."

"Hen, that's a lot of money, right?"

He pressed the call button for the elevator several times.

"After fifty years," he said, "if you took care of it, you could have millions today."

"But you said Mr. Benham doesn't have millions."

Tess threw fuel on Frieda's young fire. "Some of the richest people in the world live really cheaply so they don't attract attention. They don't buy stuff. They just collect tons of money."

"Like Smaug," Frieda said, nodding her understanding.

Henry looked at Tess to see whether she had picked up on the reference.

"Exactly," Tess answered. "Like a dragon."

The elevator pinged its approval before Henry could express his own.

As the trio approached the nurse's station to ask for directions, they were interrupted by a familiar voice.

"Tess! Henry!"

Further down in the intensive care ward, Bernadette stood alongside a uniformed police officer. The nurse behind the counter wore glasses on her head and a second pair at the end of her nose. Her eyes followed the group bypassing her station, squinting and using none of the lenses.

"Constable Stubbing was here to ask Ron about what happened," Bernadette said. The police officer smiled only with his mouth as he nodded his agreement and scanned each of the newcomers.

Henry tore himself away from the police officer's stare to ask, "How's Mr. Benham?"

"He's talking this morning and doesn't remember a lot. The whole thing's been too much for him." Bernadette's voice cracked. "They're saying that he had a heart attack. Maybe more than one. They say he's too old for a cardio-myo-some-thing-or-other, so they want to put a pacemaker in."

"Can we see him?" Tess asked.

"They're doing some pre-screening for the surgery in a bit, but you can go on in." Bernadette pointed at the closed door behind her. The curtain in the small, square porthole window was drawn shut.

Henry put his hand on Frieda's shoulder and spoke to the severe-looking man in uniform. "Do you work with Officer Tipton?"

"Constable Tipton. Yes, she said you'd have something for me?"

Tess disappeared alone into the room as Henry pulled out the papers that Frieda had found and explained. They listened as Frieda recounted seeing the stranger on the lawn, the car, and the license plate. The officer took the papers, made notes, and even asked Frieda to draw the shape of her "K-Car" on his pad.

"Why didn't you mention this before?" Stubbing asked.

Frieda's drawing became jittery. She shrugged without looking up. "I didn't remember." She initialed her drawing with only an *F*.

Constable Stubbing looked over the drawing, pointed at Frieda with his pen and spoke to Henry. "And this is your daughter?"

"My niece. My ex-wife's sister's daughter."

The officer turned his head and looked at Henry from the

corner of his eye. "So, she's not your real niece."

"Fuck you!" Frieda shouted, loud enough to make the nurse sitting at her station jump to attention. The young girl started to cry.

Henry bent down and put an arm around Frieda. "You know what? I think we're all getting hungry. Let's you and I go to the cafeteria and grab sandwiches for everyone."

Stubbing's face was flush. He winced in apology. "I still need the young girl's address."

Bernadette inserted herself between Henry and Frieda, whispering, "I've got her. Let me grab my purse."

Instead, Henry pulled a twenty-dollar bill from his wallet. Bernadette slipped it into her pocket without taking her attention from Frieda. And, with that, she whisked the crying girl toward the elevators.

Henry took the notepad and began writing. His irritation with the situation cleared when he overheard a bit of Bernadette's conversation with Frieda at the elevator.

"Yeah, fuck him for sure," Bernadette said, a little too loudly. "But you still can't say that."

Henry returned the notebook with a grin. Stubbing had heard as well.

Ron Benham's room was large enough to hold a second patient. Instead, on the far side of the silver steel mechanical bed were two chairs. Nearer to the door, a massive cream-colored machine looked ridiculous compared to the tiny six-inch black-and-white screen, which showed Benham's heartbeat and a stream of numbers.

Tess laughed at something as she stood up and walked around the foot of the bed. She lifted a purse from one of the chairs and sat. Benham coughed as he caught his breath.

"You must be Henry."

"I am. It's nice to meet you, despite the circumstances." The old man's hand was thin and weak, but the skin still bore the callouses of an active life.

"Likewise. I'm sorry to have caused such a fuss. Where's Bernie?"

"She and my niece have run down to the caf."

Henry turned to Tess, backlit by the window. The view of the city was reminiscent of Henry's old office, only ten stories higher.

"Thanks for bringing my things," Benham said. "They only have soft toothbrushes here. Nothing that cleans worth a darn."

Henry pulled the spray and pill bottle from his pocket. "I picked these up, too."

Benham's frail hand took the spray. "Those aren't mine." He waved at the orange bottle in Henry's hand.

Henry turned the bottle over in his hand. The prescription label was faded, the name illegible.

Tess cleared her throat. "I was waiting for you."

Benham sat up further in his hospital bed, frowning at each of them, on either side.

"That sounds serious. What've you got for me?" he asked.

"We know that someone came to visit you yesterday."

"What of it?" The old voice was slow and creaked with skepticism.

"What happened?" Tess asked.

"Pardon?"

"Did he harm you?"

A sigh, followed by coughs. "Nothing happened. He left. I must have fallen, or taken the wrong pill, or something. Whatever you expect us old people to do."

"Who was he?" Henry asked.

"What is this? The Spanish Inquisition?"

"Look," Tess picked back up, putting her hand on Benham's

leg. "We think he's been hanging around. Henry's niece saw him in the hallway and saw him leaving your place."

"I don't know him. He knocked and he had the wrong house, so he left. He had nothing to do with my heart attack. I'm old. It happens." He wagged the nitroglycerin spray bottle that Henry had given him. "This stuff is a lifesaver."

"Do you have a lot of those?" Henry asked, pointing at the spray in Benham's hand.

"These? No. The pharmacy never lets you fill more than one at a time. Cheap buggers."

"And you've told the police that you just had a heart attack."

"That's right."

"Care to tell us what really happened?"

"You've got a hell of a nerve."

Henry held up his hand. "Before you say anything more, here's where I'm coming from." He walked back to the door to the hallway, glanced outside, and closed it. He came back and stood over Benham.

"Your oxygen is next to your chair, so you were sitting there when you had your so-called heart attack. You knocked over your coffee, so you could reach your table. But someone stopped you from getting to your nitro spray. Isn't that right?"

"What makes you think—"

"The cap. You wouldn't have replaced the cap."

Benham turned the spray over in his hand.

"But the cap was open on this one." Henry held the orange pill bottle out at arm's length and watched as the light of recognition flickered in the old man's eyes.

"Let me see that," he said. "Is there a name on there?"

"No, just a prescription number." Having got Benham's attention, Henry returned the bottle to his pocket. "Why is this guy interested in you?"

Benham leaned back into his pillow. "You're making something out of nothing. Just a random kook."

"Did he say anything?"

"Yeah, sure. I don't remember a lot. But it was just a bunch of garbage." He rubbed the stubble on his chin with the back of his hand. "He thought I was someone else."

"That's it? Did he use a name?"

"Sure. K-something. I don't remember."

"Cooper?" Tess suggested.

Again, Benham's eyes failed to hide surprise. "No. He kept saying nonsense, like it was safe to come home. Gobbledygook. High as a kite, I'll bet. That's all."

Tess nodded. "The man from your apartment dropped a bunch of papers on the lawn. We read them and did a bit of digging on our own, to figure out what he was looking for. Well, it turns out that he's some kind of treasure hunter."

Henry watched Benham for a reaction: confusion, denial, bewilderment. Nothing. Stone.

"Is that it?" the old man said in a low, steady tone.

"This guy," Henry said, "is looking for DB Cooper."

Benham locked eyes with Henry; a wall of resolve had gone up. "I don't know any Cooper."

"But you're familiar with the story?" Tess asked.

"Young lady, everybody alive heard about that when it happened. But there were a lot of hijackings in those days. That was before airport security figured itself out. Now the pendulum's swung the other way and you can't even bring a sneeze on board without them searching through your tissue."

Tess produced her phone and brought up the old military picture. "Can we ask you about this?"

"He had it?" Benham asked. His right hand held the phone awkwardly, a monitor clipped to his index finger. With his free hand, he tapped the young airman's face. He scrolled from side to side to his old compatriots' faces.

"Oh no," Tess said. "I just took a picture of this when I popped in to pick up your things."

Benham stopped scrolling. "Why?"

Henry tried not to sound absurd. "The guy who attacked you followed a trail to Richardson Street, looking for Cooper and the ransom money. He found you." Henry pointed at the phone. "You've jumped from planes before. Where were you in November 1971?"

Benham's mouth cracked. He handed the phone back to Tess.

"You think I'm Cooper?"

Tess shrugged.

"What will you do if I am?"

Henry looked to Tess for the answer to Benham's question, only to find her returning his lost expression.

"Well, don't get your knickers in a twist," Benham said. "I'm not. Help me sit up."

Tess shifted pillows behind the old man's head, as Henry adjusted the tilt of the bed.

"I'll tell you," Benham continued. "In 1971, my life was the pits, sure. The economy was in the tank. My wife chucked me out of the house, and I had to move into the Cambie Hotel for a time. But I sure as hell never got so desperate that I hijacked a plane. I still had plenty to lose. My two young girls, Jane and Bonnie."

Tess rested her hands on the bed next to Benham's hip as he spoke. "You think Cooper was desperate?"

"Yeah, I do. Lots of people were being put out of work, losing homes. Lots of young men from the States were moving up here to get away from the draft. It didn't help that those young men who survived their tours in Vietnam weren't coming back to parades. Just the opposite. The Cold War was at its peak. I'm telling you those were crazy times. And, while I never got as close to the edge as that myself, can I imagine a man getting pushed so far that he's got a grudge to settle no matter what? You bet I can. The 'peace-love-dove' of the 1960s was over and for many people it was every man for himself, unfortunately. Crazy times."

He patted Tess's hand.

"You've seen my place. I'm not Cooper. If I had that kind of money, I'd have a bigger TV."

The mood lightened, Tess and Henry laughed along with Benham, although not quite as hard.

"I'd love to see these papers that this guy dropped, though," Benham said. "Do you have those on you as well?"

"Henry gave them to the police," Tess said.

"The police?" Benham's raised voice lifted Tess to her feet. Even Henry straightened. "Why would you do that?"

"Well, he dropped them," Tess said.

"They've got nothing to do with me."

"You said you couldn't remember much," Henry said. "Is there more?"

"You can't involve the police."

"You just told us yourself that they attacked you. If there's an intruder around the house, then we have every right to know."

"It'll be your word against mine and you weren't even there." Benham looked quite satisfied with this logic.

On cue, the machine next to Henry gave a small beep.

"What's the problem?" Henry asked. "He should be caught."

"I'm telling you he came looking for someone and he didn't find them. So he's gone and he's out of our hair."

"And what if he's not? What if he comes back?"

"If he comes back..." Benham winced and looked at Bernadette's purse on the chair with a melancholic affection. "Then he's trouble, isn't he?"

"So, let's involve the police."

"I can't"

"Why not?"

"That's not for you to know. Find out who he is."

"What are you thinking? This isn't a game. I have a thirteen-year-old girl staying with me."

"Get rid of her. She must have other relatives."

"No," Henry said, aware of how defensive he sounded.

"Why not?"

"That's my business."

"Quite a standoff," Benham concluded. He looked out of the window, appearing to ponder the gray, heavy clouds that were advancing over downtown in the distance. "I'm sure I don't need to tell you that Bernadette is sick. It would be too much for her to have the police crawling all over the house."

He turned to Henry. "I'm sure you wouldn't like it either."

"I've not done anything wrong."

"None of us have, Henry. Tess . . ." This was a plea now. "The police are a system to enforce rules. And a system has no conscience; it shouldn't go digging into the past. You see?"

The puzzled silence was interrupted by a nurse tapping on the door as she entered. This one had no glasses but wore a navy smock covered with rocking horses and teddy bears; a fashion choice that Henry presumed was meant to amuse children.

She strode with authority to the machine that had pinged and began pressing buttons. "We're getting you ready for your tests now."

Tess circled the bed and took Henry's wrist. "We were heading out anyhow."

Benham grabbed Henry's other wrist and tugged. Unsatisfied with Benham's final, enigmatic note, Henry eagerly bent down.

"You get it, right?" Benham whispered. "This is why Bernadette chose you."

The nurse interrupted by tapping Henry on his shoulder.

Mr. Benham thanked them for coming as they left.

CHAPTER TWENTY-FIVE

Henry's mind was distracted by Tess's hand as they returned to Richardson Street. Her fingers lightly clinging to his arm above his elbow.

"I said, do you think they'll catch him?" Frieda asked in a loud voice. She looked back at them over her shoulder as she walked.

"Sure," Henry said, unconvinced. "You gave a good description, and they'll get more details from the café. If the guy is dropping papers behind on the lawn, then who knows what else he left."

Would they, though? Unless Benham confirmed the attack, there was little likelihood of the police digging deeper. Henry repeated to himself Benham's enigmatic words.

A system has no conscience.

Birds chirped and dove recklessly between the trees lining the sidewalk. The trio walked through back lanes and quiet residential streets, coming across little traffic.

Tess broke the silence. "What did he say to you in there?"

"When?"

"You know when."

"Besides telling us we shouldn't go to the police? He said Bernadette chose me. Whatever that means."

"That's what I told you last night, isn't it? She chose you. Why, do you think?"

Henry only shrugged. It was a hell of a guilt trip. And he was fearful of sounding paranoid.

"The police won't look into this," Tess said quietly, so that Frieda, kicking leaves behind them, wouldn't overhear.

He nodded at the painfully obvious.

"What do you know about the management company, Hen?"

Henry understood each of the words she had used, but he only registered the use of his nickname. "Pardon me?"

"The page that Bernadette kept." She let go of his elbow to produce the paper from her back pocket. "It wasn't just Mr. Benham's name that's circled on here. Who is 121702 BC Ltd.?"

"Where did you get that?" Henry asked, coming to a halt.

"It was sticking out of Bernadette's purse, along with the card with all the numbers. Between her reaction, and Mr. Benham's . . . Looking into them ourselves just felt like the right thing to do."

"You talked to him about DB Cooper?" Frieda held her arms high over her head, her eyes wide. "Without me?"

Henry remained fixated on Tess's light-fingered success.

"It's an index card of some sort. It's got our address on it, but I can't imagine what it means. And, as for the list, there's something interesting." Tess pointed at her own entry.

Unit 3 Tess Honma (& daughter?)

"You have a kid?" Frieda asked.

"No, Fred," Henry said. "I think that's you. I think he's been watching the house, learning about us. And when you ran upstairs, he assumed that you were with Tess."

"How many papers are you missing, Hen?" Tess asked.

Crosswords, he managed to not speak aloud. "Three."

"So, he's been watching since Sunday."

"Which makes sense if he's the treasure hunter who came into town on Saturday."

"So, *he's* DB Cooper?" Frieda asked, excited.

"Not sure how you got there, Fred, but no," Henry said. "In fact, I've been thinking about the ransom since Tess mentioned the money found in the 1980s."

"Me too."

"Not like that. I mean that it's impossible that any of Cooper's ransom money could have entered into circulation without kicking off alarm bells. I don't see how it could be spent."

"Isn't that what money laundering is for?" Tess asked.

"Normally, the bottleneck with money laundering is the layering stage, where it gets disassociated with the illegal activity. It gets funneled through a legitimate business or something. In this case though, because of the tracking of the bills, you wouldn't even be able to get it placed in the system to start."

"You know how to launder money?" Frieda asked. Henry couldn't tell whether she was impressed by her uncle's criminal wherewithal, or disappointed that he had been holding out on her.

"Kind of. No. More how to track it down. It's the sort of thing I had to look out for at the bank."

"What if he deposited it?" Frieda asked.

"The bills would have turned up. The FBI would have traced them. Badda bing, badda bang, he's caught."

"What if he bought diamonds?"

"Same."

"What if he just put it in a safe?"

"That's what I'm saying. In a safe, you can't spend it. You can't grow it. You can't do anything with it. He might as well never have got on the plane. And I can't believe that someone would just sit on a pile of cash like that. I'm saying that if Cooper survived with the cash, he'd have been caught by now."

"What if he has been caught, but the government is hiding him?"

"Creative, Fred."

Tess started walking again, her pace slow and deliberate. The others followed. "Have you ever met anyone from the company, Hen?"

"No," Henry said, drawing out the word and ending it with the inflection of a question. "Bernadette showed me around when I came to look at the place. She met me with the contracts when I signed the lease. And I slip checks through the mail slot." Henry made clicking sounds as he thought. "What about you?"

"Exactly the same. So, what is Bernadette hiding? She knows what connects this company to Mr. Benham. There could even be a link to what happened."

Frieda climbed on board with Tess's suspicion. "We should find out who's behind the company."

"Whoa," Henry said, loud enough to scare a few birds out of the hedge next to them. "'Behind the company'? This isn't a movie. We aren't detectives."

"Henry," Tess said. Already he had gotten used to her using his nickname, and the sound of his full name was jarring. "The police are not investigating the company. Bernadette took this because she doesn't want them to investigate it. But what's the harm in finding out for ourselves?"

"Harm? Plenty. Look at Benham in a hospital bed. And I'm looking after Fred."

"Maybe she stays—"

"Don't even," Henry interrupted.

"Look," Tess said, her tone stern now. "Someone broke into my home and hurt my neighbor, who may or may not be DB Cooper."

"Isn't," Henry said.

"May or not be. And if he isn't, then it's all a bunch of harmless dead ends anyhow, right? In the meantime, two neighbors want to keep information from the police, and another neighbor is a strange, anonymous corporation. You want to take care of Fred? Then let's figure out what's going on. How do we feel safe unless we understand what this person was after? What if it wasn't Mr. Benham they were looking for? Doesn't that mean that this could happen to any one of us?"

Tess froze with her arms wide, her raised eyebrows challenging Henry for a more reasonable answer. Frieda mimicked her expression.

Henry felt the silence heating the surrounding air. He swallowed and breathed through his mouth.

"I need to know," Tess said, her hand on her chest.

"Okay. Let's see what we can find out about the numbered company."

Frieda and Tess cheered. Their enthusiasm seemed undiminished by their poorly connecting high five.

"Here's the catch," Henry said. "I'm ninety-nine percent certain we're not going to find anything on the internet. There's only going to be information online if that company has ever issued securities under a prospectus or has made the news for some reason."

"English please," Frieda said.

"Okay, if our company had shares on a stock exchange, there would be publicly available documents. Financial statements, information about directors, etc. Chances are that this '121702 BC Ltd.' is a private company. It doesn't need to disclose its information publicly."

Frieda shook her head. "That's how corporations steal and don't pay taxes."

"No, not at all." Henry counted out on his fingers. "Private companies still have shareholders that own the shares. They still have directors who run the company. They still have to pay tax. They still have to make annual filings—"

"Can we get those?" Tess asked.

"Hen can," Frieda said. "Right?"

He looked at the pair of them: their similar expressions, their eyebrows raised in hope.

"Bits of it. There is a registry for BC companies."

"Let's do it," Tess said.

"We can't just open an account. It takes days. I used to have access through the bank."

"Use your old one," Frieda said.

Henry squinted hard. *The sooner this is cleared up, the better, right?*

"Alright. Tess, are you up for a low-level misdemeanor?"

CHAPTER TWENTY-SIX

Henry watched Tess dodge between traffic as she jaywalked across the street and into the coffee shop where they waited. She hadn't been gone twenty minutes.

"How'd it go?" he asked.

She dropped into her seat and laid several printed pages on the table.

"Piece of cake," she said. "The guy at the internet café register barely looked up to sign me in. The username and password you gave me are still active and the site was pretty intuitive. The toughest part was that I had no idea what I was looking at. So I printed out everything."

"I thought you had a business degree," Henry said.

"Marketing," Tess said by way of explanation.

Henry flipped through the papers. The top of the first page read *"BC Corporation Summary - 121702 BC Ltd."*

"The company was incorporated way back on December 1, 1971," he read, skimming and flipping sheets. "The only director of the company is R. Benham."

"Mr. Benham owns our building?" Tess asked, surprised.

"Not necessarily." Henry's eyes scanned the remaining document as he spoke. "Shareholders own a company. Directors just sort of make decisions. They don't have to be the owners, too. It's possible, though, but it makes no sense." He tapped the table with his index finger. "The registered office's address is Unit 2, 1584 Richardson Street, which is no surprise. Although, I've never seen anyone picking up mail from there. Have you?"

"I've never seen anyone going in or out, ever," Tess said. "What's that other address?"

Henry frowned at the page.

Why is this familiar?

"1501 West Broadway." He looked out the window, mentally walking through a map of the city.

"Why are there two addresses?" Tess asked.

"The records office is different from the mailing address of the company. Lots of companies keep their corporate records at their lawyer's offices." He typed away on his phone. "Lawyers. There's only one law firm in that building. Whoever the shareholders of the company are, they are using Tolmie Douglas & Associates, upstairs."

"Let's go up there and pretend we work for the company," suggested Frieda.

"Nice try, kiddo," Henry said. "I'm sure that's illegal for some reason. Plus, I know those lawyers. You remember my friend, Alex? That's his firm."

"Just ask him, then."

Henry winced. He couldn't stop now. He also couldn't just ask Alex to violate a client's privacy. Tess and Frieda sat in silence as Henry weighed the consequences of putting a friend in a compromising position versus the cost of not knowing the answer.

"Alex does trusts and estates, not corporate work. But I think I know what I can ask, without actually asking. First, I need to figure out whose client the company is. There are three possible corporate lawyers there and maybe we can find out who we should talk to. Two of them I know only by name, from work we did with them at the bank. The third, Tolmie, is a tyrant. We'll get nowhere if it's his client."

"Let's hope it's not his, then. Who's Alex?" Tess asked.

Henry punched in Alex's number without thinking. "A friend from university. He's also handling my divorce." He heard the phone ringing and held a finger to his lips.

"Alexander Irving speaking."

"Hey, Alex."

"Hey yourself. I thought you were going to be busy all week having fun. What's up?"

"I'm just trying to get a hold of someone at the management company for my apartment. I lost the contact info, but I remember them saying that they use you guys for their corporate work."

"Oh? Do you recall whose client it is?"

"I don't. I think it was either Nolan or Mya. The company is 121702 BC Ltd."

Henry waited. He shrugged at Frieda and Tess and continued. "The thing is, Bernadette's my usual person, and she's away right now. I think she might have gone on vacation or to see her family or something."

The response was slow in coming.

"Really?"

"I know. You'd think she would have left a contact number. She might have mentioned it, in fact, and I guess I just missed it."

Henry waited. He thought for a moment they had been disconnected. But Alex spoke again.

"Why are you asking?"

Henry tried to sound as nonchalant as possible. "I'm just trying to track down another contact at the company. I figured you guys could put me in touch with one of the owners."

"Huh. I can't help you."

Henry rolled the dice. "Is it possible that Nolan or Mya might know? Or Tolmie?"

"What the heck is this, Henry? What are you really asking about 121702 for?"

Henry's mind raced. Corporate structures ran through his mind: holding companies, trusts, shareholders, trustees.

That firm must have hundreds of corporate clients. Why would Alex be aware of this company off the top of his head? Why this reaction?

Henry pulled the ripcord. "Hey, I must have misheard that it was one of your clients. Sorry for wasting your time. I'll just leave a message for my usual person to call me when she gets back."

"Yeah, don't worry about it." There was disbelief in Alex's tone. Still, he seemed willing to play along.

"Hey, by the way, have you heard about Ron Benham?"

"You can't ask me this shit, Henry." Alex growled. "I don't know what you're up to, but you're going too far this time, even for you. This conversation never happened." A loud, clattering sound followed as Alex hung up.

CHAPTER TWENTY-SEVEN

H enry lowered the phone from his ear. The pieces fell into place.

"Well?" Tess asked.

"The company is owned by a trust," Henry said with confidence. "If Alex is the lawyer, then either he is the trustee or, at least, he's legal counsel to the trustee. Whatever the purpose of the trust is, by his reaction, I'd guess it's hush-hush."

Henry leaned back and crossed one leg over the other. "Using a trust would be a simple way to obscure ownership of the company. You continue to operate the company just as you'd like, based on decisions you make when you set it up. Then lots of the directions are set in stone and anyone else can run it as the trustee. The big question is: where did the trust come from?"

"And you can find that out, right?" Frieda asked.

"I don't know that we can." Henry shook his head and rubbed his temples as he spoke. "I hope I haven't burned a bridge there with Alex, too. That's going to take some explaining. If he's the trustee, he's accountable to the people who benefit from the trust. The beneficiaries. We have no idea who they are, and there is no way in hell that he's going to tell us."

Henry polished off his coffee, now cold, in one long swig. "I mean, it's possible that the trust is some long-dead person's estate. But it's just as likely that someone living set it up for themselves."

"To hide something?" Tess asked.

"Maybe." He shrugged. "It fits, right?"

"Mr. Benham," Frieda said, under her breath.

"Could be," Henry said. "Anyhow, I think the trust successfully prevents our figuring out who owns 121702. This is a dead end."

Henry leaned one elbow on the table and flipped through the corporate information again.

"That was enough law and accounting for me for one day," Tess said.

"We can't be stuck," Frieda said and pouted at the window.

Tess placed the card from Bernadette's purse on the table. "This is all we've got." She pulled out her phone and looked to the service counter for the posted password to the WiFi.

The three of them fumed in their own ways. Eventually, Frieda dipped into her satchel, offered them all gum, and joined Tess with her own phone.

"You took a pic of the chat?"

"I'll send it to you."

Henry's phone beeped a receipt, and he listened as the conversation turned more intently to the subject of DB Cooper. His own eyes passed again and again over the small card Tess had lifted from Bernadette's purse.

"Hang on," he said. "Where are you guys?"

"We're looking at the Net-Tectives site again," Tess replied.

"Did you know that DB Cooper left his tie on the plane?" Frieda asked. "It wasn't even a real tie. It clipped on. How cool, eh?"

Henry read through the conversation again between *treasurehunter1971* and *juliancaesar*.

"So, we're confident that Mr. Creepy is Keller, or *treasure-hunter1971*, right?"

"Because Frieda pointed out that he had out-of-town plates," Tess said.

"Right. But who's the other guy? Who did our stalker come here to meet? And for what?"

"Holy sh—" Tess caught her language and looked at Frieda. "Smokes. We went down the rabbit hole with the Cooper-Benham thing, but we've still not looked at the other side."

Henry turned back to his laptop and brought up the Net-Tectives site. He brought up the *juliancaesar* profile. Member for thirty days, no posts to his name, most recent history was the same DB Cooper hijacking forum. And a name.

"Julian Corbeau," he said. "At least it's not Ron Benham."

"Corbeau means 'crow' in French," Frieda said, leaning most of her body across the table to see Henry's screen. "And he's from here, right?"

Henry googled the name, followed by 'Vancouver'.

"And we have a hit." He looked up at Tess. "Julian Corbeau, it seems, is the owner of Corbeau Silver & Gold, right downtown. Not much of a website, but we've got a phone number."

Henry dialed the number. No answer. He looked at his watch. "It's past five-thirty."

"Where is it?" Tess asked. "We could go in tomorrow and talk to this Julian guy."

"This is crazy." Henry's shaking hands made and corrected mistakes as he typed into the laptop. "East Hastings. Right downtown. Why not? We'll go in the morning. He doesn't know who we are. We're just customers. It'll be an adventure and, if we learn anything, we'll pass it on to the police."

Frieda leaned in very close to the screen. "Could you switch to street view?"

Henry switched map views, so the screen showed the street right in front of the pawnshop. There to the left of the barred windows was a small store with a green sign that read *Welcome Pharmacy*.

CHAPTER TWENTY-EIGHT

I n the hallway of 1584 Richardson, they agreed to order pizza and immerse themselves in Cooper lore. Henry watched Tess climb the stairs in lithe hops. She would fetch her laptop, and probably lose her socks and shoes.

Inside Henry's suite, Frieda scooped Shima into her arms before the cat had fully emerged from the bedroom.

Henry leaned with his back on the door and surveyed the situation. Despite the drama and sirens of the night before, despite the lingering scent of new furniture, despite everything, he felt a long-unfamiliar calm. There would be no permanent damage to his friendship with Alex. The decision to walk away from his professional designation felt more right the more he thought about it. And Frieda? He could look after her, and he couldn't ask for a better house guest.

He dared wonder whether the worst was behind him.

Before Henry could find the number to call for delivery, the apartment door burst open, knocking him forward.

Tess rushed in, barefoot and crying.

"He was here."

CHAPTER TWENTY-NINE

"Lock the door behind us. Don't let anyone in. If you hear me shout, call 911."

Frieda, with Shima still in her arms, nodded in the bedroom doorway as Tess and Henry went out into the hall.

Henry stopped cold as his foot hit the first stair to the second floor. "He's gone now, right?"

"I think so," Tess said.

They crept up together, wincing at each creak of the old stairwell.

From the hallway, through the open door, Henry could see books and papers littering the floor. Further on, in Tess's bedroom, sheets and clothes were piled on the floor. Every drawer had been opened and emptied. Whoever had been through the apartment had invaded every imaginable space.

"This is the worst bit," Tess said.

In her studio, a bottle of ink was upturned onto the hardwood floor in one dark pool with spatter in all directions, looking like a murder scene from a black-and-white film. A single brush lay staining her yellow chair, discarded after having been used to write on the wall.

The letters were a dark, dull black, the ink having soaked into the paint and plaster.

THIEF

Henry stared at the word.

"Why me?" Tess asked.

Henry opened his mouth but had no words. They studied the message together for a long moment.

Henry whispered. "Do you notice how nothing looks broken?" He turned on the spot. "Other than the ink, there's a mess but nothing's wrecked. Why?"

"Maybe he was trying to be quiet?" Tess said.

"Maybe," Henry agreed. "Or maybe he was angry when he attacked Benham. And here? Here he was just looking for something?"

They looked back at the writing on the wall. The characters were tall, evenly spaced, of equal size.

"It's not scribbled, is it?" Tess said as she leaned in to look at the letters. "He even went back to the well a couple of times for more ink."

"So, what does he think you stole?"

"His papers?"

Henry shrugged. "That's the only thing I can think of."

Tess's pale look told Henry that she was thinking the same thing. Her 'daughter' Frieda was the thief.

"What's so goddamn important about those papers?"

"Whatever it is, he wants them back."

"And he can't have found them, because there was nothing here."

"You're sure?"

"We had all of it last night. It's all downstairs. Which means . . ." She looked out the large window at Richardson Street. There were neither cars outside nor pedestrians. Even the café appeared empty.

"I was thinking the same thing," Henry said. "There's a good chance he's coming back."

"Augh!" Henry turned quickly from the window and made fists in his hair. "We'll have to call the police. Again."

"What do we tell them?"

"What do you mean, what do we tell them?" Henry's eyes were wide. "This could mean Frieda." He pointed at the writing on the wall. "We tell them everything."

"We can't, though, can we? Are you going to tell them we held back a bunch of pages? Or that we used your bank password to get information about the numbered company?"

Henry rubbed his eyes. He paced in a circle, stepping on paper, avoiding books.

"And what about Mr. Benham?"

"Okay," he said. "Let's get our stories straight."

They spoke for several minutes before they heard sirens. Henry looked out the window and saw a police cruiser pull up in front of the house. One of its front tires rested on the curb. Its front end nearly touched the lamppost and faced against the direction of traffic. A familiar figure in uniform got out of the passenger side of the vehicle and stood looking at the building.

"Did you call the police?" he asked.

"No. I've been with you the whole time."

"Well, Stubbing and Tipton are here."

"Fred must have heard you shout."

Henry tipped his head back to the ceiling, groaning.

"You go see Fred," Tess said. "I'll meet our friends."

A second car pulled up behind the first.

"And their friends, too," she added.

CHAPTER THIRTY

S ergeant Khatri was a towering, full-bearded figure, several
inches taller than Henry. He fairly filled the doorframe
leading to the hallway. The Sikh officer wore his turban low on
his forehead, dark blue and cheerless to match his uniform
jacket. Only when Khatri smiled could Henry surmise that he
wasn't scowling.

"My colleagues are just finishing with your friend upstairs.
Would you mind if I asked you a few questions in the meantime, Mr...?"

"Lysyk. Henry Lysyk." Henry waved Sergeant Khatri into his
apartment.

The Sergeant gave Henry a sidelong glance as he entered.
"Have you lived here long?"

"Only about half a year."

"And you are dating Ms. Honma?"

"No, we only just met."

"But you've lived here for months?"

"Yes. I keep myself busy."

Henry held out a mug and kettle. Khatri shook his head and
continued walking around the room.

"Do you have keys to the other suites in the house? Maybe Ms. Honma's?"

"No."

"But you do find her attractive. I mean, you're a single man, and she's a young, single woman."

"I beg your pardon. What kind of question is that?"

Khatri looked at his note pad. "And your niece? She is staying with you?"

"That's right. Her folks are away for a few more days."

"Where is she now?"

"In the bedroom with my cat. He's a little spooked by all the activity."

"She saw the man on the lawn?"

"Yes."

"You don't mind keeping her in the house where your neighbor was attacked downstairs?"

Henry looked at the closed bedroom door. Frieda would be pressing her ear to the other side.

"Well, I don't like it, of course. But what happened to Benham has nothing to do with me."

"What about what happened upstairs?"

"What?"

"You saw what was painted on the wall?"

"Yes. *Thief.*"

"If you had to guess what the person who wrote this was referring to, what would you say?"

Henry blinked and tried to read into the scowling Sikh's eyes.

"What would you say that you do for a living, Henry?"

"I'm between things."

Khatri broke off and paced into the kitchen. He stopped in front of the large window and blocked out a great portion of the view.

"Where did you tell my colleagues you were yesterday, when Mr. Benham was attacked?"

Henry spoke to the man's back.

"I said that I was taking care of something. Something personal."

Khatri turned slowly. The heel of his boot squeaked on the hard wood.

"This is what you said. Is this what you did, Henry?"

Henry blinked questions at dark eyes that probed back.

"What?"

"I've read about you in the papers, Henry. You went rogue and turned against your employer, didn't you? You got yourself quite a bit of attention."

Khatri took a seat at the far side of the table and leaned forward on his elbows. He looked more at home here than Henry.

Henry wiped his hands on his lap.

"Would you like to tell me about the bank, Henry?"

"That has nothing to do with this."

"But they are accusing you of being a thief, are they not?"

"There's no thief in that picture," Henry said, pulling out a chair opposite Khatri. "Maybe you and yours should be looking into the information that we gave you."

"Specifically?"

"Have you looked into the online conversation, the one we gave to Constable Stubbing? To see who he was speaking to, and why?"

"Who is 'he'?"

"Well, whoever did this," Henry waved his arm up and down. "To Mr. Benham and Tess."

"How do you know it was the same person from the messages?"

Henry took a deep breath. "It's not for me to investigate this. That's your job."

"Right," Khatri said, leaning back. "I'm curious, Henry, about your niece. You seem quite certain that she is safe here."

"Do I?"

He nodded. "I don't hear that you're worried about what might have happened if our villain had come into your apartment instead of Tess's. I don't hear that you've even thought about taking the girl to stay with her aunt instead."

"Who said anything about her aunt?"

As though in answer, the front door opened. Tess walked in without knocking, slowing down as she neared the men at the table.

"Hey," she said, "we're done upstairs."

"Did you tell the police that I should take Fred to Sarah?"

"No," she said, clearly having expected a different question. "Yes. But not to hijack your visit."

Henry bristled at her choice of words. Had she said something so that he would continue with this ridiculous Cooper thing?

"I couldn't tell them anything else and I'm leaving them with the run of my place," she continued. "So, I thought that I would pull the chute and hang out with you guys until they're done."

Angry though he was at Tess having mentioned Sarah, her signals were getting through.

I'm slow, but not that slow.

"I think she's right, Sergeant. As you yourself have pointed out, I should probably spend some time with my niece. Make sure she's alright. It's time for you to go."

Both men rose.

"Mr. Lysyk, would you be willing to come downtown to continue our conversation?"

Tess let out a small gasp.

Henry had heard this question once before. Only then it was a plain-clothes officer, and he was in one of the bank's boardrooms. He responded just how Alex had instructed him to that first time.

"Am I being detained or arrested?"

"No. I'm asking you to meet voluntarily, so we can speak at length. You may remember something else."

"Then I will pass, thank you."

Khatri's stoic composure masked any annoyance. He nodded and walked past Tess to the front door.

He looked back over his shoulder and spoke, holding the door by its knob. "If we find out that you are the one terrorizing your neighbors, or if you are this 'thief' and we find out you are messing about in our investigation, this will not end well for you."

"Thank you. Bye."

"And, Mr. Lysyk, if you aren't involved, and you care at all for your niece, you will take her to stay with her aunt."

"Thank you. Bye."

As Sergeant Khatri closed the door behind him, he offered one last piece of advice.

"Get a lock on the front door."

Henry and Tess both spoke at once.

"What was that about?" "You told them about Sarah?"

Tess waved his question away. "They asked how long Fred was staying with you and whether there were any other family members. They said Bernadette had already mentioned an aunt. What was I supposed to say?"

"Bernadette?"

"She's the property manager's contact, right?"

Henry scowled.

Tess continued. "They think this is because of you, Hen. They asked if I knew about you and the bank."

Henry picked up on the question in her tone, and the conspicuous absence of her typical directness. He was acutely aware of Frieda behind him, listening from the doorway to the bedroom.

"It's nothing to do with me. I'm not a thief. What was with the Cooper references?"

"They've not looked into the Net-Tectives at all. Constable Tipton was here again. She told me they've only investigated as far as finding out that it was from a forum for amateurs investigating cold cases. They're monitoring the site for further messages, but other than that they've stopped there."

"Well, the fact that they're monitoring means they aren't completely buying Benham's story about not being attacked."

"Sure. But other than that, they just turned their nose up at it. There's no love lost between the pros and the amateurs it seems."

"So, no one is looking for DB Cooper?" Frieda spoke from the doorway of the bedroom. Shima's dark eyes reflected out from her cloak, bundled in her arms.

"No one except us," Tess said.

"And whoever broke in," Henry corrected.

"What does this mean? Are you still up for the pawnshop?" Tess asked, her voice skeptical.

"Are you?"

"I'm not stopping," she said.

Henry pressed his lips together and stuck a hand in his hair.

"As long as they think you're the person they're looking for, Hen, I think they're on the wrong track."

He opened his mouth to speak and closed it again.

"If you're worried about Fred, then you guys should stay."

"But you could use our help," Frieda said.

"I could."

"The way I see it," Henry said, "our best bet all around is to get the police on the right track. We know that our villain is the

American that was meeting Julian at the pawnshop. Therefore, Julian cannot be our guy. But, if we play our cards right, maybe we can at least find out what our guy is looking for."

"Agreed," Tess said. "But what about..."

Henry and Tess looked at Frieda. She looked especially small right now, as panicky tears welled in her eyes.

"No, Hen," Frieda said.

Henry took in a deep breath.

There was nothing Henry could do about getting a lock on the front door tonight. Taking Frieda to Sarah's, though, was in his power. Even if the thought made him sick.

CHAPTER THIRTY-ONE

Tess sat at the kitchen table as Henry put away the rest of the takeout Thai food; their working dinner. Laptops were still on the table, making the place look like an improvised command center. Frieda's laptop was a notable absence, though, having taken it with her to Sarah's. Henry imagined Frieda would still be up, likely poring through the Net-Tectives site in bed. Probably cursing him, too.

"Jeez, 1971 was a gong show," Tess said. "Vietnam, the Pentagon papers, massive layoffs. There was even a riot in Gastown."

"Hmm." Henry watched Shima's chest rise and fall on the chair next to his own.

"And Godzilla burned Disneyland to the ground."

"Hmm."

Henry flinched in surprise as Tess poked his arm.

"Sorry. I was thinking about Fred," he said. "I hope she doesn't have nightmares."

Tess brushed his arm before taking her hand back.

"She's tough. In fact, I'll bet if she has any trouble sleeping it's because she's excited."

"No. She's disappointed and angry."

The discussion with Frieda about going to Sarah's had gone as poorly as Henry expected. Tears were followed by the silent treatment. It was cold comfort that she didn't want to go any more than he wanted to get rid of her. There was just no way, as far as Henry could see, that he could look after her. The police saw the break-in to Tess's apartment as a one-off. Henry wasn't as confident this would be the case.

He tipped his head back and emptied the last of his glass of wine. "She doesn't want us to go to the pawnshop without her." He poured some more.

"Can you blame her? In her mind, we're solving a mystery and we've cut her out."

"Is that what we're doing? Solving a mystery?"

"Whatever. There's an element of excitement."

"It's dangerous."

"And she trusts you to keep her safe and, to be honest, I think she has fun with you."

"Whose side are you on?" Henry closed his laptop. He scrubbed the sides of his head with his fingers in frustration. His fine hair became fluffy over his ears. "She's still holding something back, though."

Tess dipped a middle finger into her glass, just breaking the surface of the wine. "What makes you say that?" she asked, putting the tip of her finger to her lips.

"Do you believe that she forgot about the car? Or that she had those papers on her and forgot to mention it?" Henry instinctively looked to make sure the bedroom door was closed. "No way. The Fred I know would've run upstairs with the cross-word the minute she found it. She'd have been dancing around with it."

"Because she solved your mystery of the missing crossword?"

"Because then you couldn't call me crazy. Furthermore, it

would prove that it had nothing to do with Sarah and her boyfriend."

"You think she's hiding something."

"Something. Yes."

Henry studied his glass. The wine was dark, more burgundy than red. *But we still call it red.*

"Is she so bad, your ex?"

"To be honest, I don't know. She wasn't always. But it makes me wonder whether you can ever really know someone."

Tess started to speak, but Henry picked his glass of wine up from the table and gestured with it at the half-full bottle and then the living room.

She closed her laptop in agreement and picked up both her own glass and the bottle. She flicked off the light in the kitchen with her elbow. Her bare feet padded after him to the couch.

Henry scooped Shima up with his free hand and dropped the old cat onto his lap. Shima made a groaning sound, turned in circles and appeared to decide for himself to settle down right where Henry had placed him.

"Speaking to the police this afternoon, her re-telling of the car was different."

"Was it?"

"Maybe," Henry said, with less certainty. "At first she said the car was parked right next to the diner. Then, she tells Constable Tipton that she didn't see the man's face as he got in. If the car was right in front of the diner, the car would be facing us; the man would have to face the house in order to get in the driver's side. If she didn't see his face, then he was parked on the other side of the street."

Tess poured more wine. "Wow, Sherlock. How did you just let her get away with that? You've busted her wide open."

"I know, I..."

Henry caught the look of sarcasm on Tess's face, the mischief of wide eyes and the beginning curl of a smirk.

"Good one," he said. "I'm serious. Why would she lie?"

Tess shrugged. "Maybe that's why. Because you're so serious. I'm not saying it doesn't matter. But maybe what she needs from you, though, is just to feel safe." She turned her back to him and curled her feet onto the couch, leaning against his arm.

"Safe, eh? I'm trying."

Henry looked at the cat curled up in his lap, the tip of its tail beating a quiet tattoo against Tess's back. Henry settled his own body against hers.

"Don't get me wrong," Tess said. "She's exceptional, and I know she means a lot to you. Well, take the good with the . . . teenager. Just hang out with her when this is all over."

"It's not that simple. She will not let this go."

"Sure, she's got her teeth in this as much as we do and she's going to want to know what's going on." Tess sipped and took air in through her lips before swallowing. "Did you want to get rid of her?"

The dread that had come over him in the restaurant, when he first learned of Frieda's visit was now so unfamiliar. "Of course not."

"But you did."

"I had no choice."

"Didn't you? What do you want?"

Henry rested his lips against the rim of his glass. The wine smelled old, like earth and vines. It tasted of refinement and time spent learning about vintages and varietals. The ones he chose always smacked of fruits and berries.

"It's too late," he said.

"Is it?"

"I don't know."

"You don't know what you want? Or you're afraid to say?"

He sighed and tried to explain his loan repayment scheme, getting fired, and the bank's aggressive claims against him. "So,

I don't know where I'm going to be in a year. I might be here. I might be in Toronto. If that's the case, I may not see her again for a long time."

"That's rather sly, Mr. Goody Two Shoes." She patted him on the knee.

Henry swelled a little at her approval.

"All but the Toronto bit," Tess said. "Doesn't that feel like running away?"

"Or I've got nothing left to run away from."

"Does Fred know?"

Henry bit the side of his cheek. After a moment, he answered, "No."

"Ah. You'll miss her."

"I think I would miss a few people."

Those last words hung in the air as they sat quietly. Henry managed sips of his wine, navigating the glass over Tess and the cat. As the trickles of wine passed through his throat and into his chest, so did Tess's observations.

She broke the silence. "I'll drive tomorrow."

"I didn't even know you had a car."

"There are a lot of things you don't know about me, Mr. Lysyk." Henry could hear the grin in her voice. "I'm an artist, sure, but I'm not starving."

Henry looked over at the door to the empty bedroom. "So, you think we should take her tomorrow? To the pawnshop?"

"No," Tess said after a pause. "I don't think so, but it's your call. We don't know this Julian guy and we're coloring outside the lines here. We gave the police the chat sessions, but we held back the index card. Then again, Fred's as much a part of this as we are. Sure, it's not the week of movies and Kool-Aid that you guys had planned, but maybe it's the time together that you have."

"Escape room," Henry said.

"Pardon me?"

"We had a reservation for one of those escape rooms today. You know, like the games?" He mimed playing on a phone with his hands. "You get locked in a room for an hour and have to find a hidden key and let yourself out."

"That sounds awful," she said, laughing.

"Probably."

Shima jumped down and headed to the bedroom. He nudged the door open with his nose and slipped inside.

"I guess we were too loud." Henry's arm lay on top of Tess's and he felt her intertwine their fingers. She gave his hand a squeeze.

Although they knew they were the only two people in the house, they spoke in hushed tones. The one light, a cheap paper column floor lamp, seemed to dim as their eyelids grew heavy.

CHAPTER THIRTY-TWO

H enry woke on his couch with the pasty grogginess that comes only with having slept fully dressed from the day before. He pushed away the small, wool blanket.

Too hot. What is this?

He opened his eyes and saw that it was Frieda's cloak. Next to him on the couch, Tess was curled up with a proper bedsheet. She made a light snoring noise, not unlike Shima. He sat up and craned his neck to see into the kitchen. Frieda knelt perched on a chair at the table, pen in hand, looking deep in thought.

She noticed him and waved with the pen. "G'morning, Hen."

He rolled off the couch, careful not to disturb Tess, and whispered, "What are you doing here?"

"I want to come today." She put the pen down and faced him.

As confused as he was, Henry felt pleased to see her. "Did Sarah drop you off?" He looked in the cupboard for a tin of cat food.

"I fed Shima and there's coffee."

"Have I told you you're the perfect house guest?" Henry

joined her at the table where she had been working on the crossword. "Wow, I haven't seen one of these in a while."

"I got up early and I saw the paper guy come. It wasn't a paperboy. It was a grown man."

He sipped at the coffee, swirling steam from the mug with his breath. "Thanks," he said, perhaps for the coffee, the cloak, or something else altogether. She had filled in the odd word here and there in the crossword. One answer was crossed out and written over more than once. "You made a good dent in it," he said, ruffling what was left of her blue brown hair with his fingers.

"Did Sarah drop you off?" he asked again.

"Don't be mad, Hen."

He tried to erase any look of concern from his face. Tess's words from the night before echoed in his brain.

"After you dropped me off, I didn't go inside."

"What do you mean you didn't go inside?" he asked, covering his reaction by bringing his mug to his lips.

"I knocked and no one was there. I went around back, but it was locked. You drove away and I came back here."

"Sarah wasn't home?"

"She flaked."

"You don't have a key?"

Frieda shook her head as she sipped on her coffee.

"You could have picked the lock."

"I forgot."

They stared at each other in a stalemate.

"Where did you—"

"In the bedroom. You were out when I got back. I figured you were getting dinner, so I finished the pizza and went to the bedroom. I texted Sarah already, too."

"You were here all night?"

She pursed her lips matter-of-factly and nodded. "Are you mad?"

What had she heard last night? He thought about Tess's comments about his being so serious. He had to admit he was glad to see Frieda.

"No," he said. "I just want you to be safe."

Frieda was clearly happy to change the subject. "Is Tess staying for breakfast?"

"She's more than welcome to."

"Did you have sex?"

Henry choked on his coffee in mid-swallow. He coughed in loud barks into his elbow. Unable to speak, he shook his head.

No.

From the couch, Tess asked in a sleepy voice, "Is everything okay?"

"Hen's choking, but he'll be fine. Are you having breakfast here before we go downtown?"

"Well, good to see you Fred. I'd love a bite." She was suspiciously unfazed by the young girl's unanticipated appearance. "You're joining us?" The question was directed as much to Henry as Frieda.

Frieda nodded. Henry didn't disagree, adding, "We're a team."

"Like a crime-fighting family," Frieda said.

"Alright then," Tess said with raised eyebrows. "Let me just go freshen up. I'll be back down in a sec." With that, she sat up, pulled on her pants and headed upstairs, carrying her socks and shoes.

Henry blinked as he processed that she had undressed at some point. *Had she known Fred was here?*

As soon as he heard the click of the door latch, Henry took the seat across from Frieda.

"Things don't move that fast."

"Well, I don't know," she said, shrugging. "They do in movies."

"Well, I don't move that fast. We must watch different movies."

"No. Kyle Reese and Sarah Connor fall in love and they have sex right away. And I saw that movie with you."

Henry managed to down this mouthful of coffee without gagging.

"*Terminator*? That's what you took away? Adults hook up quickly? That's not the message I got."

I'm going to have to re-watch that and be more careful with future movie choices.

"How about: 'Don't make robots smarter than humans?'" Henry said. "That's a good message. Besides, Sarah had a son who would save humanity. Real life doesn't need another hero because it already has you."

"It's true." Frieda puffed out her chest. "I made coffee this morning."

"Well said."

Henry's phone hummed to life on the table. The caller was from Toronto, Ontario. He picked it up and hesitated before answering. Frieda sipped her coffee across from him. What did she know?

He shooed her to the bedroom with his free hand, messing her hair as she passed. "Get dressed, hero. It's a quick breakfast then straight downtown." The phone continued to buzz.

"It's going to be an interesting day."

CHAPTER THIRTY-THREE

Downtown, Frieda slid the seat forward so that Henry could get out of the blue two-door Tercel. Practical and compact, Henry couldn't imagine a more appropriate car for Tess. Frieda had been on the ball and called shotgun. Last night, driving to Sarah's, there had been no such fun.

It was a one-block walk to the East Hastings pawnshop.

As they approached the building, the economy of the population changed around them. People huddled in groups on the sidewalk, next to shopping carts heaped with everything from sleeping bags to guitars covered in stickers, and well-worn suitcases.

Henry and Tess cleared the sidewalk, stepping into the street for a young, shirtless man on a bicycle. In one hand, the cyclist carried a massive clear plastic bag full of bottles and cans over his shoulder. With his other hand, he navigated the bike while holding onto a second, equally full bag.

They spotted the pawnshop on the opposite corner and crossed the street.

Bars covered the windows and the lights inside were off. The internet listing had said that the shop opened at 9am. Henry looked at his watch. Just about eleven-thirty.

He rattled the gate over the front door. Locked shut.

"Well, that's not right," he said.

"What do we do now?" Frieda asked.

They took turns peering in the windows. Only Frieda could get her face between the bars, close enough to press to the dirty glass, between the bars.

"Do you see anything?" he asked.

"Nothing. It looks closed."

"Google says they should be open."

Inside, Henry spotted an accumulation of flyers, mail, and several copies of the free Vancouver Metro newspaper. "No one's been here all week."

Frieda rubbed dirt from her nose. "Why do they call it a pawnshop? Why don't they just call it an antique shop?"

"They don't just have antiques," Henry said. "They'll take anything that has value. The big difference – what makes a pawnshop a pawnshop – is that they can loan you money. You bring something in, say, a diamond ring, and they give you cash now. When you pay them back, you get your ring back."

Frieda looked doubtful. "So, how do they make money?"

"They charge interest. Maybe there's a fee, like if they loan you a hundred bucks and you pay back a hundred and twenty. Or, if you don't pay them back after a certain time, they get to keep whatever you've left them. If they're smart, they've loaned you less money than they can get for selling your stuff."

Frieda spoke more quietly. "Why wouldn't someone just get a loan from the bank? Or get a job?" Her eyes darted for a fraction of a second to the young woman lying in front of the shop.

Henry looked at the figure stretched out on the ground, her head using a blue hiking pack for a pillow. He dropped his volume down a little. "Banks won't loan to just anyone. Sometimes it's hard, like if you don't have a job. Pawn shops can make smaller loans, like a hundred bucks. And the owners can make their own deals based on whether they want to take a chance on a particular person. They get to know the value of stuff better than most people, and that's how they end up with some unusual things as security sometimes." He pointed at the mounted buffalo head in the window.

"Banks are more... mercenary."

Frieda thought about this and studied the motley collection of items in the window. "Maybe they're out to lunch?" Frieda smiled at her own use of the *double entendre*.

"Well, now what?" Tess asked, looking up and down the street.

"Maybe they have gone for lunch," Henry agreed. He stepped backward away from the doorway and looked up and where the sign had been. "Maybe they'd gone out of business?" Fluorescent bulbs sat bare and unlit in its place.

"Why don't we . . ."

The business next to the pawnshop was much narrower. A brief sign spanned the width of its door and single window. *Welcome Pharmacy*.

Henry slipped his hand into his pocket and removed the small, orange plastic bottle.

"That's from Mr. Benham's place," Tess said.

"I never looked at this closely," Henry said, "because I thought it was his."

He raised his glasses from his nose to read.

"It's for something called Xypresta. The name's gone, but I can just make out the prescription number, and the pharmacy address. It's in Everett, Washington."

"Keller's from Washington," Frieda said.

"If these are his, then maybe we can find out his name."

"What is it for?"

"I don't know," Henry said, pulling out his phone.

"Are you googling it?" Frieda asked.

He shook his head.

"What, Hen?"

"Better." Henry smiled and lifted the phone to his ear. "I know who we talk to next."

CHAPTER THIRTY-FOUR

Commercial Drive was a humble antidote to the downtown core. Small cafés, patios, and a thriving arts community gave the lengthy neighborhood a distinct feel. The pharmacy on Commercial was no bigger than the one next to the pawnshop. But the absence of layers of street grime on the window and door illustrated the difference that a seven-minute drive could make.

"Why didn't we just take it to the pharmacy back at the pawnshop?" Frieda asked.

"This sort of information might be confidential," Henry said. "So, we have to take it to someone we know, if they're going to tell us anything."

Past the cashier, in the very back of the store, a pharmacist dressed all in white spoke to a young woman over the counter. His salt-and-pepper hair looked too old for his stylish glasses and smooth bare face.

"Is that his real name?" Frieda asked, pointing at a large, framed certificate, hanging squarely on the wall behind the counter. "Dr. Well?"

"Peter Well, yes."

"Cool."

At the sound of his name, the pharmacist glanced up. Recognition flowed into his face, and he gestured them over, with a wave.

They wandered through the aisles, waiting for the young woman to leave. Dr. Well found them arguing over licorice. Sweet? Or salty?

"Henry," Peter said, holding his arms out and getting a hug. "Jen told me you'd called. It is good to see you. Have those bastards left you alone yet?" He checked himself and looked at Frieda. "Sorry."

Frieda shrugged.

"Ongoing," Henry said. "They're tenacious."

"They are buggers. Greedy buggers. Come on back to the coffee room and I'll make us some tea."

Peter led them behind the counter. Two chairs and a small corner table were somehow enough for this large closet to earn the title of "coffee room". A small mirror leaned over the sink from which Peter filled an electric kettle, and there was just enough room to stack boxes as stools for the rest of the guests. "Don't worry, it'll hold," he said as he indicated Henry should sit.

After introductions, chit-chat, and once everyone held a mug of Earl Grey ("Sorry, no milk") Peter explained to Frieda how his business had been saved by Henry from foreclosure.

"Six months ago, I didn't even know your uncle. He just called me out of the blue and warned me that the bank was going to exercise its right to call my loan. I couldn't believe my ears. It's not like I wasn't good for it. I'd just fallen behind. The pharmacy didn't have that kind of money all at once. I would have had to fire everybody and shut my doors."

Frieda drank with both hands on her mug and listened intently.

He continued. "Henry read to me some fine print in the terms of the loan agreement. All it would take to hold the bank off was a small payment. Any payment. I had no idea why a guy from the bank was telling me all this, but what could I do? I had to believe him. Sure enough, it held off any collections and we negotiated something new that this little pharmacy can manage."

"Six jobs, Henry saved. Good-paying jobs. Not even including me." His eyes watered as he remembered his close call.

"So your uncle's a hero," he said.

"It was nothing, Peter," Henry said, rubbing the back of his neck and happy to change the subject. "I wish I could say that we dropped in just for a visit. But in fact, we have a bit of a puzzle I'm hoping you can help us solve."

Henry pulled the orange pill bottle from his pocket.

Peter put his mug on the sink behind him. The direct steam condensed a small patch on the mirror in the already muggy room. He pulled his glasses down a little further on his nose, took the bottle from Henry, and squinted at it.

"These aren't yours," he said.

"Right. And I get it if you can't tell us anything. I'm not trying to ask you to do anything unethical."

"Well," Peter said, suddenly professional. "I'm relieved these aren't yours. Whose are they?"

"We aren't sure. We think their name is Keller. That's part of what we're trying to find out, hoping something you can see might help."

"Okay. This is Xypresta. It's the brand name for a drug called thorpazoline. We don't see it much in Canada, but in the States, it was licensed to treat schizophrenia and psychotic disorders. Specifically: productive symptoms such as automatism, hallucinations, and delusions."

"What was that first one?" Tess asked.

"Automatism? Think of it as unconscious action. When someone doesn't know what they're doing. You've seen in movies where someone says, 'I just blacked out and such-and-such happened'? That's a kind of automatism."

The looks on the faces of his audience spurred Peter into continuing.

"It's okay," he said. "That's what this is for. It's manageable once it's diagnosed."

"But we have their pills," Henry said. "Whoever this belongs to is off their meds."

"We don't use that expression," Peter said, scrunching his nose.

"Does that mean they're crazy now?" Frieda asked.

"No," Peter said. "That's one reason it's an awful term. Maybe this patient has other medications. Or maybe they're getting another form of treatment or support, like cognitive-behavioral therapy."

"Can you tell us anything about this person, Peter? I know it's a US prescription, and there's a question of confidentiality. But I wouldn't ask if it weren't important."

Peter thought for a moment before rising. "Give me a minute."

Cool air poured into the small room as he left, and Tess kept the door ajar with her foot.

Long minutes later, Peter returned and closed the door behind him. He pulled up his box, sat.

"Much of what I can say, you already know. It's from the US, and it's an anti-psychotic."

He turned the bottle over in his hands and showed them the worn-away label.

"A bit of the prescription ID is gone, but I tried a few until I found the match."

Numbers had been added, in pen, on the label.

"You're right about the name. It belongs to a Jack Keller. But no one has filled this prescription in at least a year."

"A year?" Henry asked. "Did they just get a new prescription?"

"No. There were still three more refills for this one. But it looks like the patient lost their insurance."

"What?" Tess asked. "So, this Keller just stopped taking his drugs?"

"It happens," Peter said, shrugging. "Without insurance, each refill of this is fifteen hundred dollars. That would last a month."

"Holy crap," Henry said. "But whoever's this is . . . They're fine, right? I mean, there's still one pill in there, so they've been on top of it. Right?"

Peter shook his head. He opened the bottle and brought it to his nose. He leaned back, reaching for his mug on the sink, dumped out the tea, and shook the pill onto the table.

The pill with its squared-off but rounded edges rolled to a stop in front of Frieda. It was a soft, familiar off-white.

"I know what that is," Frieda exclaimed.

"Clever girl," Peter said, impressed.

Everybody jumped as Peter smashed his mug down onto the pill like a hammer.

Only a splash of white powder remained, looking as though a tiny white meteor had crashed onto the table from space.

Frieda rubbed her finger through the damage, rolled it with her thumb, and held it to her nose. She sniffed.

Even from where Henry sat, the familiar smell of mint and vanilla was unmistakable.

"It's a Tic Tac," she said.

Peter nodded grimly. "Someone's only pretending to take their medication."

CHAPTER THIRTY-FIVE

Over lunch, they debated whether to return to the pawnshop at all. Tess and Frieda finally won, mollifying Henry with the argument that it would probably be closed anyhow.

Sure enough, as they stood outside, nothing had changed since this morning. Their handprints on the glass door were perfect and undisturbed. Even the young woman with the blue backpack seemed an exception to the passing of time.

Henry blew into his hands as he looked at her and worried whether she was alive.

"Excuse me?"

"Yes?" She appeared surprised to be seen, let alone addressed. She looked at the three people standing around her. Her eyes stopped on Frieda, and she nodded and sat up.

"I don't know how to put this," Henry said. "Have you been here for a while? That is, what I'm trying to ask is, have you seen anyone coming or going from here in the last week?"

From her seat on the ground, the young woman turned to look over her shoulder into the shop. She answered in a thick French-Canadian accent. "This place, it has been closed all week. Usually, Jules, he is good for a coffee or something. But this week, he stays in there."

"How do you know he's in there?" Tess asked.

"The lights, they are on at night. It's kind of nice. It means I can read."

Henry pulled a five-dollar bill from his pocket and placed it in the cup next to the backpack.

"Maybe we should check around back?" suggested Tess.

"What if Keller is there?" Frieda asked.

Henry scanned the cars on the street. "Let's keep an eye out for your K-car, Fred. If we see any sign that Keller is here, then perfect, we call the police."

The young girl blew up her already round cheeks and blinked in thought.

"We'll just knock and see if Julian is there," he added.

Frieda made a little groan.

Tess stepped in. "If you want to go back to the car, Fred, I understand," she said. "Me, I need to talk to this Julian guy, though, so we can get the police on the right track."

"I want to help," Frieda said.

Henry repeated himself. "We'll just knock."

The three walked around the corner and up the hill to the alley which provided access to the back of the shops on this block of East Hastings. Except for the usual dumpsters and telephone poles with an absurd number of wires attached to them, the alley was empty.

"No cars," Frieda said.

The back door to the pawnshop was easy to find, metal, and next to a large garage-type door that opened vertically.

Henry knocked several times without a response. He held out his empty hands, suggesting they leave.

"Want me to pick it?" Frieda asked.

"That's not necessary, Fred. I also think it's breaking and entering."

Tess spoke, and Henry turned to see her standing with the door open and one foot already inside the back of the shop.

"It's unlocked," she said, repeating herself.

"Wait." Henry shot out his palm, his fingers spread wide. "We were just going to knock. Why would it be unlocked? Maybe someone's in there."

Tess leaned in the door and shouted, "Hello?" After a second, she shrugged at Henry.

"Tess, what if we set off an alarm?"

"Then we call the police ourselves. We ask to speak to Tipton or Stubbing and explain that we were following up on the chat room conversation that we handed over. They should thank us for doing the leg work for them."

Tess disappeared inside.

"Yeah, they should thank us," Frieda added, following Tess as though attached by a string. "Are you coming?"

Deep breath.

Henry looked up and down the alley once more. There wasn't even a breeze to stir the bits of garbage or sway the knots of power lines. Nothing moved.

Still skeptical of the merits of this plan, his priority was watching after Frieda. He followed the pair through the door.

The lights in the back of the shop were already on. Still, the room was dim, as the towers of shelves blocked out most illumination that wasn't directly overhead. Right next to the door was a heap of random furniture: desks, tables, and chairs.

"What are we looking for?" Frieda asked.

"Anything that tells us something about Julian or Net-Tectives," Henry said.

"Or Cooper," Tess added.

Tess and Frieda disappeared into the stacks of pawned items.

Henry proceeded straight into the front, retail area of the shop. The ceiling was lower, but the gray light that filtered its way through the dirty windows made it easier to see than in the back. He bent at the mail on the floor. Today was Thursday. Each of the Vancouver Metro newspapers from Monday through to this morning was there. The shop had not been open all week.

He looked around at the walls covered with guitars, leather jackets, and the occasional framed hockey jersey. Glass cabinets held X-Boxes and other video game consoles. The glass counters had hundreds of watches, rings, and other jewelry. Large displays of knives were kept behind the counter.

One floor-to-ceiling showcase contained military surplus and police memorabilia: helmets, bayonets, handcuffs, and stun guns.

Henry returned to the back and spotted each of Frieda and Tess in the rows of shelves.

"How are we doing?" he called out. Shouts of "Fine" and "Good" echoed back.

In the very back of the shop, near to where they had entered, Henry walked over to a couch. It was covered with so much nylon sheet that it looked more like a nest than a bed. A bundle of clothes made a makeshift pillow.

"I think someone's been sleeping here," Henry said, loud enough for the others to hear.

Frieda emerged from the stacks of shelves to join him. "What kind of sleeping bag is that?" she asked, pointing at the drab, gray sheets.

"It stinks." She kicked at the folds of fabric on the floor.

Henry lifted it with his foot and pulled some of it to the ground. The material had long, strong seams, and bits of cord had been trimmed off the edges. "I think this was a parachute. There is a bunch of army and police surplus in the front. Whoever is sleeping here must have borrowed this chute from there."

"Ohmigod," exclaimed Frieda, picking up a bundle of nylon in her arms, mildew and odor instantly forgiven. "It's Cooper's."

"I don't think so," Henry said. "It's too new."

"Then maybe he thinks he's Cooper because he's crazy, right?" she suggested. "That's why he attacked Mr. Benham. Because he's off his meds." She caught herself. "I mean, because he's not getting help."

She turned the thin nylon over in her hands. It looked woefully inadequate for a blanket. Even the young girl on the sidewalk had down-fill in her sleeping bag.

"Why can't he get help, Hen?"

The irony of delivering a life-lesson in the middle of breaking and entering wasn't lost on Henry.

"I wish I knew, Fred. There could be a million reasons. I'll bet that a few of the people we passed on the way in here could be helped if they got solid medical attention."

"But they can't?"

"They can't, or they won't. I don't know the answer to that. Everyone has a different story."

He watched her taking this all in. The world was a big, complicated place.

"I'm going to copy this down as evidence." She had found a label on the parachute. She knelt, pulled her notebook from her satchel, and began writing.

And, just like that, the learning moment's over. He, too, had once borne that youthful resilience. *So, whose lesson was that?*

Henry walked over to the stacks of familiar banker boxes. Each looked just like the one he had packed his office into under the watchful eyes of his former boss.

The dates on the boxes reached back years, the stacks tall and leaning on one another. Gravity and entropy were gradually turning an organized record-keeping into a single solid mass.

He moved the top boxes to see how far back they went.

"1973. When was DB Cooper again?" he asked aloud to no one in particular.

Frieda had wandered back into the stacks.

Tess's voice said, "November 24, 1971."

It didn't take a minute to find the right box within the deceptively well-organized mound.

Inside were envelopes containing receipts and invoices, as well as three ledgers. A shoebox contained cards like the one that Frieda had found on the lawn.

He read one of the cards.

June 29, 1971
DJ Dudley
660 Jackson Ave, Apt. 314, Vancouver, BC.
Men's watch. Breitling. 17 jewels.

On the back, *$12.00* had been written and crossed out in pen. A stamped date read *CLOSE July 12, 1971.*

Each card was a separate pawn loan. The ridges on the side indicated where the ticket was torn off and given to the customer. There were hundreds. It was going to be much faster to start with the ledgers.

At the bank, the old ledger binders were no longer in use, but every so often there would be some reason to look through old records. Those binders always had stiff, leather-bound covers. These here were thin, flimsy cardboard. He pulled out the one labeled September 17 – December 31, laid it out on a large freezer, and flipped through the green, lined pages.

The freezer was a little more than waist-high, and Henry leaned over onto his elbows as he read. He skimmed the neat writing and remarked at how little the pencil had faded, being half a century old.

November 24 was a Wednesday, and a slow one at that. A collection of LPs (purchased), a wedding dress (pawned), and few other items had passed through the shop's hands. If the index card with the Richardson Street address on it was a loan, it should match an entry in here.

What date was the loan?

"Hen?"

Henry shouted with surprise and twisted painfully, bending backward over the deep freeze. Frieda gave a high-pitched shriek of laughter.

"Did I scare you?"

"Oh my god, Fred," Henry said. He felt his heart beating in his chest. He sat on the ground, thinking he might faint if he stood.

Tess came running out of the stacks of shelves. "What the hell is going on? Is everyone okay?" Her eyes darted between Frieda and Henry.

"We're fine," Frieda answered, still laughing. "I was just going to say that I think you found the keys to the doors." She reached over Henry's head and grabbed the large ring of keys, hanging from the lock in the deep freeze. The key stuck in the lock, and the lid lifted open and closed a little as she wrestled with it. Cold air escaped in small bursts.

"Good eye. Hold this," Henry said, handing the ledger to Frieda. "Let me have a go."

Henry took his turn, twisting the key, lifting the freezer lid higher each time he tried to pull the ring away.

"Stand back, everyone," Tess said. Her grand solution consisted, in fact, only of removing the stuck key from the ring and all the other keys. She made a big show of it, pretending to roll up her sleeves, taking a deep breath, cracking her knuckles, and stretching the muscles on the sides of her neck.

She froze.

"Do you hear that?"

They stared at one another, barely breathing, eyes wide.

An engine shut off in the alley, and a car door opened.

CHAPTER THIRTY-SIX

"We need to go," Henry said, taking Frieda's hand. Tess raced ahead of them to the back door, opened it, and closed it again. Her face was pale.

"It's not Julian."

"How do you know it's not?" Henry said. "You mean it's…"

Tess nodded. "We have to go out the front."

Henry dragged Frieda behind him as they raced into the front of the store. Even before he finished unlocking the dead-bolt, he could see the bars of the front gate held fast with a padlock and chain.

"Stuck," was all he could manage.

Tess's mouth opened to speak, but the sound of the back-door opening cut her off.

The trio darted behind a wooden counter display of watches and rings.

Henry strained to listen. Frieda's breathing was loud as any security alarm, and Henry lifted a part of her cloak to her open mouth. She hid her entire face in the green wool.

"No," said a voice from the back room. "No!" A low, hoarse scream was followed by a loud thud and a cacophony of things clattering to the floor.

A second growl came. Closer. From the front of the store. The overhead light turned on.

Through the scratched glass of the display, Henry could only make out the large shape of a man. The hulk stood still. Listening? Surveying the room?

The suddenness with which the man moved almost caused Henry to bolt upright. He caught himself, realizing that the man was moving away from them to the far side of the store.

Glass shattered.

"Fuck," came the voice again, different. "Fuck. Fuck. Fuck."

Henry mouthed to Tess, "Is he crying?"

From the other side of Frieda, Tess nodded back.

"Not like this," the man said, moving things and rustling. "Too close. I'm too close."

Henry thought about making a dash for the back room. If he sent Frieda and Tess first, he might get caught, but they could make it out.

But the man was on the move again, passing so near to where they hid that he blocked out the light and cast an ominous shadow.

Henry rolled onto his toes and put his back to the cabinet, trying to watch to the right and left at once, eyes and ears alert.

A minute of silence, then the now-familiar sound of the backdoor slamming shut.

Henry and Tess stared into each other's eyes. Waiting, listening.

Frieda lifted her head from her cloak, and Henry held a finger to his lips in response.

He began counting, mouthing the numbers.

At thirty, Frieda started counting along.

At one hundred and fifty, Tess whispered, "I'm going to look."

Henry shook his head and made to rise, but she was already

moving in a crouch toward the back of the store. He tapped Frieda.

"You okay?" he mouthed.

She whispered back, "I have to pee."

Before he could answer, Tess's full voice came from the back room. "He's gone!"

They rose, and Frieda sprinted into the back.

Tess stood at the open door, looking out. Natural light covered half of her body and looked like welcome freedom to Henry. A flushing sound came from behind the stacks, followed by the appearance of a relieved Frieda.

One of the shelves had been tipped and leaned onto the others, dumping its contents of DVD players, clocks and boxes on the floor.

Henry stepped over the odd debris and placed the ring of keys on the freezer. Indentations remained in his palm from having gripped them the entire time.

"Let's go," Tess said.

"One sec." Henry strode back into the front of the store. The display of military and police surplus was smashed. A helmet lay on the floor. Something was missing.

"Let's go!"

"Coming," Henry shouted, and he turned to join the others. He gave the broken case one more glance over his shoulder as he shut out the light behind him.

CHAPTER THIRTY-SEVEN

S omehow, the closed doors and windows of Tess's tiny
Tercel made Henry feel safe. He twisted in the passenger
seat to face the others. No one had said a word the entire run
back to the car.

"So, that sucked."

"I didn't like that at all," Frieda said in the back.

Tess slid her seat back so she, too, could face the small
group. "We still need to find Julian."

Henry couldn't believe what he was hearing. "No, we're
done. I don't think we need to find anybody. And how do we
even know that that wasn't Julian?"

"It was the white K-car," Tess said.

"Okay," Henry said, playing along. "That suggests it was the
guy from the coffee shop, with the crosswords. Fred's Mr.
Creepy. Between the name Keller on the pill bottle and his
name on the Net-Tectives site, we're pretty sure he's the American that came to get something from Julian. Plus, he smashed
a couple cases in the front of the store to take something. Julian
owns the store, and he wouldn't have needed to do that."

"What did he take?"

Henry clenched a fist. "I don't know. I've been trying to remember what was in that case when I first saw it."

"It doesn't matter," Tess said. "Either our American guy is using Julian's shop, or Julian is using the American's car. One way or another, that's the guy that trashed my place. And now we know where he sleeps. We have to, at least, tell the cops."

"Right," Henry said. "We'll just call up and say, 'Hello, Sergeant Khatri. Remember how you warned us to stay out of it? Well, we broke into a pawn shop and found your guy. Oh, and he smashed things up a bit, but that wasn't us.'"

"We have to do something," Frieda said.

The three of them sat in silence. Henry looked up and down the street, checking for a familiar car or face.

Tess brushed dust off the dashboard with her hand as she spoke, her voice soft.

"How do we go home before they catch this guy?"

"Maybe we just leave this to the police. Maybe we just move into a hotel in the meantime."

Henry watched her stiffen, her back coming away from the seat. Her compact frame grew tall in the confined space.

"That's nice for you, Henry. A hotel?"

"If this is about the money—"

"It's not about money." She swiped the dust from her hands onto her jeans. "This is my bloody home we're talking about. This is my life. It may feel like a hotel to you, Henry. A stop-over before you move to Toronto. But I live there. Bernadette lives there. Mr. Benham lives there."

In his peripheral vision, Henry was aware of Frieda looking at him. There was no way she had missed that.

"You're moving to Toronto, Hen?"

Henry opened his mouth to speak and closed it again, unconfident that his next words would be the right words.

"Fred, I'm sorry. I was going to tell you. I've been looking for jobs and I was speaking to some people in Toronto."

"Why would you leave?"

"I didn't get the job."

"Why do you need a new job?" Her voice cracked.

"It's a good opportunity—"

"No! You're mad at Sarah, and you want to throw everybody away."

"That's not true. I'm not mad—"

"But you want to leave us."

"I don't want—"

"For a job."

"Look, Fred—"

"Don't call me that."

Frieda pulled her hood up over her head and slid against the window, behind Henry, out of his view.

"Thanks," Henry said to Tess.

"Don't blame her," Frieda said.

Henry faced forward in his seat and adjusted the rear-view mirror to see what little of Frieda that continued to poke out from beneath her cloak.

"Frieda, I love you very much. You'll understand when you're older."

Nothing.

"I'm not moving any time soon," he continued. "If I find a job somewhere else, it'll be a city like Toronto, or Montreal, and then you'd have a place to stay there. How cool is that?"

The green wool hood fell back, and Frieda's young dark eyes, defiant, met his in the mirror. "Whatever, Henry. You're not even you anymore."

Tess cut in before Henry's mind could process the deep cut.

Softly, she said, "I know this isn't what you want to hear. But maybe she should stay with her aunt."

Henry felt the window crank on the door jab into his back as he tried to create as much distance between himself and the two young women.

"That's not fair."

"For who?"

"I can look after her."

"I'm not saying you can't. I'm asking if you're running away."

"I'm not dumping her."

"I'm not saying dump her."

"You are."

"I'm talking about keeping her safe, not your running away."

"It's a job."

"I'm not talking about your job. I'm talking about you being afraid."

"Afraid of what?" He felt cornered. Confused. Exposed. Desperate. He didn't want to be an adult anymore. He didn't want responsibilities, a job, people who depended on him.

"I'm right here," Frieda said.

"I'll take you guys wherever you want to go," Tess said. "But I'm seeing this through."

Henry squinted, struggling to make sense of the last two minutes.

"Do you want to go to Sarah's?" he asked Frieda.

"No."

His body relaxed a little, and he unclenched his jaw. He also realized just how sharp the window crank was in his back, as he pulled away from it.

"I want to stay with Tess," Frieda said.

The stabbing pain returned.

"We need coffee," Tess said, pointing at a little sandwich board, sitting in the middle of the sidewalk toward the end of the block.

"Sure," Henry said, grateful for the reprieve. "But let's find a different neighborhood."

Several wordless blocks away, the affluent tourists of Gastown crowded the sidewalks. The trio wove between the slow-moving vacationers and settled on a table in the first café they found. Henry watched Frieda and Tess talking as he ordered.

He left the saucers at the counter, in order to manage all three mugs in a single trip. As he balanced his way to the table, he noticed a change in atmosphere.

"Tess has a plan," Frieda said.

"Actually, Fred came up with it."

"Do tell." Henry's words came out slowly.

"We don't have to go to the police. We don't even have to go after Keller."

As he sipped, Henry gave an approving but dubious grunt.

"If the police caught him in the act, then it's all over, right? So, all we need to do is lure him back to Richardson, with the police waiting for him."

Tess continued with her pitch.

"I know, because Constable Tipton told me they are monitoring the Net-Tectives messages. We need to get him a message that we have what he's looking for. Whatever that is. He shows up, the police show up, and bingo-bango." She clapped her hands once in conclusion.

Henry looked at each of them over the rim of his coffee mug, his head unmoving. They were serious.

"No," he said, setting down his mug.

"No? It's perfect," Frieda said.

"It's not. One, I don't like leading him back to the house. Two, how do we know the police are even going to see the message? Three, how do we even get the message to him? Four, Sergeant Khatri already thinks I'm some criminal vigilante. What kind of trouble are we going to be in when they see us baiting a trap?"

"Well, come up with a better idea," Tess said. "I'm doing this."

Henry could tell this was true. Patience didn't appear to be in her vocabulary. If she played backgammon, her strategy would be aggressive, stretching out her pieces in fast, bold moves. It was exciting and fun to play this way sometimes, but it required luck to win. And this wasn't a game.

"A trap?" he said.

Frieda leaned back in her chair and crossed her legs.

Where did she pick that up from?

"Tess's certain they're looking at the messages. We just create a new anonymous user that the police can't trace to us, and we don't even have to be there."

"Shima's there," Henry said.

"I thought of that, and we keep him in a carrier in the car."

Henry shook his head.

"No. It shouldn't be at Richardson Street." He tapped the table with the point of his index finger. "What if we ask him to meet at the pawnshop? Even then, the part that doesn't work is the anonymous user message. Chances are the police are monitoring the messages between these two guys. Not every message on the board."

"Then we get someone he knows on Net-Tectives to pass the message along," Frieda said.

"Pass it along to who?" Tess asked. "To *treasurehunter1971*? Or to *juliancaesar*?"

"Now you're assuming they'll use these boards, so the police can intercept it," Henry added.

"I've got it!" Frieda said, coffee waving over the back of her mug and onto the table as she sat forward. "We make Julian send Keller the message. Then the police have to come."

"Sure," Tess said. "But I think Henry makes a good point. We don't know that Julian will pass the message on using Net-Tectives."

"No. We make Julian send the message," Frieda said, adding

air quotes to the word *"make"*. "We hack in. It looks like Julian sent the message."

Henry said nothing. He didn't like where this was going.

"Cool, but I don't know any hackers, Fred," Tess said.

"Henry does."

"You do?" Tess asked.

"No," he said, quickly.

"He does."

"I don't."

"You do."

"I did. I don't anymore."

"Come on, Hen," Frieda said. "Please."

"Who are we talking about?" Tess asked.

Henry just looked at Frieda. Was this her revenge for his not telling her about Toronto?

Frieda answered for them both.

"Stewart."

———

"Who's Stewart?" Tess asked.

"Henry's friend," Frieda said.

"No." Henry looked at Frieda. "Not anymore."

"Please, Hen." Frieda held balled fists against her chest.

Tess was clearly confused and yet still too polite to enquire.

"We *were* friends," Henry said. "We met in university; we hung out; I got him a job at the bank. We had a falling out."

Frieda filled in the gaps. "Stewart and Sarah are moving in together."

Tess's eyebrows shot up.

"He could do it, though, right, Hen? Stewart could send a message as Julian."

He could. In university, Stewart and Alex had once taken over Henry's email in order to ask out a series of female classmates in an uncharacteristically bold manner. In fact, it was how Henry and Sarah started dating.

Henry looked at Frieda. "No" took shape on his tongue. But before it could come out, he saw Tess in his peripheral. Her admonishment from the car still burned.

What am I running from, when I know I can make this right?

"Yeah. Stewart could do this."

The hope in Tess's face spoke volumes.

"So, we have a plan?" she asked.

"We have a plan," Henry said.

CHAPTER THIRTY-EIGHT

Henry was taking a chance by dropping in without calling. Stewart's apartment was in North Vancouver, a little over forty minutes from downtown, and there was no guarantee he'd even be home. Worse, there was no guarantee that Sarah would not also be there.

Henry's stipulation was that he would go alone. Tess's demand in return was that he should take her car. Although he refused at first, he was grateful for the little Tercel as he drove up the long, steep hills from the water that made up most of North Van.

The last time Henry was at Stewart's was the Tuesday before he learned of the affair. Tuesdays were a longstanding poker night with the two of them, Alex, and a pair of Stewart's neighbors. The cards hadn't gone Henry's way that night, and Stewart thanked everyone for their money as they left.

He punched Stewart's apartment number into the intercom at the front door and waited. Behind him, the view of the street and the roofs of the apartment buildings, down the hill to the Fraser River, was an awkward sort of familiar. He'd probably never be here again.

A scratchy, "Hello?" came from the slits in the metal plate next to the door.

"Stewart, it's me, Henry. I need to talk."

An understandable pause. Stewart would be no less weirded out than Henry by this situation.

"Why didn't you call?"

"I couldn't. Can we talk?"

"Okay. Talk."

For fuck's sake.

"Not here. Up there. Face to face."

"Are you going to hurt me?"

A pause, this time Henry's, but no less understandable.

"No."

"Promise?"

"Promise."

The door hummed and clicked. Henry pushed his way through and went up to the second floor.

Stewart stood, waiting in the hallway.

"You're alone?" he asked.

Henry checked behind himself.

"Yes. Are you?"

"Yeah. What did you want to say?"

Stewart stood blocking the door, ajar, with his body. Henry didn't want to speak in the hallway, but if Stewart was lying about being alone . . .

"Not in the hall, Stewart. Come on."

Stewart backed into his apartment and held the door open for Henry.

Inside was chaos. Moving boxes lay open and half-filled. Clothes, books, and superhero collectibles were piled here and there. Much of the large furniture—the ugly floral print couch, and the cool green 1950s style table and chairs—was gone. The door to the bedroom was closed. Henry didn't want to know, and he didn't ask.

"Is there anywhere left to sit?"

They went out to the patio which still held a couple of wooden folding chairs, and from which they had a clear view of the Fraser River.

"It's good to see you, Hen."

Henry ignored this, diving in.

"I heard you got fired."

Stewart nodded and swallowed. "They said that I helped you with your . . . thing. They think somehow I tried to cover your tracks."

Henry laughed.

"Cover my tracks? The only thing that I did to cover my tracks was delete a few emails and dump my phone log. But that wasn't for me. That was for the clients. I'm not ashamed of what I did."

"Well, you weren't really happy there, anyhow."

"True."

"I sort of think you might have been trying to get fired."

"I was finding a way to sleep at night, you idiot."

"Well, whatever. I was happy there."

Henry bit his tongue so as not to share his personal thoughts about Stewart's happiness.

"The point is, it's not right that they've wrapped you in with my thing. You didn't help."

"I know, but they say I did."

Henry found it hard not to feel sorry for Stewart. He was an uncomplicated guy, with limited ambition or drive. He had chosen computer science in university solely because finding a job would be easy.

"I want to help you get out from under this."

"I don't think I can get my job back now, Hen. They've already bumped Jeremy up to take my place."

"No, the job is gone. But if you can prove that you weren't involved, then you can at least clean things up, so that you're not tainted goods when you apply for other jobs. Maybe you even get a wrongful dismissal suit out of it."

The mention of legal action seemed to distract Stewart further. Maybe it was a reminder of whose side Alex had taken.

Henry continued. "Before I deleted everything from the server and my laptop, those emails were backed up. Those emails would show who I spoke to and when. They've got the data that the national office sent about which loans to collect. They've got information that I sent myself when I was reviewing specific loan histories. Essentially, they show each and every loan I chose, how I chose them, and who I contacted."

"You backed it up?"

"Yup. And all of that would show how I did all that on my own."

Stewart gave him a puzzled look. "And you've still got these?"

"I'm not saying that," Henry said. "I don't work for the bank anymore and, if I had access to the bank files or if I had sent them outside of the bank's systems, that would be a serious violation of the Privacy Act."

Stewart slumped in his chair. "Well, that does me no good, then. Does it?"

Henry stood.

"But when they found out, they went code blue. I was instantly out of the system, off the network. They flipped a switch and locked my phone. Security watched me pack, escorted me out, and if I'd had to pee, that guy would have followed me into the can."

Nothing.

"Do you understand what I'm saying, Stewart? Instead of taking back my phone, the bank just locked it. But everything on that phone still exists. I don't have access to what's on it, myself, but it's all still there."

Stewart caught on, excited.

"Where?"

"You understand that I can't give it to you?"

"Okay."

"But if you were to find it, that would be something else."

"Okay."

"But you would need to be strategic. Give the information to your lawyer. You can't just hand it over. You have to make sure that they can't go back on the businesses, the borrowers."

"Right."

"Use it like a bargaining chip."

"I heard you."

Henry looked at the man he'd known for a decade and a half. He searched for the friend within the stranger before him. The uncomplicated joker that everybody liked. The relaxed guy who coasted through life with neither failure nor success in his wake. Back when they were inseparable. Before everything.

Henry had little choice. He walked into the apartment, speaking. "Could you tell Sarah that I think there is still a box of my stuff in the garage in the back? I think it's everything that I took from my office when I got canned."

Stewart looked back at him from the patio with eyes wide.

"Why are you helping me, Henry?"

Henry took in a deep breath. The apartment still had that musty, bachelor smell, even though this was no longer true.

"Because they're accusing you of something you had no part in. You didn't do this. And, I guess, I don't want you associated with it."

"Because it was wrong."

"Because I know it was right."

"Thank you, Henry."

Stewart missed the point, but Henry moved on without missing a beat.

"Now, I need to ask you for a favor."

Stewart paused with one foot in the apartment and foot on the deck.

"This is a trade, then?"

"No," Henry said. "It's not. You have everything. You don't have to help me. You can say no, and that's okay."

"Are you in trouble?"

"No. Kind of. That's not what this is about. I just need to send someone a message." Henry pointed at Stewart's computer and the three monitors still set up on his desk in the corner of the living room. Like any good geek, this would be the last thing he would take down in a move. It would also be the first thing reassembled in order to ensure the least amount of time possible disconnected from the rest of the world.

"And why do you need me?"

"I need this message to be sent as someone else."

"If I do it will this help make up—"

"Don't even go there," Henry said.

Stewart was uncomplicated and naïve in the realm of relationships, but never stupid. He nodded his understanding and walked over to his desk. His gaming chair, with USB ports in the arms and speakers in the headrest, may have been the most expensive thing in the apartment.

"Is it hard to do?" Henry asked.

"Maybe," Stewart said. Serious now. All business. "Where are we sending it from?"

"It's a message forum on a site called Net-Tectives."

Stewart's body relaxed, and he flopped into his seat. His mood shifted up several notches. The screens lit up to greet him. Programs were open across the screens: email, internet, a paused game of chess, YouTube. Henry glimpsed Sarah's hair in an image on one of the desktops, poking out above the windows. His stomach groaned.

"Is that all?" Stewart asked. "Jeez. I thought you wanted me to send a Gmail or something from a work account." He began typing.

"It's easy?"

"Probably. Who's the sender?"

"Juliancaesar"

"So, we find out the email associated with this account, and it should be easy."

After a couple of minutes, Stewart looked up. "The registered email account is hidden."

"So, not easy?" Henry asked.

"It's substantially harder. Maybe beyond my skills. With an email address, all I've got to do is check to see whether it's been exposed in any hacks on other sites. Then, if it has, I just head over to the Darknet, find the database of stolen information from that hack, and get the password used there. Most people use the same passwords over and over for everything and never change them."

Henry pulled out his phone and checked the Corbeau Silver & Gold website. Under *Contact Us*, he saw Julian's name and an email address.

"Try *julian@corbeausandg.ca*," he said.

Stewart entered the address into the database of hacked accounts.

"Nothing."

Henry looked back at the website. There was one more address: *office@fullartonbros.ca*. He flipped back to the main page and read that the pawnshop was under new management.

"A name change explains the sign in the shop."

"What?" Stewart asked, confused.

"Try *julian@fullartonbros.ca*," Henry said, and he spelled it out.

Stewart typed. He turned and grinned.

"Three hits. This one was exposed in three different hacks. Three is the magic number."

When Henry's text arrived, Tess and Frieda were standing in front of the new releases of comics at Golden Age Collectibles in the shopping center of downtown. They'd been reading books from the shelves for an hour, under the increasingly darkening scowl of the shop staff. One of the employees had recognized Tess when they entered, and it was down to this and the fact that she'd signed a dozen copies of *Time Doctors* that they hadn't already been tossed out.

Tess looked at her phone.

Mission accomplished. Package delivered. On my way!

With the afternoon traffic, they would have at least forty-five minutes before Henry would get downtown. Her stomach cringed at the idea of more coffee. She'd have to switch to tea.

"He's done," she said. "It sounds like it worked."

"I knew Henry could do it. We have no way of checking, though, do we?"

"We don't if he sent it as a private message from Julian, which is the whole point."

"Now what?" Frieda returned a *Robin* comic to the shelf, careful not to crease the spine.

"Now, we meet up with Henry at Blenz Coffee. Then we wait. It's not even three and the pawnshop set-up isn't until five."

"I don't think I can handle any more coffee, Tess."

"Me neither. Let's just kill time down by the water and then what would you say to sushi for dinner?"

Frieda's cheeks rounded out as she grinned. "I'd say, 'Hello, sushi.'"

They collected their bags and headed up to the front.

Tess was a little embarrassed to be buying one of her own

comics, but she had already signed the *Enigma Team 6* hard-cover for Frieda.

Frieda made amusing exaggerated expressions of exertion as she struggled to fit the book into her satchel. A well-worn, red, cardboard binder already filled much of the young girl's bag.

CHAPTER THIRTY-NINE

Henry hated answering his phone in a restaurant. But the caller ID read *Vancouver PD* and, besides, they were just about the only customers in the place.

But this wasn't the plan.

The plan was for Tess to telephone Constable Tipton later that night, under the guise of looking for an update on her break-in; the expectation was that they would hear how the police had trapped Keller at the pawnshop.

The phone buzzed again.

Henry looked across the plates of half-eaten sushi at Frieda picking stray rice from her soy sauce. An hour ago, he had listened to her talk with her parents. ("Everything's great!")

Buzz.

"Hello?"

"It's Sergeant Khatri, Mr. Lysyk. We met before."

"I remember."

"It's time for us to have a talk."

"Sure. Fine. Go ahead."

"It would be better if we could do this face to face."

"I'm sorry, I don't see why—"

"There has been a development. If it's a question of transportation, Mr. Lysyk, I can send someone to pick you up."

"It's not that. I'm just unclear why you can't tell me what this is about over the phone."

"It's simply a matter of procedure. We may have something for you to look at or sign. Shall I send a car?"

"No. I told you—"

"Are you afraid to come in for any reason, Mr. Lysyk?"

Afraid? "No."

"You know where the Cambie Street station is, of course."

"Sure. I—"

"Excellent. I will expect you within the hour. If you're not here, we'll send that car to collect you at your house, alright?"

The Sergeant hung up before Henry could respond either way.

The call had been brief; but long enough, and enigmatic enough, to quash Henry's confidence in a simple plan carried off smoothly.

"He told me to come into the station," Henry said to Tess and Frieda.

Tess put down her napkin, flattening it on the table as she pondered this. "You? Or all of us?"

"Just me, I think. He only mentioned me."

"Why just you?"

Henry shrugged. His phone, face-up on the table, blinked off.

Did Stewart mess up? Had Stewart called the police?

"When?"

"Now."

"Now?"

"Within the hour."

"That's good, right?"

"I don't know."

"What do you mean you don't know?"

Henry only winced in reply.

"Did he say why?" Tess asked.

Henry shook his head.

Frieda had a grain of rice stuck to the back of one of her small hands. She chewed on the end of a chopstick as she took this all in.

Rachel and Tomas are going to be so upset.

Tess clucked her tongue. "Did he say anything at all about the pawnshop?"

"No. He just said that there's been a development."

"What development?"

"I don't know. I didn't get to ask."

Henry searched their faces in vain for encouragement, hope, excitement, anything.

"Maybe it's a good thing?" Tess offered. "Like they want you to pick Keller out of a lineup."

"Yeah," he said. "It could be a good thing."

It didn't feel like a good thing.

Both Frieda and Tess looked back at him as though they were saying goodbye.

The police station was as typical a building as one might find in Vancouver's Mount Pleasant neighborhood, at the southern foot of the Cambie Street Bridge. Two floors of street-facing brick were topped with several more stories of cookie-cutter glass office tower. Only the sign and the dozen cruisers parked outside distinguished it from the other buildings in the area.

The trio had chosen not to split up. Constable Tipton was waiting for them at the station when they arrived. Henry hoped she might flash him a comforting smile but got nothing.

They passed through a gate beside the front counter, and weaved past numbered offices, unlabeled metal filing cabinets, and open workspaces equipped with printers and computer monitors due for upgrades. They rode the elevator to the fifth floor in silence and followed Tipton deeper into the labyrinth. The doors here were nicer, unpainted, wood instead of metal. The corridor opened up into a waiting area the size of Henry's bedroom. These adjoining offices all bore name plates. Ladner, Reinhardt, Khatri.

Copies of *National Geographic* and *Reader's Digest* adorned a low coffee table, the bare minimum of hospitality. Two small couches lined either side of the space. The thin cushions were the same dark blue as the officers' uniforms and looked only comfortable enough to forestall complaint.

Henry's favorite cop, Constable Stubbing, got up from one of the couches. He and Tipton conferred quietly with each other to the side, while the trio watched in silence. Henry felt the weight of Frieda's arm as she held onto his sleeve. He patted it to reassure her, and himself, that everything was fine.

Stubbing directed Henry into Sergeant Khatri's office. Henry gave one last look over his shoulder at Frieda taking a seat between Tess and Constable Tipton, before Stubbing closed the door behind him.

Keller tossed his room key over the counter as he walked out of the Lampert Hotel. The manager failed to catch it, constrained by the buttons of his shirt, which might have fit him twenty pounds ago. As he bent over to retrieve the key, the manager squeezed out, "Doors lock at eleven."

Even though the couch in the pawnshop was softer than the bed here, he'd passed out right after arriving. The Lampert Hotel was somewhere to hide, somewhere to collect his thoughts. It was the kind of place where you chose to stay only because they were used to people paying in cash and not carrying ID.

He couldn't see them, but he knew that, far to the west, were the familiar pawnshop and drugstore.

His hand reached into his backpack and felt around for the plastic square bottle of pills. He shook one into his mouth. A brief taste of mint crossed his mossy tongue. There was no waiting until his old bottle turned up. Already, the stories were creeping into his thoughts.

The girl had followed him to the pawnshop. And, earlier today, he had imagined a message from a dead man. This had to end. Forces conspired to lead him astray, but he knew better. Everything required caution now. It would be as unforgivable to lead them to the end as it would be to fail.

He wandered along several blocks of East Vancouver until he came across a coffee shop advertising free WiFi.

Inside, no one turned to look at him as he entered. Even the girl at the counter couldn't be bothered to look him in the eye as she took his money and filled a huge paper cup with a burned smelling brew. He was running out of money. But, at his stomach's insistence, he took a day-old muffin.

He settled down in a corner, facing the door, and booted up his laptop. The coffee was too hot to drink. Crumbs and seeds spilled onto his shirt.

On the Net-Tectives site, there were no new messages. He clicked on the last message, to read it again.

To: @treasurehunter1971
From: @juliancaesar
I have what you lost. Meet me at my shop at 5. Come in the back.

He looked around the coffee shop. No one was looking his

way. His eyes bounced to the corners of the rooms but saw no cameras.

The words floated off the screen.

Had he imagined this? Had he imagined the rest of it? Spies in the store?

It wasn't possible. He had slept at the pawnshop for most of a week. Julian was . . . unfortunate.

He was trying to keep me from you, Dad. They all are.

So, it had to be a trap. There was another mystery hunter in this now. But what did they want? To capture his father? The money?

He was too close. Now he knew he wasn't the only one. How close were they?

Find you, find the money. Get back over the border, get home.

Keller shook half of the pills from the bottle into his mouth. The coffee burned as it washed them down. It was just lucky that he'd been able to find them at the pharmacy, and he'd bought all that they had.

Had they found his car? It was hidden in an alley, but he had no idea whether police checked these sorts of things.

There were too many unknowns. There was no time.

Julian told the police.

No. Julian is dead. Isn't he?

Keller knew he could figure this out. What stones were still unturned?

He closed his eyes and tried to tune out his thoughts, but a small tinny voice kept getting through. Was that Julian? No. He looked at the source of the noise.

A young woman at a nearby table was picking up messages on her phone with her speaker turned up.

She was just like that woman, Tess. With the thief of a daughter.

That bloody house. That bloody company. The one with the door that never opened. Where no one went in or out.

There might be police there, after last night. Maybe. But they wouldn't stop him either.

Keller knocked the rest of the coffee onto another seat as he jammed his laptop into his bag. He stuffed the remainder of muffin into his mouth, breathing from his nose as he tried to walk calmly to the door.

This is it.

He couldn't wait for the right time.

There is only now.

He felt his heart hammering in his chest as he walked to the alley where he'd left the car.

Those liars are going to show me the truth. If I'm too late to save Dad, I'll see them pay.

I'm getting what I came for.

CHAPTER FORTY

Sergeant Khatri was out of uniform but no less intimidating, even seated. His tan turban matched the blazer hanging on the coat rack in the corner as well as the occasional stripe of his tie. He watched Henry, undistracted as Stubbing pulled two chairs away from the wall and dragged them over to the desk.

"Have a seat, Mr. Lysyk," Khatri said, his voice deeper than Henry remembered.

Henry sunk low into the chair so that he was looking slightly upwards at the sergeant on the far side of the desk. He resisted turning to see whether Stubbing, seated just over his right shoulder, looked as awkward in his chair as Henry felt.

"Thank you for coming in."

Henry nodded. "Anything to help. You needed my fingerprints?"

"As your niece has been left in your care while her parents are away, we will need you to sign something so we can get her fingerprints, too."

"Frieda's?"

"Please. It's a formality. We'll also be asking Ms. Honma for hers. To eliminate them from others we've found. It's common. You've seen this sort of thing on TV, I'm sure."

He had. The words were well rehearsed, along with the sergeant's patient, compassionate expression. Henry had also seen that it didn't always work out well for the guy on TV.

"And you said there's been a development. Does this mean you caught our guy?"

"No. Not yet."

"But you know who it is?"

"We might."

"You might? So why did you want to speak with me?" Police hierarchies were surely like those in any bureaucracy, bank, or business. You can only ever speak with the lowest level person who can handle your situation. Even in Henry's lack of police-specific knowledge, it was unfathomable that a sergeant would be necessary to take fingerprints.

"I appreciate that you cut to the chase, Henry." Khatri stroked his thick beard as he spoke. Flecks of gray hair rose to the surface and disappeared again. "I wanted to ask you about someone else."

Please don't let it be Stewart.

"What do you know about Julian Corbeau?"

Henry turned to look back through the office window at Tess. Stubbing stood stiffly in the way of the window, never having sat down.

Why didn't we discuss what we would say?

He shouldn't have to lie. They hadn't done anything wrong. Except the breaking in. And the email. And not calling the police.

Shit.

"I think... I don't know, but I think he's one of the people in the online conversation that Frieda found on the lawn."

"What else?" Khatri scratched quick, staccato notes without

looking directly at the pen and paper, which Henry had not noticed before now.

"Not much. I googled him, so I know he works at a pawnshop."

"Have you ever spoken with Julian Corbeau, Henry?"

"No."

"Have you ever communicated with him?"

"No. Never." Not a lie.

"Have you ever impersonated Julian Corbeau?"

Henry hoped that his pause could just as easily be interpreted as confusion over such an unusual and specific question.

"No," he said with surprising steadiness. Technically, not a lie. Stewart had done all the typing and hit send.

"Have you ever been to Julian Corbeau's pawnshop?"

"Look," Henry said, knowing that couldn't keep this up indefinitely. "I want to do whatever I can to help catch whoever attacked Mr. Benham and broke into Tess's apartment. But I think it's only fair if I know why you've asked me here."

Khatri's eyes looked over Henry's shoulder for a moment. Stubbing shuffled audibly. Khatri set down the pen and leaned back into his chair. His hands rested on the desk, ready to pick up where they'd left off.

"Julian Corbeau's mother reported him missing a couple of days ago." Sergeant Khatri paused to let this sink in. "So, we've been monitoring his email and various social media. Do you know what we found?"

"What?"

"A message."

"Okay. That's good for you, right?"

"No."

"No?"

"It's a mystery, Henry. You see, this evening we found Julian Corbeau dead."

"What? You think this is related to what's happened on Richardson Street?"

"We are looking at that possibility, yes."

Henry pulled at his hair as he thought.

"Suffice to say," Khatri continued, "we've been trying to get a hold of Julian since your niece gave us that same paper, the private messages. Until now, no one, not even his family and friends, knew where he was."

"Where was he?"

Khatri's dark eyes registered Henry's confusion. He picked the pen back up and scratched out more notes before answering.

"At his store."

"The pawnshop?"

Khatri nodded. "We thought we'd had a bit of luck when we read that he was arranging to meet someone there. After he didn't show, we looked in on our own. Imagine our surprise when we found his body."

He went to the meeting? Did we walk him into his own death?

Henry's stomach turned. The perspiration forming on his brow distracted him from being able to piece together quickly what he was hearing. He fought against the urge to dab at the beads of moisture.

"Was it the person he was supposed to meet?"

"We don't think so. You see, his body was found in a large deep freezer. He was killed days ago. Days before the meeting was even arranged. Could you imagine such a thing?"

Henry's mind raced.

Already dead? How did we miss this? Deep freezer? I touched it. Did Fred touch it? I think she only touched the keys. Tess touched the freezer for sure.

"Are you alright, Henry?" Khatri asked. He got up from his seat and walked around the desk.

Henry blinked to clear his head. *Why is he calling me Henry now?*

"I'm fine," he said. "Where's Frieda?"

"She's right outside with your friend and one of our other officers. Do you need a glass of water?"

Henry followed Khatri's gaze through the window. Frieda and Tess were still sitting on the bench, carrying on what appeared to be an intense discussion.

"No," Henry said. "Do I need a lawyer?"

"I don't know, Henry," Khatri said. "Do you?"

"I think I'll speak with my lawyer before volunteering my fingerprints."

Khatri froze, a look of shock on his face. His eyes wide, he spoke to Constable Stubbing. "Haven't we—"

"The machine was busy." Stubbing's voice had shrunk, buoying Henry's spirits. "I was going to take them down right after this."

Henry watched Khatri's glare intensify, the silence long and deafening.

Khatri strode to the far corner of the office. Stubbing hurried to follow. The two spoke in hushed tones.

On the bench, Frieda and Tess hugged one another.

Henry kept his eye on the two men conferring angrily with one another as he slid his phone from his pocket and typed.

GO!

From the bench where they sat, Tess and Frieda could see inside the office. The sergeant stood up and walked around the desk toward Henry; the first time either had moved in what seemed like a long time.

The station had all the white noise of an ordinary office:

printers, telephones, talking, doors. It filled the periods of silence that might otherwise have seemed long or awkward.

"It's not as exciting as it seems on TV, eh?" Tess said.

"Why did you mention Sarah?"

"What? Pardon?"

"To the policewoman, we were talking to. You mentioned my aunt Sarah. Everyone thinks I should go stay with Sarah."

"Well, we don't know what's really going on, do we, Fred? Mr. Benham's in the hospital, and someone broke into my apartment. That's some scary stuff. Maybe the right thing, the safer thing, would be for you to stay with your aunt."

Frieda twisted her pursed lips to one side.

"You know that he's just trying to do what's best, right?" Tess said.

"You didn't know the old Hen." Frieda slouched on the bench, her arms crossed. "He used to love adventure. And fun. Why does he want to move?"

"I don't know. His work situation sounds . . . complicated."

Frieda shrugged her shoulders as only a teenager can.

"But maybe I won't see him again."

"Henry cares for you a great deal. I can see why. He thinks you're pretty cool."

In a small voice, Frieda said, "I want Hen to think you're cool, too. Then maybe he'll stay."

Tess put her arm around Frieda's shoulders and gave her a squeeze. Frieda squeezed back.

"Henry and I will keep an eye on each other," Tess said.

"I really don't want to go to Sarah's."

"Fred, don't you like your aunt?"

"Of course I do. It's just now all she ever wants to talk about is the baby."

Tess pulled back and spun in her seat, bringing one knee onto the bench between them. "Say again?"

"The baby she's having. Plus, Stewart is moving in. He's

okay. No, he's weird. But everything with Sarah is about the baby."

"I didn't know that." Tess held her hand over her mouth as pieces fell into place. "Does Henry know?"

Frieda looked at her like she was crazy. "Uh, yeah. That's why he moved out."

"It's Stewart's baby?"

"Who else's?"

"The same Stewart?"

Her phone buzzed in her pocket. She didn't text many people. It was probably an ad, or a phishing scam.

It wasn't.

Before she could read it twice, Tess grabbed Frieda's wrist and yanked her from the couch.

"What?" the young girl objected.

"Henry's orders," Tess said, as they headed toward the elevator.

Constable Stubbing withstood the sergeant's flak for another minute before there was a knock on the window, startling Henry so much that he almost shouted. Khatri broke his glowering conference with a wave of disgust at the castigated Stubbing, and the door opened.

Behind Henry, Constable Tipton's voice spoke up. "Linda Fullarton is here, sir."

"Thank you," Khatri said. "We won't be too much longer."

"And," Tipton added, her voice sounding confused, "Ms. Honma and the girl have left."

Khatri and Stubbing both snapped their heads to look out the window at the empty couch. Khatri lowered his head and pinched the bridge of his nose. Stubbing seized the opportunity. He whispered something brief to Tipton and slipped out of the room.

"Can I go?" Henry asked after the door had closed.

"Do you know who that is, Henry?" Khatri asked, his voice soft with exhaustion. They were alone together in the room now. Any facade had dissolved.

"No."

"That's Julian's mother." Khatri hunched as he leaned his elbows onto the desk. "I have to tell her about her son now."

"That's awful."

"It is."

"Are we in any danger?" Henry asked.

"Surely you see that there is some danger to you." Khatri took a deep breath before continuing. "Unless you know who did this?"

"I had nothing to do with any of this."

"I didn't say that you did."

"I inferred. I feel as though you don't trust me, Sergeant Khatri."

"I don't know you, Mr. Lysyk. I only know your reputation as someone who enjoys making their own rules. I believe you have more to share than you are letting on."

"I don't."

"I hear you saying that. Are you protecting someone?"

"Look, Sergeant, I appreciate where you're coming from. But perhaps, it would make the best sense if one of your men were to watch the house…"

Khatri was already shaking his head.

"Seriously," Henry said. "We have another neighbor to consider. There's an elderly woman upstairs. Someone has to stay there to keep an eye on her."

Still shaking.

"Ms. Pruner has already agreed to stay with Mr. Benham's daughter," Khatri said.

"Ah." Henry wasn't expecting that. When had they spoken?

"Look at the situation here, Henry. There has been an assault, a break-in, and now a murder. If you grasp this, and I think you are intelligent enough to do that, then I have to ask myself why you continue to drag your niece into it all?"

"I'm not dragging her—"

"You're not exactly putting her safety first, though, are you?"

"Her parents are away."

"Does she have to stay with you? What about her aunt?"

The silence in the room was almost perfect. Just the slightest sound of voices from the other side of the door.

"Sure," Henry said. "But none of this has anything to do with me. I can still look after her. It's complicated. That's why we need you to catch this guy."

"Listen to yourself, Henry."

"No. You listen to me." He raised his voice. "Looking after Frieda is my responsibility and you can keep your nose out of it. Stay in your own lane and do your bloody job. The online chat, it's from an amateur detective forum. But do you know what it's about?"

"Henry—"

"The man who was communicating with Julian is named Keller. And this guy is looking for DB Cooper and the money, isn't he? He's not looking for me, or Frieda, or Tess, or Bernadette or even Benham. Maybe Julian knew something, and that's what got him killed?"

Khatri's face darkened into a scowl. "Mr. Lysyk, please do not presume that the Vancouver PD and the RCMP haven't already looked into these things. I'm told that colleagues who have been working on the assault on Ron Benham also considered the connection to the infamous DB Cooper."

He walked to the far side of the desk and rested against it with his hip. Henry craned his neck to look up at the man.

"You have problems enough already, Henry. If it turns out

you had anything to do with any of these crimes, or if I learn that you interfered with our investigations, your niece may be visiting you in jail."

It was Khatri who broke eye contact first.

"It may help you, Henry, to know that the FBI is not interested. We've already shared with them what we know about Keller. They agree that Ron Benham isn't DB Cooper. And the RCMP is only interested where these messages suggest that it was someone from the United States who came up to meet with our victim.

"We've been able to contact Keller's ex-wife and, other than her, he appears to have no other family members. It seems his last living relative was his father, Ryan Keller, who passed away in 2017."

Henry blinked, unsure whether he had heard correctly. "You're sure of that? That his father died in 2017?"

"Yes. According to his ex, his father died about a year after she and Keller were divorced. Keller had pulled him out of a nursing home, and the two of them were living together. We are keeping in touch with her, in the hope she can provide us with more insight."

"Thank you for that." Where did that leave them?

"That means we still don't really know what this villain is after." Khatri paused to look out the window where Tess and Frieda once sat. "Do you see where I'm going with this?"

Henry merely listened.

"What I'm saying is we don't know why this man has taken such a keen interest in your neighbors and your house on Richardson. We don't know why Julian Corbeau was killed. And, until we know these things, I cannot say that you and your niece are not also in danger."

"I will not embarrass myself and my department by chasing down a fifty-year-old ghost. We will patrol your neighborhood, and I trust that you and Tess will look after one another. But, as for the girl, this is no place for her."

"Am I being detained or arrested?" Henry asked.

Henry could feel the heavy, dark gaze of the sergeant on him, as the man gave his last warning.

"Frieda has an aunt in town. I recommend you take her there until this is over. Only a person guilty of these crimes, or a selfish fool, would do otherwise."

CHAPTER FORTY-ONE

J ack Keller studied each car parked on Richardson Street as he cruised past the coffee shop and house.

None of these look like stakeouts.

It seemed that the police hadn't left anyone behind to watch the house. He'd seen the girl and her daughter from upstairs leaving together, carrying bags, ten minutes ago.

Keller parked in a quiet-looking side street nearby. Nice and close, and not too visible. Yesterday, the police had gone into the café across the street; they would have his description.

But had they seen the car?

If the police knew about the car, he'd be cooked. The Washington plates, for sure, would give him up.

I just want what's mine, and then I want to go home.

Keller walked down the laneway that ran parallel to Richardson Street. The narrow, gravel road was wide enough for a car, and the fences on either side were taller than he was. It was a poor place from which to watch the old house, but perfect for approaching it unseen.

The fence in the back of 1584 Richardson had an uneven shape, forming a notch in the yard for a parking pad that might accommodate a single car. He hadn't seen this before and was a bit put off that his surveillance had missed that one of the tenants might have a car. It had to be the woman upstairs. The Henry guy downstairs biked everywhere.

The gate was unlocked. A flagstone path wound its way around a vegetable garden with two weather-worn chairs at the far side. Keller oriented himself to the house in front of him.

The guy's place is on the right. The company's office is on the left, the east side.

There was no movement that he could see in any of the windows. His heart pounded as he headed toward the left side of the house. He was already breathing heavily, and, rather than running to avoid being seen, Keller only raised his shoulders and ducked his head a little as he walked.

The windows that would open into the company's unit started nearly seven feet up. Keller could reach the sills but was unable to see inside. Even then, the goal wasn't simply to peer in, but to get inside.

He tested the strength of the frames around the windows, but they were old and wooden.

Too weak to hold my weight.

He looked around for something to stand on.

Seeing nothing on the side of the house, he returned to the back.

There was a small greenhouse on the far side of the yard. Even though the walls were misty with dew on the inside, they were clear enough that he knew there was nothing there he could use. His eyes finally settled on the two Adirondack chairs in the garden and, one at a time, he carried the large wooden seats to the east side of the house, his head and shoulders still scrunched together.

Stacking the chairs, with the legs of one on the arms of the other gained him four feet.

High enough.

Horizontal blinds still prevented Keller from looking in. He tried lifting the window, but it was locked. Standing on the arms of the top chair, he went into his bag and took out a hunting knife. The four-inch blade was fixed open to the equally long plastic handle.

He turned his head away from the house and, with the butt of the handle he smashed a hole in the glass. Using the serrated spine of the knife, he pushed jagged, broken pieces into the house, making the hole large enough to put his arm through. He reached in and unlocked the window. It stuck, and he wondered if he was going to have to shatter the pane entirely to climb through. Shattering more glass would risk attracting more attention, so he tried lifting the window again. It came free with a loud crunch of wood on wood.

Keller stopped and listened for sounds coming from inside the apartment. Nothing.

His hands shook with adrenaline. He took a deep breath and wiped his moist palms on his chest.

All those fakers online, pretending to be detectives, pretending to solve mysteries. They're all just playing.

This is my life.

This is real.

It was amazing to have come this far. Still, his heart was racing too fast.

He rooted around the bottom of his bag until he found two of the small, familiar pellets, which he popped into his mouth and swallowed.

Keller straightened out the blinds of the window and turned to face the room. His eyes adjusted to the dim lighting and he blinked several times.

Empty.

There was a fireplace on the far side of the room, with a mirror built into the mantle, and a closet with narrow gaps into the walls. But the room was devoid of contents.

He rubbed his eyes and took it all in again. Nothing was

different. Keller walked quietly to the door to the rest of the apartment. He listened. Hearing nothing, he opened it.

No one lives here.

No one does anything here.

What might have been a living room was bare, as was the kitchen. There were appliances in the kitchen, but the fridge and freezer doors were open and not cold.

A small pile of mail lay at the foot of the front door. He picked it up and sorted the flyers from the single envelope addressed to *Resident of 2-1584 Richardson Street*. He tore open the envelope. It was a form letter from a realtor. *Sell your home while the market is hot!*

Keller turned his back to the door, surveying the room. Confusion became frustration, which swelled into anger.

They cleared out?

Did they know he was coming?

He tore the flyers and the form letter to pieces and threw them into the air. They fluttered to the ground, disturbing the light dust.

Something nagged at him. He didn't know what he was seeing, but he felt certain that there was something there.

There isn't a week's worth of mail, but there is dust in front of the door. It's not been opened.

It was as though he had a key but didn't know what it opened.

Keller scanned the room for answers. He walked back into the first room, the closet, the fireplace and the broken glass. He returned to the living room. Paper littered the floor. Someone had tacked up a long black cloth over the mail slot to prevent people from peering inside.

Keller unlocked the door and leaned out into the hallway. Directly across was the door marked *Unit 1*.

I'm close and someone doesn't want me to find it.

In the kitchen he looked at the wide horizontal blinds that

covered the windows to the front of the house. The fridge was off, the pilot light on the stove was unlit, and the pantry door was closed.

He'd not looked in the pantry. The door was as tall as an ordinary door, but only three quarters wide. He looked at the floor by the pantry; dust had been swept aside, in a perfect semi-circle.

His hand trembled as he opened the pantry door, and he heard his own gasp as he saw inside. There were no shelves, no preserves, and no stores. There was nothing to suggest it had been a pantry in a very long time.

There was only a narrow, spiral staircase that led upstairs. Upstairs to the old lady's suite.

CHAPTER FORTY-TWO

Henry waited until he was several blocks from the police station before checking his texts. It was only ten blocks down and ten blocks over to get home, assuming that's where Frieda and Tess had gone. Maybe they should go to a hotel instead?

There were two unread messages. Both were from Tess.

Safe.

The second was more cryptic.

OV Skytrain.

He had been walking away from the Olympic Village Skytrain station. As a measure of caution, he looped around a block rather than retrace his steps north.

The damp in the air becomes apparent in Vancouver as soon as the sun sets below the horizon. This evening was no exception. Henry pinched the top of his peacoat closed as he approached the station.

Past the ticket machines, the escalators disappeared below

ground in the direction of the water. Henry stood with his back to the wall and looked about. Was he supposed to get on? Was he supposed to wait here?

A tall, thin woman leaned up against the wall next to him, in his space. She wore a long coat past her knees, a knit wool cap, and sported the acute-angled eyeglasses of an architect. He left his post. And, from the corner of his eye, he could see the woman following.

Cop?

He felt sure she wasn't a Skytrain Officer, but he made to leave the station anyhow. It wouldn't do to get a fine for loitering right now.

"Buy a ticket, Henry," she said as she strode to one of the turnstiles and swiped herself through with a pass.

He was so distracted by her thick accent that he almost missed the words themselves. He snapped out of it when she looked back at him, making eye contact, before stepping on the escalator and disappearing down from view.

Henry tried to appear calm as he bought a three-zone ticket for as far as the train would go and followed the stranger through the same stile and escalator, for trains heading north.

He found her seated in the last car and got on just as the doors closed. There were only a half dozen other riders, mostly wearing headphones or earbuds, all paying the customary zero attention to anyone else's business.

He sat with one space between them, and, when she spoke again, he decided that her accent was Russian.

"I'm supposed to tell you that I will take you to Kat Hunter."

Bernadette dimmed the lights in the hospital room. Ron snored lightly. Her eyes took a bit of adjusting until she could again see Ron's daughter, Bonnie, seated in one of the two chairs on the far side of his bed. The doctor was gone for the night, but the nurses would soon be making their rounds. She figured that the small subterfuge with the lights might keep them from being thrown out after visiting hours.

The family resemblance between Ron and Bonnie was undeniable in the half-light.

Ron's surgery had lasted four and a half hours, during which time Bernadette had managed to eat only an apple from the cafeteria and skim through every issue of *Maclean's* magazine from the last six months. Bonnie's company was much appreciated.

"It sounds like he did pretty well," Bonnie said. "Still needs plenty of rest, though."

"I was supposed to see him you know," Bernadette said in a whisper. "That day, I mean. I was going to get him out, go around the neighborhood or something. Maybe I could have found him sooner, or maybe this wouldn't even have happened if we weren't home."

"You can't go down that road." Bonnie shook her head. "If you had been there, then maybe the two of you might even be sharing a room." She reached across her father and placed a familiar hand on Bernadette's arm. "There's no reason for you to go beating yourself up, Bernie."

"I need to show you something," Bernadette said, walking around the foot of the bed and taking the seat next to Bonnie. She picked up her purse and rummaged through it, squinting in the poor light. "The man who did this. He dropped some papers on the lawn and Frieda picked them up. Where'd they go?"

"Your tenant's niece?"

"What? Yes. Why can't I find them?" Bernadette bent to look under the mechanical hospital bed, pain pinching in her waist.

"Did you lose something?" Bonnie asked, standing.

"There was a card. And a list. One of the pages that this

criminal dropped was a list of all of us in the house. I think we can infer that someone's been watching the house and trying to figure out something."

Wherever they were, the papers were not in the room.

Bernadette sensed old feelings coming back. It seemed like they'd only just stopped looking over their shoulders.

"Don't go there," Bonnie said. "We all know the FBI stopped looking for Cooper in 2016. It's over."

"Is it, though?" She lowered her voice again. "This is someone who doesn't know us. They're gathering information on us, and they are particularly interested in your father and the company because their names were circled. A part of you must have been thinking it, because you went there right away, didn't you?"

Bonnie looked at her father, sleeping, exhausted from the surgery. "I just took for granted that everything was wrapped up in a perfect bow."

"Me too. I guess knots can be undone."

Bernadette placed her hand lightly on Ron's chest. It rose and fell steadily, but weakly. "I'm so sorry," she said. "You're strong, old man. You're going to make it."

She saw Bonnie reach out to take Ron's hand.

They stayed like this until a nurse came in, unfooled by the turned-down lights, telling them it was ten o'clock and time for visitors to leave. Bonnie had dozed off with her head on her father's arm. Bernadette was still sitting in the same position, her mind running over all the things that had transpired to bring them here.

She knew in her heart that her chance meeting with Ron in 1971 was one of the best things that ever happened to her.

Bonnie rose, groggy, and fumbled with her coat. "I should get going anyhow. I'll come by tomorrow."

The two women embraced with the intimacy of decades of sisterhood.

"Can I call for a cab?" the nurse asked Bernadette.

"No, that's all right. We live close enough that I can walk. I'll just be another minute."

"You're sure?" Bonnie asked.

"I'll be fine."

"You can come both back any time after eight tomorrow," the nurse said.

She wrote some numbers from the various machines onto a clipboard, considered each of the liquid-filled bags hanging next to Ron, and slipped out, closing the door behind her. Bonnie followed.

Bernadette shuffled over to the chair that Bonnie had been sleeping in and felt it still warm. Ron's skin was pale, fitting in with the white walls, curtains and sheets. She pressed her lips against his arm.

"Ron?" she whispered. His hand was cold and didn't return her gentle squeeze. She held onto him, willing her warmth into his limbs. Unconsciously, her breathing matched his mechanical rhythm as she stared out the window.

"If I had to live alone all these years, old man, I'd have gone mad."

The lump beneath her ribs ached and felt larger. It had been quiet through the evening, as she worried through Ron's surgery.

She shifted in her seat, leaning back, one hand never leaving Ron's. With the other, she turned her phone off, removed earplugs from her bag, and pushed them in. She rested her feet on one of the bars beneath the hospital bed and let her chin fall to her chest. Her free hand pressed into her side, which somehow provided comfort to the dull pain.

She would stay until Bonnie could come back after work tomorrow. In the meantime, she closed her eyes and gave thanks that the worst had passed.

CHAPTER FORTY-THREE

The spiral staircase was well made but it was so narrow and tightly wound that it couldn't have been original to the house; the design suggested secrecy over utility. Keller emerged from a similar pantry in the apartment above that of the numbered company.

This is the old lady's apartment. What does this mean?

He walked through Bernadette's kitchen with soft, deliberate steps, laying his feet down first on their sides, then rolling onto them carefully with his weight. The house made no sound, though. The apartment was bright for the large open window in the kitchen.

Outside, he looked across at the café, where he had spent hours upon hours preparing to get this far. He imagined himself sitting there at his booth, eyes peering into the apartment, and saw this version of himself inside looking back. He felt exposed and backed away from the window.

At the first sense of anxiety, Keller's hand instinctively reached into his bag for his pills. Finding nothing, he crouched on the floor and rummaged through the crumpled papers.

Dammit!

A lump rose in his throat as he tried to take a deep breath.

His hand shot to his mouth and Keller bit down on the back of his middle finger, hard, trying to distract himself from the panic rising in his chest, moving into his head. He sucked deeply on his knuckle until the fire began to subside.

He needed to finish this and get some more pills. He took several long blinks and tried to settle.

Bernadette's apartment.

She knows something.

He opened and closed drawers and cupboards, slamming each with increasing frustration, uncertain as to what he was looking for.

His eyes rested on an old answering machine on the counter next to the telephone. It was the kind with micro-cassettes.

Keller remembered bringing home an almost identical version once. It had been state-of-the-art then, with the ability to pick up your messages by calling in from another touchtone phone and entering a code. His wife thought it was extravagant, but she was more than happy to show it off to her friends.

An LED number flashed on the corner of the machine: 3. He pressed play and listened.

"Hi, Bernie. It's Bonnie. I'm heading in to work today. I figure that you're going to VGH to see Dad, but I just wanted to confirm. If you're not, could you please give me a call? Thanks. Love you."

A long beep separated the messages.

"Hello, Bernadette. It's Pam calling from VGH. I'm not sure what time you're planning on visiting Mr. Benham, but I thought I'd let you know that we'll be moving him out of ICU and onto seven this morning. Take care. Bye."

The third and final message.

"Bernadette, it's Tess. Call me."

Useless. Why was he looking in the kitchen?

In the living room, a black cat had been watching him silently from the couch. *Unpredictable, sharp little beast.* Keller slowly reached into his bag for his knife. Keeping a measured distance, the cat coolly leaped from its perch and trotted into another room.

His knife out, Keller scanned the living room. It would take him all day to search this apartment. He needed to speed things up. Eventually the police would spot his car parked on the side street. He wondered when Bernadette was coming home and whether he should just wait for her here. That would be easier than searching everywhere.

She's got to have some answers.

Keller walked into the next room, as though he were stalking the cat.

Her bedroom.

A double bed was at the far side of the room, beside a short bedside table, with a lamp and a small pile of books. Keller read the titles: *Treating Your Cancer Naturally*, *Balance: Nature's Way to Heal the Body*, and *Fifty Shades Darker*.

He pulled the drawer out of the bedside table and emptied it onto the bed. An eye mask, ear plugs, hair elastics, and night creams. Nothing of interest or use.

Across the bed, next to the door, was a roll-top, dark wood desk. He'd walked right past it, coming into the room. He had never seen one in real life, only in movies. He tried rolling back the top, but it was locked. Each of the drawers was locked, too. His heart pounded.

This must be it. People lock up secrets.

Keller jammed the knife between the desk and the roll-top, below the lock, and leaned hard on the handle. Everything was moving so quickly for him now. There was a loud snapping noise, and the knife slipped a little in his hands. The lock was broken.

He rolled back the top of the desk, skimmed a few papers and tossed them aside. He broke the lock on one of the drawers and opened it.

More papers?

The drawer contained stacks of bank statements in the name of 121702 BC Ltd. He flipped through the pages. None of these pages were the hundreds of thousands of dollars that he should be finding. He wiped his forehead and licked the moisture on his top lip.

Where is it?

I could wait until she gets home, and she'd give me answers. If the old man isn't Dad, this old bag will know what's going on. The trail leads here.

He spun left and right. Nothing was jumping out at him, telling him where to look.

The bill takes me to this house. The house takes me to the company. But why?

I'll tear this place apart.

He kicked the other drawers which remained resolutely closed. He stabbed the desktop with his knife, carving deeper and deeper scars into the wood. Screaming, he grabbed the back of the desk and toppled the entire thing into the middle of the room.

He stopped cold.

The knife dropped from his hand.

An envelope had been taped to the back of the desk.

The tape was yellow with age and it fell away in stiff strips as Keller peeled the envelope away. He couldn't catch his breath. Sweat dripped from the end of his nose and onto the paper as he tore off the end and shook the contents out into his hand.

CHAPTER FORTY-FOUR

Henry's first impression of Luba was one of confusion; his own, that is.

Her stern Russian accent suggested she was a deadly super-spy, but her demeanor was too playful, and she was clearly amused by all the subterfuge. She introduced herself briefly on the Skytrain as a friend of Tess's and explained that they were going to her place, in Yaletown. The ride lasted only minutes as they emerged on the other side of False Creek. She spoke as fast as she walked, leading them among the tall glass condo towers and along anachronistic cobblestone streets which belied the industrial history of the neighborhood. Tess had asked, she said, if they could spend the night.

"You were not so long with the police as I would have thought," she said.

Luba's condo had a design to match her fashion aesthetic. Beneath her coat, she wore all white, in contrast to the gray concrete floors and black furniture. The walls, meanwhile, were littered with brightly painted covers and pages of various comic books. By their size, Henry presumed this was all original art. It stood to reason there was more to his Russian host than met the eye; Henry knew how Tess lived as a comic artist and he wondered whether someone could fare so much better as a writer alone.

He was overjoyed to see Frieda and Tess, and particularly touched by the group hug. "Thank you," he whispered, his lips close to Tess's ear.

Relief sank in as they both peppered him with questions. He wondered how much of Frieda's joy was from seeing him, and how much came from discovering her element among like-minded women.

Henry was too emotionally exhausted to attempt to decipher his Slavic host who sat cross-legged in a huge leather chair. He just sipped gratefully at the hot ginger tea Tess had made for them as Frieda and Tess filled in their side of events. "So, we put food down for your cat, packed up some overnight things, and here we are," Tess concluded.

"I brought your backgammon set," Frieda added.

Henry thanked them both and recounted the interview with Sergeant Khatri. Everyone feigned sympathy for Stubbing's gaff with the fingerprints. What little Henry knew about Julian's death was met with silence.

As she listened, Luba picked quietly from a bowl of bright orange Cheezies, which sat alone and out of place on an expensive glass coffee table.

"Maybe," she said, looking at Henry but speaking to Tess. "Maybe he is not a paranoid after all."

She slapped her palms against her thighs in decision. "There is room here. You will stay until the police catch this person. Tomorrow you even get your cat, yes?" Pleased with herself, Luba popped a Cheezie into her mouth, crunching and smiling.

Henry instinctively started to protest, but he had nothing better to offer. A hotel was the best he had come up with. And, now that Luba was already caught up with the whole story, it was a moot point. This was a better solution. Tess had saved them.

"Wouldn't it be incredible, though, if your neighbor was this hijacker Cooper?" said Luba.

"But he isn't," Henry said. "Our villain is Jack Keller. It's some guy with a massive, untreated chemical imbalance. He may think he's on the trail of Cooper and his ransom money, but he's just delusional."

"It's not impossible," Luba persisted.

"There is a resemblance," Tess said, pulling her phone from her jeans. "I've got an old picture of Mr. Benham."

Frieda got on board. "There's so much information online, it's crazy," she said, retrieving her laptop from her backpack. "There might even be something that you can use in *Time Doctors*. Like, if the team went back to 1971 but their hop-pods were broken. So, in order to get back—"

"*Stop.*"

It had come out impulsively, louder than Henry expected. Even Tess froze, her hand poised over her phone.

Henry gave an unconvincing smile at their host.

"I appreciate your letting us stay here, Luba. We've had a long day, though, and Frieda should get ready for bed."

"Hen," Frieda protested.

"I'm tired, too. Maybe let's pick this up in the morning," he said, hoping they might forget.

Luba showed them the bathroom and the spare room where Frieda and Tess could stay. Henry would sleep alone on the couch, she suggested, speaking directly to Tess.

Henry and Frieda brushed their teeth in silence. Frieda pouted in protest, and Henry tried to figure out how to play down his outburst; Luba's curiosity was to be expected. And, he still had Frieda.

When they emerged from the bathroom, Luba made the couch into a bed, and Tess and Luba retreated to the kitchen.

Both women opened their computers and started on a bottle of wine. Henry and Frieda went to say their goodnights.

Before Henry could utter either his goodnight or his excuse, Tess spoke excitedly.

"Look at what Luba showed me."

She switched tabs in her browser and showed them the cover of a comic book. A pilot with a maple leaf on his helmet looked back at the screen, his arm raised as though about to give a thumbs up. An oxygen mask covered much of his face. A second jet was flying parallel in the background. In bold, bright gold and red, the title read: *Dan Cooper: Les Rochers de la mort.*

Tess's head cocked to one side. Henry squinted at the screen from where he stood.

"The Adventures of Dan Cooper is an old Belgian comic about an air force pilot," Luba explained. "A Canadian Air Force pilot."

"Like Benham," Tess said.

"Interesting," Henry said, recognizing he was being baited. "But we already know that the RCMP and the FBI are certain that Mr. Benham is not DB Cooper."

"Oh, right," Tess said. "Would they tell you? Or would they be afraid to kick off a massive treasure hunt for the money?"

"No." Henry refused to bite. He wagged his finger in the air.

"Okay, that doesn't matter so much. I know you don't want to hear it, Hen, but look at this."

She held her phone up next to her laptop. On the computer, the artist's rendition of DB Cooper looked back. Henry had stared at the image so many times that every bit was familiar: the small stern mouth, the widow's peak, the sharp chin. On her phone, Tess showed him the 1959 photo of Ron Benham with his Air Force buddies.

"I see it less and less," he said. "Maybe if he wasn't wearing his cap."

"No," Tess said. "Not Benham. Look at this guy."

She pointed at the shortest of the three men in the photo. His jaw was sharp, closer to Cooper's. Even the smile was diminutive compared to the others. Henry squinted at the name: *Kevin F.*

Tess's middle finger was dark at the tip, presumably from her wine.

Lovely hands.

"Closer," he said. "But who is he?"

"He lived in your apartment before you."

Henry and Frieda spoke at once. "What?"

"You just noticed this?" Henry asked.

"Honestly, I think we were so focused on Mr. Benham."

"Is it possible," Luba asked, watching Henry warily, "that what your criminal is looking for is in your apartment?"

Henry was stunned. Once Frieda went to bed, he should go back to the apartment to pick up Shima.

"Who is he?" he asked. "What happened to him? And who is the third guy, Bryan D?"

"I've never heard of the other guy, I'm sure," Tess said. "But Kevin Fullarton died just last year."

Henry snapped back from the table as though hit with a cattle prod. Tess flinched in surprise, splashing wine into her lap.

"Henry!"

"Fullarton." The name stuck in Henry's throat like a barbed hook.

CHAPTER FORTY-FIVE

Henry took Tess's wine from her hand and downed what remained in two gulps, pacing in a circle. He gesticulated with the empty glass as he spoke.

"We know the pawnshop as Corbeau's Silver & Gold, which is what it's called because that's Julian's last name. But, when Julian's mom came to the station, Sergeant Khatri told me her name was Linda Fullarton. Furthermore, when we were in the pawnshop, there was a sign for 'Fullarton Bros. Silver & Gold', which was the shop's name under the previous owner. I'll be damned if Julian isn't Kevin Fullarton's nephew."

Tess stabbed at the table with her finger as she spoke. "This means that his—your—unit has to hold the key."

"Does it?" he asked. "My gut tells me the key is the pawnshop."

He tapped his chin with the rim of the glass. "A pawnshop is a cash business, so there should be some means of laundering the money, but I still don't see how. Sure, some of the money might have got into circulation and never been detected. But all of it? It's not possible."

Henry looked at his palms. "The answer was right there. I had it in my hands. There were records of the purchases and pawn loans going back decades. I was literally holding the answer when Keller showed up."

Frieda ran from the room.

"Now you think Kevin Fullarton could be DB Cooper?" Tess asked.

"No. I think there's a link between Ron Benham and that pawnshop. Therefore, there's a link between Julian's murder and the house on Richardson. Damn it." Henry pressed the heels of his palms into his eyes as he thought of their finger-prints on the freezer. "And, we can't say anything to the police without admitting we were there."

"Hen?" Frieda's voice interrupted his musing.

Henry's vision sparkled as he blinked to take in what he was seeing. Frieda was holding the book he had handed to her in the pawnshop: the red leather-bound ledger for 1971.

"Is this what you're looking for?" Her beaming smile said that she already knew the answer.

"You've been carrying this around the whole time?" he said with amazement, taking the book.

"I sort of forgot about it, except that it's kind of heavy."

Henry opened the book to the middle and started flipping through the pages. The light from the chandelier over the table shaded as everyone crowded around.

He found the entries for November 24, 1971, and they read the list of transactions. Purchases, sales, property taken in, and loans made.

"What does this tell us?" asked Luba.

"This tells us nothing without matching it to our index card," Tess said, diving back into her bag.

"Actually," Henry said, "there's already something inter-esting here. Look at the writing on all the days. It's the same penmanship."

Tess produced the index card and laid it on the table. "The card matches, too."

"So what?" asked Luba.

"So," Henry pointed at the book, "the person who wrote all of this couldn't have been hijacking in the States if he was working in Vancouver on November 24th."

"An employee?" Luba suggested.

"Anything's possible," Henry said. "But it's the same writing in the entire book." He flipped through the pages, stopping at odd intervals. "I'm thinking only one person would be authorized to make loans. The owner. If I'm right, then Kevin Fullarton is also not DB Cooper."

Henry picked up the card and turned it over.

"This one's different from the others I recall seeing in the pawnshop. The others were typed, not handwritten like this one."

The back had numbers beginning at fifty and counting down. "And this appears to be a loan for fifty bucks."

"I found it," Tess said. "That's not fifty bucks."

In the ledger book, the entry read,

WFT Duffel & Jackson $50,000

Henry pulled out his phone and punched in numbers. "The index card is an amortization schedule for a loan. Fullarton loaned someone fifty grand and got repaid a thousand bucks a month over four years." He looked back at the ledger and the card.

"Holy..." Henry again typed onto his phone. "When I first read the card, I thought that Duffel and Jackson were the people who had sold or pawned something. But look at the columns in the ledger." Henry pointed at the other entries on the page.

"WFT is the name. Duffel and Jackson are the things that WFT pawned in order to borrow fifty thousand dollars."

"Getting lost here, Hen," Frieda said.

Henry became hyper-animated, his fingers spread wide as he waved his arms.

"What did Cooper get away with, Fred?"

"Money."

"More specifically."

"Two hundred thousand dollars."

"More specifically."

"Twenties."

"Yes. How many?"

"Augh," Frieda groaned.

"Ten thousand," Tess said, picking up the index card.

Henry smiled.

"Right," he said. "And who is on the US twenty-dollar bill?"

"Andrew Jackson," Tess said. "So, the card says that WFT brought a duffel bag into the pawnshop with nine-thousand three-hundred and eighty twenty-dollar bills."

"Or, one hundred and eighty thousand six-hundred US dollars," Henry said. "The rest probably either came loose after Cooper jumped from the plane, or it got spent. We know some of it turned up in a sandbar down in Washington State in the 1980s."

"Why would they get a loan for less money than they had?" Luba asked.

"Good question." Henry flipped back and forth between the front and back of the pawnshop card.

"You said the cash was worthless, right?" Tess asked.

"You cheeky bastard," Henry said, handing Tess the card and taking over her laptop.

"Excuse me?"

"No. It's clever," he said as he searched through the Net-Tectives site. "The ransom is all traceable by the serial numbers. So the challenge with laundering this cash starts right with getting it placed into the system without leading the authorities right to you. But, until you do this, you can't go through the next step of legitimizing the source of the ransom. The laundering. Cooper, or whoever, solved the placement issue by never depositing the money into the system to begin with. Look."

He pointed at the screen. The two familiar drawings of Cooper were part of a larger wanted poster, including a physical description and reward.

If you have information regarding the identity or whereabouts of this individual, please contact the FBI in your area.

"The FBI were offering fifteen thousand dollars for information. Fullarton couldn't spend the money, either. But if the loan wasn't repaid, Fullarton could have handed the money in and claimed a reward. You couldn't spend the cash, but it was far from worthless."

"Fifteen is not fifty," Luba said.

"Right," Henry said. "And who would pay more than the FBI? If we look long enough, I think we'll discover that the insurance companies for the airline would have been desperate to get their money back. I'll bet they would have paid at least fifty thousand dollars." He searched further. "Fullarton would just say that fifty thousand was all the customer had asked for. Even fifty thousand dollars was a king's ransom in 1971. Very decent seed money to start building a fortune."

Henry didn't even bother to hide his smugness. The plan was simple, and beautiful in its simplicity.

"But who is WFT?" Frieda asked.

The room slowed to a standstill.

They stared at the pages. Occasionally, someone would pick up the index card, looking at one side, turning it over, and inspecting the other.

One by one, Frieda, Luba and Tess drifted away.

Frieda lay on the floor with her laptop. Pillows from the

bed she was sharing with Tess were piled under her chest and chin. Her short hair had dried in a burst of chaos. Luba made tea for herself and Tess, coffee for Frieda and Henry. Tess reclined on the couch in the living room, scrolling through pages of Net-Tectives evidence and conspiracy, picking at the bowl of Cheezies. Henry sat alone at the kitchen table, where the evening had got its second wind, flipping back and forth between the same few pages in the pawnshop ledger.

Luba placed her hand on Henry's back as she poured more coffee into his cup. She let out a small laugh as she read over his shoulder.

"Like the cartoon," she said.

"Pardon?"

"This man here," she said, pointing at the entry above the WFT loan in the ledger. "He sold a road runner. Like the cartoon."

"No," Henry said, irritated. "It says 1968 Road Runner. That's a car."

"Is it unusual to pawn a car?" she asked.

"Well, I don't know if it's unusual." He pictured the pawnshop in his mind. The rough corner of the downtown east side. It was possible that someone might have brought a car in. There was the loading bay in the back.

He stared at the entry.

Lee, James 1968 Road Runner OR JCL22 $850

Henry leaned backward and wrapped his arms around Luba in a sort of hug. The Russian expat held her arms stiffly at her side. He stopped just short of kissing her.

"What did you find?" Tess asked.

"James Lee," he said. "On the same day as our ransom loan, he sold the pawnshop a car with Oregon plates."

Tess and Frieda were typing furiously even before Henry had a chance to start.

"There are too many on Google," Tess said. "I'll try directories."

"There's nothing in the Cooper thread on Net-Tectives," Frieda added.

"Well, that's not entirely surprising, Fred," Henry said. It was sweet that she was trying to innovate her own contribution.

"Hen," she said.

"Hang on." Henry scrolled through a directory of Lee names in Oregon. It would require brute force and a lot of time to investigate all of them. It may even be too much work. The name was far too common.

Maybe it was time to turn in. Better to start with clear heads in the morning.

"No, Hen," Frieda insisted. "I found him." Her expression was a convoluted combination of pride and concern. Everyone stopped what they were doing and joined her on the floor.

"But it's not what you think," she said, twisting to face the others and groaning as she lifted herself to her knees. It was a Net-Tectives page, but not DB Cooper.

MissingPersons/Cold Cases/WA – Paulette Johnston
November 25, 1971 Part 2

Henry read aloud. "Washington State Patrol is asking the public for help in search of a missing woman. Paulette Johnston was last seen in Camas, Clark County, Washington in the early hours of Thursday, November 25, 1971." He raised an eyebrow. "What is this, Fred?"

"Keep reading." Her hand shook with excitement as she finished her coffee.

The missing woman's boyfriend, James Lee, was the original suspect. Ultimately, no one was ever convicted, the woman was never found, and her disappearance remained unexplained to this day. Her sister was still looking for her and had started the thread.

Tess interrupted the silence, her tone skeptical. "So what? Lee hijacks the plane, drives to Canada, sells his car, leaves the money with Fullarton, and returns to Washington State to be interviewed about his girlfriend going missing?"

"Look harder," Frieda said.

Henry scrolled and came to a photo. An image of a long-haired brunette in her twenties looked into the camera. She wore overalls and leaned on a shovel as she laughed.

"She is familiar," Tess said. "Where have I heard about this?"

"You wouldn't have heard about it because Paulette Johnston changed her name to Bernadette."

Tess snatched up the laptop and held it close to her face, squinting. "That's *her*?"

"I'm with Fred on this," Henry said. "I saw an old picture of Bernadette in her apartment. If it's not her, it's a dead ringer." He shook his head. "The timing with Cooper is ... suggestive."

"Of what?" Tess asked. "First Ron is Cooper, then Kevin, and now Bernadette?"

Henry waved his hands.

"It would make sense if Cooper was working with someone. Someone who would meet him on the ground. Remember, he jumped from the plane in just a business suit and an overcoat."

"If Bernadette was involved, then why isn't she rich?" Tess asked. "We've seen Mr. Benham and Bernadette's apartments. Those aren't people with money."

"That could just be someone not spending money," Henry said. "What if Fullarton was holding onto it until the investigation was over? Maybe they never expected the FBI to keep hunting Cooper for forty-five years." Henry's hand rubbed his chin. "Invested right, it might be worth hundreds of thousands, even a million dollars."

Henry ballooned his cheeks.

"Could it be in the company?" Tess asked.

The air blew out of his mouth fast.

"That would explain what Bernadette has been trying to hide."

"And Keller had the information about the numbered company. If he didn't get what he was looking for from Mr. Benham . . ."

Henry nodded. "He's going to keep working his way through the house until he finds it." Henry thought of Shima. "Maybe he's even made the Fullarton connection, which means he could be tearing my place apart right now."

The old cat was clever and would hide somewhere if necessary.

But if anything happens to my boy...

"And if he doesn't find it there?" Tess asked.

Henry dialed Bernadette's phone. Everyone watched him as it rang and rang. He shook his head.

Tess called Bonnie next, the conversation brief.

"Bonnie says Bernadette was going back home."

Henry tried Bernadette again.

"Her phone must be off. Whether we're right or wrong, someone has got to warn Bernadette. I'm going."

"Not without me," Tess said.

"Or me," Frieda chimed in.

Tess stopped. "You should stay here with Luba."

Frieda held Tess's gaze. "Nope. I kept the red book. I found out Bernadette was missing."

Tess and Henry looked at one another, conferring silently.

"I'm not letting her out of my sight," he said. "We stick together."

Tess sighed. "Why break up the team? Grab your coats."

1971: THE FLIGHT

The long blond hair of the stewardess disappeared behind the first-class curtain. He waited another moment to give her time to get into the cockpit.

Brenda didn't seem too scared. He was glad for that; she was a good kid. She had managed to lighten up and joke about all the money. She even made a good wisecrack as he cut cords away from one of the reserve parachutes. Maybe because she realized at that point that the extra ones weren't for her.

The man who had given his name as Dan Cooper tugged at his knots, the pink nylon cords running through his belt loops around his waist and ending at the heavy bag of twenty-dollar bills. He wove the slippery cords into a netting around the bag. Three good-sized bundles of cash, held together with elastic bands, slipped out of the bag onto the floor of the aisle. Cooper made a growling sound and wound more cord around the mouth of the bag, tying it as tightly as he could before stuffing the errant wads of twenty-dollar bills into his pants pockets.

With Brenda gone, the cold of the vacant, unpressurized cabin stabbed through his business suit, a harsh reminder of what was to come. He took the book of matches out of his breast pocket and cursed under his breath. Empty.

He lifted a foot onto a seat in the back row, his elbow resting heavy on his knee. The intensity of it all was exhausting; adrenaline gave way to reality, like ground rushing up to meet him. The negotiations had gone well, but still not according to plan. It had taken an hour and a half to refuel the plane; a frustrating delay just to play out the ruse that their destination was Mexico. In the end, they had taken on enough to make it as far as Reno. This would do.

Still, he had to hurry; the stairs weren't down, and he would have to operate them himself.

Cooper shifted his jaw back and forth to pop his ears as the plane continued its ascent. Brenda had secured the aft door of the cabin open, so that only the rear staircase stood between Cooper and the world outside of the plane. However, it meant that the entire cabin was unpressurized. Even though the pilot was supposed to stay below ten thousand feet, the air was noticeably thinner, every effort more tiring.

The noise from the tail engine above the aft stairs had made conversation difficult when Brenda had given him instructions for lowering the stairs. She didn't want to open them herself, for fear of being sucked out and into the old sky. Even in the storm outside, flying at such a low speed, and with the landing gear down, the Boeing 727 flew smoothly. It was a decent pilot up there, and this was a solid aircraft.

The best.

He tore away his clip-on tie and tossed it next to the briefcase on what had been his seat.

The three remaining parachute rigs they'd delivered were a mixed bag. Right away, he had identified the pack that would hold the most familiar canopy—a military-style round-type chute—and his hands went to work on the straps and cords mechanically. His mind wandered. He'd stood in 727 cabins just like this one as they sat on the factory floor.

These are our drawings and dreams come to life.

All that he'd given, all that so many had given, and they were tossed easily aside when the going got tough. Money was the only thing that mattered to companies like Boeing these days. Loyalty meant nothing anymore.

Now he was speaking to them in a language they'd understand.

The plane dipped, and Cooper shot his hand out against the rear door of the cabin to steady himself.

He knelt over the remaining front, reserve chute. It had no rings or straps that agreed to the military C9 rig on his back. Moisture from the storm outside, seeping in, joined the sweat beaded on his forehead. He was running out of time. He should be gone already.

Cooper stood up and kicked the smaller chute hard into the stairwell. He only needed one chute anyhow and, if they'd sabotaged one, they would have sabotaged the lot.

From a green paper bag, he took out a wool hat and a pair of leather gloves. Already, they offered some relief. Outside, they would be invaluable. He stuffed the bag into his pocket.

Leave no trace. Just disappear.

He took one last look at the cabin. Through the nearest small porthole window there was only the gray-black of night and clouds, flickering with the exterior lights from the plane. Rain streaked in defiance of gravity across the glass. It was fine. He was ready to say goodbye. Even though he was late by hours, he was more relaxed and ready than he'd expected. Still, one last cigarette and bourbon would be swell.

In a minute, he would know if they had kept their word and were traveling at the correct speed. If they were going too fast, the parachute could be ripped to shreds on opening.

He stepped into the tiny alcove between the passenger cabin and the aft stairwell. The tail engine growled directly overhead, voicing its displeasure with the awkward flight speed. Vibrations rippled up through Cooper's feet and into his teeth. The discarded reserve chute rested at the bottom of the first few steps, where the stairs folded back on themselves. Cooper took a deep breath and, with both hands, pulled on the red lever.

Nothing.

He pulled again. Still, nothing.

His head swung around, eyes searching.

She said red.

He tried one last time before moving back into the cabin. He grabbed the intercom receiver roughly from the wall and spoke to the crew in the cockpit. They wouldn't have trapped him like this on purpose. Surely, they must still believe that he had a bomb.

Over the engine, he strained to make out the faint voice through the receiver. "Say again?"

"The stairs won't open."

"Hang on."

Cooper pictured himself: a grown man, wearing an overcoat, a suit, sunglasses and a parachute. Standing alone in a dark airplane cabin. Holding a phone in one hand and a cloth bag filled with cash, wrapped in pink parachute line, tied to his waist. A briefcase at his feet. Without a doubt, in all of human history, he was unique.

He spoke to himself as he waited.

Picture that first cigarette. Imagine landing on the deep, four-star hotel mattress, sleeping all day, rising only for dinner.

Salmon. I'm going to order the salmon.

The plane's altitude adjusted. It leveled off flat, much to the disapproval of the engine, directly overhead.

The small voice returned.

"The . . . gravity . . . try again."

Cooper returned to the red lever, again took in a deep

breath and pulled. A blinking orange emergency light accompanied the rush of cold air as the stairs lowered away from the plane's tail. The pressure was fine. He allowed himself a smile. A gaping, dark maw opened at his feet. The reserve chute was gone.

He set his briefcase on the floor; the briefcase he'd carried every day for eleven years. He didn't need it anymore. Its worn corners and repaired handle spoke of years of faithful service, even tonight. But that life was over. Under his left arm he cradled almost twenty-five times his old salary.

His black loafer nudged at the leather case and it slipped down the stairwell. Halfway down, it took off horizontally, as though shot from the plane, and disappeared into the storm.

He took his first steps down the stairs and turned to look once more into the lit cabin behind him. This was fine. It was just balancing the scales. They'd taken from him. Now things were even.

The power of the wind was unnatural; exactly why he couldn't afford to use chutes with automatic opening devices. He had to pull the cord himself. Even through the gloves his hands were chilling.

The railing became too cold to hold onto as he neared the end of the stairs. Wind whipped around and up his pant legs. Rain, which seemed to come from all directions, already soaked his socks. He turned up his coat collar, pulled his cap low, and tried in vain to pull his sleeves lower over his wrists.

Cooper squeezed his prize close to his body and his right hand made the sign of the cross over his chest and the ransom both.

With that taken care of, he leaned forward.

Farther.

The wind pushed back and kept him on his feet.

He knew that on the other side of the dark below there were

rivers and forests, and people waiting. In only minutes, a new life.

Farther, Cooper leaned, his knees bending.

Accepting the offering, the weather plucked the tiny figure from the back of the plane and devoured him whole.

CHAPTER FORTY-SEVEN

The muted sound of a nurse entering the room brought Bernadette back from a dream. She fumbled with her earplugs, ready for the inevitable negotiation about visiting hours. The sound of closing curtains was followed by an unfamiliar thunk. Bernadette half-opened her eyes. A shadow of a man stood at the door, one hand still resting on the deadbolt.

He flicked on one of the overhead lamps. Though dim, the light took some getting used to.

He wasn't a nurse. The chest and armpits of his shirt were damp with sweat. He stared at her with wide eyes that made her feel exposed, naked. He closed the curtains to the hallway.

Bernadette made to stand, and the man produced from behind his back something that looked like a carpenter's stud finder. He pointed it at her and the chair.

"Sit."

Bernadette rose anyhow, still drowsy from her insufficient nap.

"Sit," the man said again, with greater insistence.

As he took a step toward her, a crackling and popping noise filled the room. Bright strings of electrical current shot across the jaws of the device the man pointed at her. A smile broke across his face, so wide that it seemed all his teeth hung out.

Bernadette's knees buckled in obeyance, and she dropped into her chair.

She hadn't seen a stun gun in real life before, but she wasn't clueless either. This had to be the maniac who had attacked Ron in his apartment.

She met his eyes.

"What do you want?"

"I just want what I came for, then I want to go home."

"What have you come for?"

"I thought I was coming to find my father. But he isn't my father, is he?" He pointed at Ron with the weapon.

Bernadette winced at how close the stun gun was to Ron's chest. She tried to keep the conversation moving. "No. He's not your father. Maybe you have the wrong room."

The man's laugh was over-exaggerated and forced. "No, Pollie. I have the right room." His eyes focused on her with greater determination.

The familiarity stung. She tried with desperation to compose herself, even though a part of her thought this madman might see her heart pounding through her blouse.

"You must have the wrong room," she said with as much steadiness in her voice as she could manage. "My name is Bernadette."

"No," the man said. "I know you. Your name is Paulette Johnston. I want to know who this man is." He tapped Ron's chest with the electrical tips of the weapon.

Bernadette tried not to look at the device, to keep the man's attention on her as much as possible. She had heard of people being killed with stun guns; people younger and less frail than Ron.

She cursed herself. She had grown so accustomed to her life, with all its benefits and restrictions that this day had become unthinkable. Paulette was never supposed to return. She needed time.

"So, you know the name Paulette Johnston. So what? Who are you?"

"My name is Jack Keller." He looked at her as though he was hoping for a sign of recognition.

Bernadette kept her expression only interested, without emotion. She tried to sound as inviting and motherly as she could, "Why exactly are you here, Jack?"

Keller's eyes softened. "My parents are Ryan and Janis Keller. I grew up in Everett, Washington. My dad was a mechanic. He was in the Air Force in Korea before that, and he came home a hero. He was buying us a new house in a new neighborhood and I was going to a new school. Then the bank wanted to take away both our houses.

"It wasn't right. My dad was a hero and they wanted to kick us out of our home. My dad knew what it was to be a man, though. He tried to take care of us. He knew how to get what the country owed him, what it owed him for his service.

"But he couldn't come home. Mom said that he wanted to come home, but police were after him. He had to stay away until it was safe."

In the same, soft voice, Bernadette asked, "What did your dad do, Jack?" If she kept him talking long enough, maybe a nurse would find them.

"He took over a plane. He pretended to have a bomb, but he didn't have one. My dad would never hurt people. So he got everyone off the plane and asked for hundreds of thousands of dollars. All the money we needed to keep our house and be a perfect family again."

"Jack, how long ago was this?"

"It was 1971," he spat. "You know this. You know him. He's famous. The police and the newspapers call him DB Cooper. But his actual name is Ryan Keller." Pride shone in Keller's wide, red face; he stood taller, his shoulders pulled back, and even his voice became more dramatic.

"How do you know all this, Jack?"

"Mom told me. She cried for days at first, when he didn't come home. She still made Thanksgiving dinner, but we didn't eat it. Then she showed me on TV. He escaped by jumping out of the plane with a parachute. He got away and they never found him. Mom used to tell me stories about what it would be like when he came home. How we would all be together again, and how he was going to buy us a real house and take us on vacations to Hawaii. She said that the longer he stayed away, the more our money was worth. It just grew and grew."

His words spilled faster. Bernadette saw control of the situation slipping away. Even his control of himself.

"What makes you think we have anything to do with your dad, Jack? We don't."

"Don't lie," Keller snapped, scowling and pointing the stun gun in her direction. "I'm not stupid. I've been searching and hunting and tracking for a long time. Then I found some of the money and it led me to you. To you and Benham here. And that numbered company. And that house."

He produced a card from his back pocket and spun it at Bernadette in the air, as a young boy might have once flung a hockey card at a wall. She missed it and, as she bent over to pick it up from the floor, the picture was unmistakable. Even though it had been years – *Twenty? Thirty?* – since she had hidden it, she knew where it had come from.

Pooling tears smeared her vision and sweat dampened her chest. She tried to hide the unevenness of her breathing as she picked the driver's license up and held it sealed between her clammy palms.

"Why do you have this?" she sobbed.

Keller smiled, making her feel smaller still. His presence

consumed the entire room. Bernadette's breathing came fast and shallow as the surrounding air grew thinner and thinner.

"You spent some of my dad's ransom money at a pawnshop. I tracked it down online and got your name from them. Your proper name. I know you tried to hide the money by changing your name and using that stupid numbered company. The company is nothing. That apartment is empty."

This isn't real.

This isn't happening.

The temperature in the room soared. Sweat soaked her scalp, and a small bead ran down the side of her throat to her breasts.

Keller pressed on. "I know that you got rich with my dad's money. I thought Benham was my dad, but he's not. Do you know my dad?"

"I don't know your dad," Bernadette said through tears.

"Did you kill my dad?" Keller's teeth clenched, widening his jaw further. He walked toward Bernadette, the stun gun pointing forward.

"No," she said, pivoting in the chair as he rounded the foot of the bed. "I swear. I never knew your father."

"Don't lie," he said, waving a finger back and forth. "Then how did you and Benham get my money? Me and Mom, we should've had that money. Not you. He was trying to take care of us."

The door hitting against the deadbolt interrupted Keller's approach. Bernadette thought about screaming for help, but Keller waved the weapon just inches over Ron's legs and pulled the trigger. The bright, strobing flash of the powerful current made his message clear.

"Okay," she said, holding up her hands and showing him her palms. Her mind still drowned in confusion and helplessness; she didn't dare hope to gain control of the situation, but maybe she could slow its spiraling descent. "Let me just see who it is." She rose cautiously. As she squeezed past Keller to get to the door, his stale musk filled her nose. It lingered in the back of her throat as she swallowed.

Keller turned out the light. He pressed up against her and his hand covered her mouth. She felt his damp warmth through her blouse and accepted the futility of resisting. They stood at the hinges and out of sight as she unlocked the dead-bolt and opened the door.

Three dark figures walked into the room, each taller than the last. When the third person had entered, Bernadette felt Keller shove her into the group as the door clicked shut. She heard the stun gun come alive with a violent cracking sound. Someone made a sort of gurgling noise as the room flashed like a bulb popping. When the lights flicked on, Keller stood with his back to the door.

There stood Frieda and Tess.

Henry lay on the floor between them.

Tess followed Henry into the dark room with Frieda in tow. They had driven the few blocks to the hospital because she couldn't wait another second to speak with Bernadette. The locked door had only increased her frustration.

She'd not had time for her eyes to adjust to the dim lighting when something struck her from behind. She felt herself press Frieda into what must have been the medical bed. There was a sound, a flash, and Henry, behind her, made a choking noise.

The room flooded with light.

There was Bernadette.

Henry lay on the floor between them.

"Hen!" Tess and Frieda dropped to their knees. His nose was bleeding, perhaps from having hit the ground. In the back of her mind, Tess registered the smell of an electrical shortage. She heard Frieda gasp and looked up.

Keller stood towering with his back to the door. Tess moved closer, putting herself between him and Frieda.

"Nobody make a sound."

The stun gun he waved at them ensured they would take him seriously. Tess recognized the weapon from a self-defense course she had once taken. She wracked her brain. Nothing in the course spoke about confined spaces with a bed, so many people, and a body lying on the floor.

"Is Hen okay?" Frieda asked.

Without taking her eyes from Keller, Tess said, "He'll be fine. He's just knocked out." She wasn't certain that was true.

"I'm so sorry," Bernadette said, to Tess's confusion.

Tess nodded but remained affixed to the principal threat in the room. "This guy isn't well, Bernadette. Don't apologize."

The less he thinks we know, the safer we'll be. I hope.

"Whoever you are, your best bet is to walk out right now. Walk out and run. We are right next to the stairs. You've got a massive head start. Any minute now, someone else will come through that door. It may be a doctor, it may be a nurse, it may be a security guard. You can't keep adding people into this mix."

Keller studied Tess, thinking.

He nodded. "Yeah. You're right." He reached into a back pocket, pulled something out, and tossed it at Tess. It flashed silver in the air, and Tess fumbled the cold metal as she caught it. She looked down and saw she was holding an old pair of handcuffs.

"Put those on."

"You're joking," Tess said, unthinking.

"Do you think I'm joking?" he said, waving the stun gun at Henry, on the floor. "Lock yourself to the bed. Both hands."

Tess stared at the cuffs.

Keller stepped toward Ron Benham, in the bed, and tapped the pillow next to the old man's head with the stun gun. "Maybe I knocked out that guy, but do you think Benham will survive a hit?" His lips curled in a sneer.

Tess did as she was told. She looped the short chain between the two bracelets around the railing of the hospital bed, leaving the cuffs loose. Keller reached across her and gave each ring a squeeze. The cuffs clicked several more times and Tess winced as they pinched her skin.

"Now you can go, right?"

"No. We stay here until she tells me how she killed my dad and stole our money." Keller gestured at Bernadette with his free hand.

Still trying to shield Frieda with her body, Tess turned to look at Bernadette.

"Killed? Bernadette, what is he talking about?"

"Her name isn't Bernadette," Keller said, dripping with arrogance. "It's Paulette. Paulette Johnston."

He knew, too.

Bernadette closed her eyes. Her shoulders sagged, as if she might die right there.

"He's right," she said. "That was my name a long, long time ago. But I haven't been Paulette for nearly fifty years. I ran away, and an angel gave me a second chance to start over."

CHAPTER FORTY-EIGHT

Bernadette tried to make her voice sound soothing, hypnotic, her eyes pleading.

"Jack, I swear that I never knew your father. Maybe I can help you understand some things, but Ron and the rest of these people here, they have nothing to do with any of this."

"The old man does," Keller said. "The two of you took what's mine. It's millions of dollars in today's money. While my dad couldn't come home, while my mom had to skip meals, you two had all our money. You ruined my family." His voice was rising, getting louder.

I have to get him away from here.

"Dad is gone," Keller continued. "Benham wasn't him. You used the money. I saw the bank accounts. You bled my life dry."

The rising anger was clear in his face. Keller's eyes darted between all the people in the room. His nostrils flared as he breathed between words. "Dad is gone. Millions of dollars are gone. All because of you. I'll never have a family again. All because of you." His face reddened and his arms shook.

"Jack," Tess said. Her use of his name appeared to stop the escalation for a moment. "How does your medicine help, Jack? Do you need your medicine?"

What is she talking about?

Keller, though, seemed to acknowledge Tess's questions.

He rubbed one of his eyes with the back of his hand, his bottom lip sticking out, like a child at the beach with sand in his eye. "Dr. Tennant said that it's so that my brain doesn't lie to me. So it tells me the truth."

"We're in a hospital, Jack," Tess said. "We can get you more medicine."

Keller squinted at Tess. His nose crinkled and his top lip curled to show teeth. "Are you calling me a liar? I took my medicine. I took my medicine this morning."

He pointed at Benham and Bernadette, spit gathering in the corners of his mouth as he spoke. "The old man is a liar. This Paulette bitch is a liar. She lied to everyone about everything. Her name is a lie. Her life is a lie. She killed my family and stole our money. I was just a kid, like this one."

He turned his attention to Frieda, watching from behind Tess, and aimed the stun gun. "You laughed at me in the coffee shop. You stole from my car. You all think you're better than me and smarter than me."

"Wait," interrupted Bernadette. "Jack, look at me." She tried to focus his attention on her. "I can't bring you back your dad, but I can give you your money."

This had the desired effect. Keller turned his entire body to face Bernadette. His bottom lip pouted, and the stun gun lowered a little.

"You can have your money. I can give it to you. Do you understand?"

He nodded. "You really took it. It's mine. I found it. I want it."

"You can have it." She stood to speak to him. "You have to understand that this involves no one else. I can take you to it, but we first have to let everyone else go. Okay?"

He looked around the room. "Where is it?" he asked.

"It's not far."

"Bernadette," Tess said, "what are you doing?"

Bernadette didn't take her eyes from Keller. She waved away Tess.

Keller knit together his eyebrows, reading Bernadette. "You might trick me."

"We are going to trust each other. All right?" Bernadette said.

"How do I know I can trust you? Did you leave me the pin?"

"What pin?" Bernadette asked.

Frieda gave a small gasp.

Out of the corner of her eye, Bernadette caught the blood drain from Frieda's face and tried to recover. "I did," Bernadette said. "Where is it?"

"No. You're trying to confuse me. You're a liar."

Bernadette watched Keller follow her attention through the air, a virtual thread connecting her to Frieda.

"She's coming with us," he said.

His long arm shot past Tess and grabbed Frieda's hair. Tess, with her hands cuffed, shouted, "No!" and kicked out at Keller. She struck him more than once, but it meant nothing to his colossal form. He pulled Frieda out of her hiding place. She dropped her satchel and tripped over Tess.

He moved the young girl about like she was weightless. Keller pressed Frieda's back against his abdomen and rested the stun gun on her shoulder. Their difference in size seemed even more exaggerated; even in her cloak, she appeared smaller than ever next to his tall, bulky frame. Frieda looked at Tess with pleading eyes.

"Don't hurt her," Tess said. "She's done nothing to you. Take me. Uncuff me and take me."

The panic from Tess only seemed to fuel and embolden him.

For the first time in months, Bernadette's side radiated no pain.

Bernadette's voice became cold and emotionless. "If you so much as harm her, Jack, you piece of shit son of a bitch, you will never know what happened to your dad. You will never get your bloody money. I will kill you."

Keller matched her stare. "Let's go."

Tess stood still in disbelief as Frieda, Bernadette, and Keller all left.

She waited for some signal from Bernadette, but there was nothing; they were leaving the hospital. Shouting and raising the alarm could only trigger him to blow up at this point. The door to the stairs was right next to Mr. Benham's room. As soon as Tess heard it close, she pulled at the cuffs, trying to force either of her hands backward through the bracelets. The skin around her wrists began to peel. She tried to deconstruct the bed in her mind.

Will the bar come off?

She was attached to the large side rail and there was no apparent way to remove it. She pulled again, as hard as she could, her wrists on fire.

As she shook the bed, Ron stirred.

"Mr. Benham!" She shook some more. "Are you awake?"

She didn't know what good his being awake might do, but any change in this situation was an improvement.

"Young lady," he muttered, "I've been awake this entire time."

"What do you mean this entire time? Why didn't you say something?"

"In case you haven't noticed," he inhaled a deep, raspy

breath, "I'm useless." His eyes were still closed, his skin still pale.

Tess shook her cuffed hands. "I'm pretty well useless, too."

"Did I hear that Henry was here, too?"

"Yes, but that monster knocked him out with a stun gun."

"My dear, you can't knock someone out with one of those things. Did he hit his head on the way down?"

"How are you so calm?" she said with frustration, pulling again at her wrists. The pain burned up her arms.

"I'm not calm. I'm unwell."

She stopped shaking the bed. He was so still that, if he wasn't making a sound, Tess wouldn't even have noticed his lips moving.

Mr. Benham spoke again. "Did he hit his head on the way down?"

Henry was still sprawled out where he had fallen. His nose had stopped bleeding. "Yes, I think he did."

"Then that's what laid him out. Wake him up."

"How?" She knocked with her handcuffs against the bedrail.

"I don't know. Water? Slap him? Pinch him?"

Tess got down on her knees, then sat on the floor. She stretched one leg out until she could just reach Henry's face with the toe of her boot. She said a quiet, "Sorry," and pressed hard into his nose. Henry made a small whining noise, like a creaking door. The harder she pushed, the more insistent and loud the noise became. Finally, his hand came up to slap her ankle.

There was hope. "Henry, are you all right?" She realized her voice sounded happier than it should under the circumstances.

Henry rolled over onto his side and looked in Tess's direction through unfocused eyes. With his jaw slack, he took long breaths.

"Hen, help me get out."

"What happened?" he said.

"He sounds worse than me," Mr. Benham said from the bed.

"Henry," Tess said, "I need you to focus. We're at the hospital. Keller was here. He shocked you with a stun gun and you bashed your head. Now he's gone and he's taken Bernadette and Frieda."

Henry shot upright. His eyes rolled back, and he almost fell on his side, his arm shooting out to save him. Tess watched him fight to clear his head.

"Where?" he managed.

"I don't know."

"I need to find her." The panic rose in his voice. "It's my fault."

"We will. But first we have to get me loose."

Henry crawled to her and studied her cuffs through blinking eyes. His pupils were like wide black drops of ink.

"Stop pulling," he said. "You'll never fit through there. We would need something to cut through the links."

They both scanned the room from the floor.

"I'm sorry," he said. "I have to find Frieda." He pulled his phone from his pocket and dialed, avoiding Tess' eyes and raising the device to his ear.

Something rang in the room.

Tess twisted to look for the sound beneath the bed. Henry peered around her and grinned.

"Are you serious?"

Henry stretched under the bed and dragged out Frieda's leather satchel. He withdrew Frieda's phone and stopped the ringing.

"I'm sorry, Hen," Tess said.

"Hang on," Henry said, fishing deeper inside the bag with one hand. "Notebook, ear buds, nail polish, cat treats, dice, and . . ." He pulled out a small leather case and held it in front of his face with a look of triumph.

He opened the case. Inside were a dozen thin metal instruments, each a different, but equally dangerous-looking, bent tip.

"Lock picks."

He poked through them and chose one with a short L-shaped tip. Handcuffs, Frieda had explained, were unimpressively easy to escape.

As she watched Henry work at the lock, her own excitement matched his. It was everything: the thought of being free, unconfined. With a click, one bracelet opened.

"Thank god," she said, rotating her free wrist as Henry worked on the second bracelet.

"Keller was here?" Henry asked.

"He doesn't think Benham is his dad any longer, it seems. Instead, he was raving about Bernadette stealing his family's money, which may be Cooper's ransom or something, and he wants it back. Keller knows her name was Paulette."

"So, he still thinks he's related to Cooper?" Henry said. "Maybe Kevin Fullarton was his dad. Fullarton looked like Cooper, but I'm still convinced that they can't be one and the same if the handwriting in the ledger was all Fullarton's. It means he was in Vancouver the whole time. Then I have to come back the possibility that, despite the drawing, our best bet is that Ron Benham is DB Cooper."

"I bloody well am not," said a weak voice from the bed above them, followed by a coughing fit.

The second bracelet opened and surrendered Tess's wrist. "Thank you," she said, hugging him. "Bernadette said she had his money and that's where they've gone. To get him his money."

"Did she say where they were going?"

"No. I'm sorry. I don't know."

Henry looked again like he might pass out. "What are you saying? We lost Frieda?" He stared at her and sat next to her on the floor. "I lost her?" Henry's breathing got louder and heavier, his eyes more frantic. "I have to find her. I have to get her back. I never should have let her come."

Tess put her arm around his shoulders, out of comfort, but also in fear that he may hit the floor again. "We don't know where they are. The only thing that we can do is call the police."

"Young lady, you don't want to do that."

Tess gasped. She'd forgotten for a second that Mr. Benham was there. They stood to speak to him, Henry leaning on the bed rail.

"Benham," Henry said, "I've had enough of all this don't-tell-the-police crap. I don't know what you and Bernadette have got going on, or what you're running from." Maybe it was because the old man was lying down, or maybe it was the concussion, but Henry felt taller than ever.

He pulled his shoulders back and stood his ground. "Don't give me some bull about doing the right thing. Keller is a murderer and now he has my niece. There is no way in hell that I'm not getting every law enforcement officer searching this city after this guy."

The old man opened his eyes. "If Bernie's taking him to the money then she's gone back to Richardson Street. That's where they'll be. Just there." He pointed weakly out the window. Even though buildings and trees blocked any possible view of the old house, the message was unambiguous: they were close by.

Ron paused only for a second, to ensure that he had Henry's full attention.

"So, young man, do you want to stay here and help the police fill out reports? Or do you want to go get this niece of yours?"

CHAPTER FORTY-NINE

Bernadette led Keller and Frieda down the hospital stairwell.

At the bottom, Keller said, "Through here," and they exited into a parking lot.

She walked in front of Keller, who held Frieda between them, until they reached an off-white, boxy car with Washington plates. Keller threw her the keys.

"You drive," he said. "We're riding in the back."

Bernadette hadn't driven in years. Decades. The license Keller had found was the last one she had ever held. Technically, only Paulette Johnston had ever had a license. Bernadette Pruner only existed in the barest of ways. She had never had a social insurance number and had never paid personal taxes. She had neither a bank account nor medical insurance. *Thank god it's an automatic,* she thought, getting in.

She adjusted the front bench seat forward as Frieda and Keller climbed in the back. As she oriented herself to the controls, a reflection in the windshield of something on the dash caught her eye. She snatched it and dropped it into her lap.

Bernadette twisted the rear-view mirror to see Frieda in the back seat. She gave the girl a wink and a smile, although there was nothing to smile about.

Bernadette looked at the object in her lap. It was the small brass brooch that belonged to Frieda. The pin was missing, but the Pepsi logo was unmistakable. The violation of the young girl's property stiffened Bernadette's spine like rebar and hardened her heart toward the bastard.

Did he go through all the apartments at the house?

"Where are we going?" Keller asked.

"My home," Bernadette said. It was only a few blocks away as the crow flies, but she'd have to weave around all the one-way streets to get there by car. She'd never once driven in these neighborhoods, in all of her years. Maybe they would have the luck of being pulled over on the way.

Keller seemed surprised. "I already searched there. My money's not there."

"You shouldn't have broken into my home, Jack."

"You shouldn't have stolen from my family."

Bernadette started the car. "I didn't steal a thing, Jack. Do you want to know the truth?"

"Tell me," he said, close to her ear, his breath warm and rotten.

She resisted looking over her shoulder as she backed the car out of its parking spot, knowing Jack's grimacing face would be right there. She waited until they started the roundabout journey through the parking garage before continuing.

"I grew up with just one parent, too. You know my name then. I was Paulette. My dear mom tried so hard to give us everything, my little sister Angie and I. Everything we did had to be better. Better than what mom had, better than how mom did. I never thought, growing up, that our life was so awful, but she did. Mom hated every minute of it. So she wanted us to go to university and become professionals. No friends. No parties.

We weren't even allowed to wear denim or leather because she said it made you look hard."

"What does this have to do with anything?" Keller asked.

"If you want to know the 'what', Jack, you have to understand the 'why'."

Keller grunted his lack of argument.

The parking attendant kiosk was empty, and they rolled past and onto the street. There would be no stopping now.

"I chafed under all the expectation and pressure. Mom and I, we fought like spiders in a jar some nights. It all sounds small now, after forty-plus years, but I guess that didn't suit me then. I've learned to accept it was just how things were.

"I had friends, despite her rules, maybe to spite them, in fact. We partied a lot, and I dated a few boys. I remember her tracking me down at a school dance. I don't remember where I was supposed to be, but it sure wasn't there. Well, she slapped a boy right across the face when she found us dancing together, right in front of the entire school. We were only dancing. She worried that I would get a "reputation". Well, I got one all right. I was the girl with 'that mom'. I couldn't get another date to save my life.

"That was when I met Jim. Jim Lee was older. He wasn't from Portland and he had a job at a mill in Camas. He had a car, a red 1968 Road Runner that would go like stink and turn heads on every block. Well, I thought it was love at first sight with Jim. Maybe it was, then. Maybe he was just my way out. Either way, we dated for three weeks before he proposed. We were happy when we were together, which wasn't that often. He took me dancing. We picnicked. He could even afford to eat dinner in the finer restaurants. Jim said, if we lived together, we could be that happy all the time.

"Well, I left a note, I kissed Angie goodbye while she slept, and I moved to Camas. That happiness only lasted about a month. Jim's house was a trailer, not even a double-wide, plunked down in the middle of a barely cleared lot on the outside of town. And there was the drinking, which pretty soon turned to violence. Like too many young girls, it took me way too long to figure he wouldn't change. A year, maybe? By that time, there was no going back home to Portland. I'd spoken to Mom once, and the disappointment was too much. Proving her right and heading back with my tail between my legs would have been even worse. I was only twenty, or twenty-one. I owned nothing except my pride. It seems even Jim couldn't beat that out of me.

"Then, come that night in November 1971."

Keller spoke up, his voice slow and drunken. "Is that the same night?"

"I don't know, Jack. It sure seems so. I was thinking of leaving him anyhow. I just couldn't figure out where I would go. It'd been over two years and we still hadn't married. Maybe it was because we both knew my bruises would have made for terrible wedding photos. Well, that night, he came home drunk as ever, but he wasn't alone. He had several of his friends with him. Jim had never brought people home before and I got spooked. I locked myself in the bathroom and I told myself—"

She reached up and turned the rear-view mirror to look at Keller. "Does that happen to you? Do you ever step outside of your own body and see yourself?"

"Yeah." He leaned forward, his eyes wide, hanging on her story. "All the time."

CHAPTER FIFTY

"I said to myself in that bathroom, if one Jim is that rough, then four or five will be the death of you. It's now or never. I walked straight out of the bathroom, made some excuse, and carried on right out the front door. I didn't have a plan past 'anywhere is better than here'.

"A terrible thunderstorm had already set in and I knew I wouldn't get far on foot. I didn't even grab a coat. I made sure, though, to pick up his keys on the way out. Boy, he sure noticed that, because I heard him screaming at me as I drove away in that beautiful, red car.

"Like I said, I didn't know where I was going. I couldn't go back to Portland. That door was closed to me. Besides, I'd heard that Angie got herself a job at a new bookstore. I told myself she'd be all right. If I had to go back to Jim, either he'd kill me, or I'd kill myself. But I knew I was leaving Camas. Do you know Camas, Jack?"

Keller shook his head. "No."

"It's a small town on the mouth of the Washougal River. Well, it was small then. I don't know about now. At the southeast end of town there's a bridge. It may have been metal once, but it always looked to me like they'd built it of rust from the get-go. As I'm crossing this bridge going into town, I see some-thing white hanging over the side.

"Now, remember, I was running. I can't imagine now that those men were sober enough to follow me, but I didn't know that then. Between my crying and the water pouring down over the windshield, I had no idea what I'd seen. Still, something compelled me to pull over. I remember 'Riders on the Storm' was playing on the radio and I felt there was some serendipity happening, some fate.

"So, I pulled the Road Runner over and walked back to the bridge. I was soaked to the bone and freezing cold before I'd even covered the twenty yards or so. It was dark when I looked over the side, and I had to rub the water from my eyes to be sure of what I saw. Hanging from the bridge was a man suspended by a parachute."

"My dad," Keller said in a whisper.

"I don't know, Jack. Maybe it was. Well, I called down and I got no answer. I could see, though, that he was hanging so low he was touching the ground. Beneath the bridge is a little island. The river runs around it on both sides. In the fall, though, the river gets low and you can walk out to it, so that's what I did. For all the rain and the cold, I might as well have swum out there.

"The way he hung, it was almost like he was down on his knees, praying. I checked him for breathing. I checked him for a pulse. He'd died, Jack. I don't know when and I don't know how. When I found him, though, his body was near frozen with chill, and he was definitely gone.

"He had no shoes. Other than that, he was dressed real dapper, in a black business suit and a white shirt. There was a bag he wore on his belly. It was like a backpack, but it was tied around him, too. It had come open and, as I was trying to get him undone, it tore open some more."

She paused to look at Keller in the mirror. "And, you know what I found."

"Two hundred thousand dollars," Keller said, nodding.

"Almost," she continued. "Some of it must have fallen out, but close enough. All twenties. I'd never seen so much money. Here I was, finally trying to escape, trying to hide, and I come upon a man in a suit, praying in a river who offers me a way out. Sort of like an angel."

"What did you do with him?"

"I couldn't bury him. Even though I'd near forgotten about Jim and his friends, it's a rocky little island. But the Washougal is a pretty swift river that empties into the Columbia. I helped him down as gently as I could. I said a prayer, and I let the current take him away."

CHAPTER FIFTY-ONE

The scraping in Keller's voice yanked Bernadette back to the present. "That wasn't for you. It's mine."

Disgusting, fine spittle shot from his mouth as he spoke. She fought the urge to wipe the back of her neck.

"I didn't know that, Jack. And, he had already died. If anyone found him, that money was going to the police. You don't need to be a detective to know that this was an unusual situation."

She looked again in the mirror, hoping to see a teary-eyed Keller. Instead, his eyes were vacant, unreadable to her. Not since Jim had she seen a look so inhuman.

They turned onto Richardson Street.

"Jack, you will want to know this. I gathered up his parachute before I left and took it with me. A bunch of the ropes to the canopy of the chute were cut. The red ones looked snapped, like someone had deliberately weakened them. If you want my two cents, I think it's the FBI or the government who are responsible for him being unable to land properly. Maybe he got blown around, or wasn't able to steer, or something."

Her suggestion had not calmed him at all. "I don't want two

cents," Keller said. "That money is worth millions today. I want my family's money."

Bernadette adjusted the mirror to once again look at Frieda. "I just thought you would find that interesting. His straps were fine."

Her eyes met Frieda's. "He had strapped himself on all right," she added, as she tugged on her own shoulder belt. She saw the young girl's eyes dart to the twitching belt and back. Frieda's eyes widened.

"I don't care now," Keller said, "I don't—"

The car's sudden acceleration cut him off. Bernadette stomped on the gas pedal, taking aim at the colossal chestnut tree in front of the house. He reached into the front seat and pulled at her arm.

In that instant, as she wrestled against Keller's overwhelming strength, Bernadette heard the satisfying click of Frieda releasing his seatbelt.

CHAPTER FIFTY-TWO

Bernadette unbuckled her seatbelt. Ache rushed in across her chest like a massive bruise.

"Frieda, are you okay?"

Keller's torso was half-draped onto the front bench seat next to her, and she couldn't see past him into the back. His head and arms had disappeared over the seat, beneath the dash. The windshield was opaque and webbed with cracks.

"I'm okay," came a small voice, followed by sounds of a door opening.

Keller stirred. In a slurred voice, he said, "You bitch. What have you done?" She felt his hand, wet, groping around her ankle.

"Out of the car, Frieda," she shouted. "Run to the house! Run!"

Bernadette struggled to get her door open halfway; metal caught on metal. Her left arm was numb from the shoulder down, where the seatbelt had restrained her. Still, it was enough for her to slide out and onto the ground. A sharp jolt in her side made her double up. She wondered for a second whether she had been stabbed, before realizing that it was the ordinary pain of her cancer. She rose and looked about. They had missed the tree and the front of the car hugged a telephone pole, which leaned at a precarious angle over the car. The engine ticked away its last gasps. From this side, she could see the dent that Keller himself had made in the windshield.

People started coming out of the café behind them.

Frieda had already reached the front steps of the house. "Come on!"

Bernadette took one last look at Keller, who had now pulled himself into the front seat, and hurried after the girl.

They held hands as they ran up the stairs and into Bernadette's apartment. She locked the deadbolt behind them. The living room appeared untouched. Some papers had been tracked in from the bedroom. She had known that he'd discovered the writing desk. Still, the violence with which it had been thrown and broken made her shiver.

Bernadette closed the bedroom door from Frieda's eyes, walked to the couch, and sat. She picked up the phone and dialed 9-1-1.

People will already have called because of the car.

They don't have a clue who they're dealing with, though.

"Frieda, what was the name of the police officer we spoke to at the hospital?"

"I don't remember," Frieda said, sitting next to her. "Ask for Constable Sonja Tipton, though."

When Tipton came on the line, Bernadette described the attack at the hospital and the accident outside. "He was out of control, and I didn't know what else to do. This was the only place that I could think of where we could get behind lock and key."

"You took an awful chance with the pole," Tipton said. "We've got cars heading your way and I won't be far behind. In the meantime, don't open the door for anyone. Are you sure he's incapacitated?"

Bernadette cradled the phone between her chin and shoulder, trying to massage feeling into her left arm as she spoke. "He's alive, but he isn't going anywhere if that's what you mean. Frieda, look out front and tell me if you see anything."

"Just a bunch of people standing around the car with their phones."

"We're safe," Bernadette relayed into the phone.

"Stay close to the phone and wait for us to arrive."

"I hear sirens," Frieda said from the window.

"We'll be right here," Bernadette said before hanging up. "That wasn't the same officer we spoke to at the hospital, Frieda. How do you know her?"

"She's nicer than the jerk at the hospital and the big guy who told Henry about the body."

Bernadette looked at her with wide eyes. "What body?"

Frieda spoke excitedly. "Julian Corbeau, who owned a pawnshop downtown. He and Mr. Creepy, Keller, met online. Keller came here from the States to get something, but he killed Julian and he's been using the pawnshop as a hideout this whole time. I think he was sleeping in the back. And Hen's friend, Dr. Well, told us that he's not taking his medication, so he could be having blackouts and not even knowing what he's doing." She paused. "The police told Hen that they found the guy's body in the freezer."

"Julian Corbeau?"

"Uh huh," Frieda said. "It means 'crow'."

He really did follow some sort of trail.

"You've been to this pawnshop downtown?" Bernadette asked. "On East Hastings?"

"Yeah," Frieda said with a cocked eyebrow. "How did you know that?"

"It's a part of the story I was telling in the car."

"You mean that was real?" Frieda's voice rose to a high pitch.

"Those were strange days, Frieda, and lots of people were doing desperate things," Bernadette said.

"People were protesting in the streets. The government had lied about what was going on over in Vietnam. The news had something fresh every day about prison riots, oil spills, political lies or police corruption. Well, I thought about all those young men who had dodged the draft and gone north to Canada. So that's what I did. I took that hotrod I'd stolen, and I tore a path up here.

"I told myself that was Jim's one gift to me, that car. I took back roads. I stopped just to wash up in Amboy and get rid of the parachute equipment and some of Jim's things from the trunk. Truth be told, I was searching the car for drugs. I didn't know what Jim kept in there, but I knew that I didn't want to get arrested crossing the border. I'd just be swapping one prison for another."

Frieda listened with wide eyes. "You didn't tell any of that stuff about money and your different name to the police."

Bernadette patted the young girl's hand. It was small and smooth, spotless even, compared to her own. "Yeah, I don't know how I'm going to handle that yet."

"I won't tell them if you don't want me to." The young girl delivered her promise with a gravity that should be reserved for later in life.

It's never been a question of whether the past would catch up, has it? Just a question of when.

"I'll never ask you to lie, Frieda, and you shouldn't lie to the police. I will ask you to let me be the first person to bring it up, though. Okay?"

Frieda nodded.

"But if anyone asks you outright, you answer them honestly."

Again, nodding. "You don't have to tell me any more about how you knew the pawnshop guy who was killed if you don't want to."

"I don't mind. I'm not going to be around forever, and maybe someone should be the keeper of the truth, eh?"

Bernadette stood and stretched her arm across her chest. Tingling had replaced the numbness, and there was a growing throbbing where the seatbelt had bit into her shoulder. Even still, given everything, she should expect to hurt worse than this. *Maybe it's the adrenaline?*

"I never met Julian, although I'd heard his name. I knew his uncle, Kevin, who used to run that pawn shop."

"Was he DB Cooper?" Freida asked softly.

"Oh, you know that much?" Bernadette said, sitting back down on the couch. "No. They were brothers."

CHAPTER FIFTY-THREE

"They were brothers."

The words were strange to hear aloud. It was years since any of them had brought it up. Time and Kevin's death didn't make any of it easier.

"The man on the bridge had a wallet, and his driver's license said he was Wayne Fullarton from Vancouver. I had no plan, but I was certain I'd be more able to hide better in a bigger city, so I followed the trail.

"When I first arrived, I had a little of my own money. I was scared to use any of the cash that I'd found because it felt like my salvation, and it didn't feel like mine. Either way, I didn't want to lose it. I could afford to stay at the Cambie downtown, though. That place has had its ups and downs over the years, and in those days it was definitely in one of the downs. It was clean enough. More importantly, it was cheap. Then I started looking for someone who might know him, the man from the bridge. That's when I met Kevin and Ron."

"Mr. Benham?" Frieda asked.

"Yes, Mr. Benham. The two of them went way back. I found Kevin because of his name on the pawnshop. It must have been obvious I was in a hell of a mess. I don't even recall how or why, but pretty soon I had given him my whole story. I told him about the body and the money, and even leaving home, Jim, and stealing the car.

"I was going to leave the money with him and carry on running. Wayne was his brother, after all. I never could tell if he didn't somehow hold it against me, what happened. Even until the day he died. But he brought Ron in, and that made us a trio. Maybe I trusted Ron because he reminded me of my memories of my dad. Anyhow, he stood out because he wasn't like other men I'd known. He wasn't down and out or anything, but he had barely enough to pay for lunch, like most folks. Ron would get dressed up, and he'd go to his job as a realtor every day, even though business was terrible and he couldn't sell a thing. He was leaving his wife and was between places to live. So I stayed, and he moved in to the Cambie, too.

"Kevin didn't have any wife and kids. Instead, he was married to his pawnshop. Wayne was his older brother who'd gone down to the States to become an engineer. That little shop wasn't making money hand over fist, but Kevin got by. It paid for Wayne's school.

"But plans get blown off course, don't they?"

She drifted off, and her attention turned to the kitchen. "Was that a noise?"

Frieda went to stand, but Bernadette's straight arm held her back. Bernadette walked on tiptoe toward the kitchen.

Shima came running from the kitchen at full speed. Bernadette gave a sharp cry, and the cat ducked under the couch.

Bernadette laughed out loud at herself. "Well, speaking of surprises," she said, picking up where she had left off.

"Each of us saw this as a chance to start over. Ron knew an excellent lawyer, and he introduced me to trustworthy people."

"So, you kept the money?" Frieda asked.

Bernadette raised an eyebrow. "We did. I did. Those two

men never treated it like it was anything other than mine. Ron was clever, and he was right. The police were looking for a man who had hijacked a big passenger jet, not a young woman.

"Ron figured they could trace the cash if I spent it or deposited it in a bank. Well, the three of us came up with a plan to clean it up and invest it well. It was clever and simple. But I could never get a credit card. I couldn't get a license or even open a bank account in my new name. Bernadette Pruner didn't exist.

"Besides moving into Richardson Street, Kevin always kept to himself. That was just his way, according to Ron. But Ron and I took each other on as family. You know, not one time, ever, did he steer me wrong. And he always referred to the nest egg we built as mine. Never his or ours."

As Bernadette thought of Ron, lying in the hospital, her body recalled all those young feelings of security, peace, and comfort. In the intervening decades, sure, she had grown confident that she was capable and could survive on her own. A part of her now felt her safe harbor beginning to fade.

"Hen figured out how you laundered the money," Frieda said.

"Did he?"

"And I figured out you ran away in 1971. That's why we were coming to talk to you."

"Is that so?" She nodded slowly as this sunk in. It was all inexplicably unsurprising. "You're as clever as your uncle, aren't you?"

Frieda gave her a proud smile. Then, "Do we have to call you Paulette now?"

"No, dear. My name is Bernadette." Some of her stoicism was returning.

"Do you miss your sister?"

"I do," Bernadette said, "and I don't. I have a family here, with Ron, Bonnie, Jane, and all of you. I've seen pieces of Angie online, and it looks like she's made a pretty pleasant life for herself."

"Can we call the hospital and find out if Henry's okay?" Frieda asked, her eyebrows drawing together.

"Of course," Bernadette said, embarrassed to have been so wrapped up in recounting her past. She picked up the phone to call the hospital.

"Maybe you could get us some water, too," Bernadette said, dialing.

Frieda disappeared into the kitchen.

As the sirens grew louder, Bernadette allowed her mind to play with the memories of those years. She danced between being a girl of Frieda's age in Portland, as her mother came home to change uniforms for her next job, and being a young woman of twenty-one, signing legal documents that she barely understood in a lawyer's office with Ron.

"Do you know what I've learned about family, Frieda?" she said. The phone in her hand made the sound of ringing on the other end.

Frieda didn't answer.

"Frieda? I said, do you know what I've learned about family?"

Frieda stepped around the corner of the entryway to the kitchen. Behind her stood Jack Keller, holding a large hunting knife to her throat. Keller's arm that crossed Frieda's chest ended in a broken, twisted hand.

"What do you know about family?" he asked.

CHAPTER FIFTY-FOUR

Henry and Tess heard the sirens from blocks away as they approached Richardson Street. Police cars blocked the street and a dozen or so people stood around, staring up at 1584. Tess turned before the house, parked at the café, and they ran together across the street.

"There!" Tess shouted, pointing at one of the police officers standing next to a police cruiser. "Constable Tipton."

Hearing her name, Tipton turned. "I thought you were at the hospital," she said.

"We were," Henry said. "Where is Frieda?"

"I spoke with Bernadette," the police officer said. "She and your niece were in an accident here, with Jack Keller." She pointed at the off-white K-car, its engine still ticking. "Frieda's inside the house now. How come you didn't call us yourselves?"

Henry ignored the question and looked at the scene. It was the car Frieda had described, only it had embraced the telephone pole, the bumper sunk deep under the hood. There were dark, wet spots on the surrounding asphalt, and the front seat was smeared with blood. Police officers had all the car doors open. With gloved hands, they were clearing the papers and garbage from the car and putting it all in clear plastic bags.

"Where is Frieda?" he asked again, his voice cracked with fear.

"Your niece and Bernadette made it safely from the car to the house. They were alone and locked in her apartment when we arrived."

"She's okay?"

"She's okay."

Henry realized he was panting and took in a deep breath.

His phone rang. The caller ID read *Rachel Duran*. He sent her to voicemail.

"Why are we out here? Can't we go inside?" he asked.

"No." Tipton looked up at Bernadette's apartment as she spoke. "I have no idea how he managed it, but Keller is with them in the apartment."

"What?" Henry's hands flew to his head and pulled at his hair.

"He wasn't there when Bernadette called for the police," Tipton said. "We're still determining how he got inside. Witnesses say they saw him just walk in the front door, but that doesn't explain why she'd let him in. We've tried calling her number, but no one's picking up. We don't know what he wants at this point. A negotiator is on her way."

"A negotiator?" Henry asked in disbelief. His mouth hung open as he looked at the house.

"We are considering this a hostage situation, Mr. Lysyk. We have to assume that Keller is armed and dangerous."

Her saccharine, soothing tone had the opposite effect.

"This is crazy," Henry said. He strained to see something in the second-story window and turned his attention back to the car. "And you're sure that Frieda and Bernadette are okay? Whose blood is that?" he asked, pointing at the accident.

"Keller's," Tipton said. "When I spoke with Bernadette only twenty minutes ago or so, she said that they were fine. I think it's safe to assume the blood is Keller's."

Henry looked at Tess for help. He didn't know what she could do about this that he wouldn't be able to. But he knew that, of all people, she wanted to end this as much as he did. Tess reached out and held his arm in reply.

"I'm going inside," Henry said. "I can trade myself for Frieda, or both of them."

Constable Tipton's shoulders drew back. Sympathy left her face, and she spoke in a dry monotone voice. "You two have done enough for today. I understand that you want to help. You're going to leave this to us. This is what we do. What I need from you are your statements about what happened at the hospital."

A loud slamming noise came from inside the house, as though someone was breaking down a door with a battering ram. People on the street looked up at the windows. Henry followed their gaze; nothing had changed.

"What the hell was that? We have to go in now, right?" Henry said.

"We don't know what that that was," Tipton said. "We have to wait for the negotiator." She may have intended for her tone to be calm, reassuring. But, to Henry, it was having the opposite effect.

The hammering noise rang out again, then again. It continued for a minute in a slow rhythm.

"You must be joking," Tess said. "You're not even going to phone inside the house to make sure that everyone is okay?"

"The negotiator will be here any minute, and it's important they make the first contact with Keller. I can tell you that we are also reaching out to Keller's ex-wife"

Henry's phone rang again. *Sarah Lysyk.*

Voicemail.

"Did you call Frieda's parents?" he asked.

"Her aunt."

"Jesus!" Henry shouted.

With no further patience, Tipton added, "Now, I'm sorry. I have to direct this scene. You need to give your statement to one of my colleagues." She pointed at a young uniformed officer, holding a paper coffee cup, leaning against one of the patrol vehicles, and laughing with a server from the café. His uniform bore the word *Reserve* across his back. Tipton shouted, "Chan!"

At the sound of his name, Chan looked back and waved. He handed the woman his cup and put his hat back on.

Turning away from Tipton, Tess whispered, "Forget that. I'm not talking with that kid."

"And I'm not waiting for some negotiator or ex-wife to arrive," Henry said. "An ex-wife will not help the situation here."

The banging restarted; slower, but persistent.

"I need to do something."

"Follow me," Tess said, and headed off down the sidewalk.

Henry kept up her pace, which would have been normal on any other day.

They got as far as two houses down the block before Tess strayed from the sidewalk, stepping over a short rock wall into the yard and heading around the side of the house. They exited the back yard via a wooden gate into the alley. "*Voila*," she said.

The alley was empty. It was a shock to the senses compared to chaos on the Richardson Street side of the homes. Without a sound between them, each knew what the other had in mind, and they ran down the alley toward the back of 1584.

Tess opened the gate only wide enough to look through. Both of them peered up at Bernadette's window on the east side of the second floor. They knew there was no back door.

"I figured that we'd climb through one of your windows to get in."

"Someone's beaten us to it, though." Henry pointed at the stack of Adirondack chairs beneath one of the east side windows.

CHAPTER FIFTY-FIVE

"It's okay, Jack," Bernadette said, holding her hands and the phone out in front of her. "You don't need to hurt her." A small, quiet voice came out of the receiver.

"Hang up," Keller said.

Bernadette placed the phone in its cradle in one slow, smooth motion.

"You had a family, and you ran away." His voice was a growl. "You abandoned your mother and your sister. But it wasn't enough for you to destroy your own family. You had to steal our money and destroy mine."

"Jack." Bernadette forced herself to hold his gaze and to not look down at Frieda. "I didn't know whose money it was. No one knew. I can't change the past, but I can do my best to help you. Your money is here. Your money is in this house."

Keller's broken hand lowered as he relaxed his hold on Frieda. Blood dripped onto the floor.

"Are you lying?" he asked, the anger in his tone softening, weakening.

"No, Jack. This is the truth."

"Show me."

"It's in the wall. We need to cut a hole."

"Where?" He looked around as though he would be able to see some evidence of patchwork. An unfamiliar expression appeared on his face; something she hadn't seen before. She thought he appeared hopeful.

Bernadette pointed to the living room wall that backed onto the kitchen. "There," she said without hesitation.

Keller staggered to the wall, dragging Frieda with him. She had not made a single noise since reappearing from the kitchen.

Bernadette stole a glance at Frieda. She willed a message to the small girl.

We are going to get out of this. It's going to be okay.

Frieda's stiff body twisted about as Keller moved, her wide eyes locked on Bernadette.

Keller tapped the wall in several places with the handle of his knife. "How do we get it?"

"It's painted and plastered over. We'll need a hammer or something."

He looked at her through squinted eyes. "I'm not giving you a hammer," he said, proud to have identified a ruse.

"It doesn't have to be a hammer," Bernadette said. "It just has to be hard and heavy. I could get a cast iron pan, if you let me." She motioned with her chin to the kitchen.

Keller weighed this. Instead, he backed up to the door of the apartment, blocking anyone's exit to the hallway. He was still closer than Bernadette to the kitchen as well; if she tried to make it to the pantry stairwell, he would catch her easily. He let go of Frieda and gave her a push with his knife hand. "Go get a pan," he said.

Frieda disappeared into the kitchen. In the living room, Bernadette heard cupboards and drawers opening and closing. Frieda came back holding a dark, cast iron pan. She held it out for Keller, who said, "Go to it, little girl." Frieda moved the chair away from the wall. "If you want to see your mom again, you'd better hope that this old bitch isn't lying."

Frieda looked at Bernadette, who nodded. "Watch your eyes, dear. It's like a hard clay stuck to some boards."

The young girl pulled her cloak off over her head and handed it to Bernadette. Bernadette felt something stiff tucked in the folds of wool as she held it in her lap.

Frieda took a batting stance next to the spot where Bernadette had pointed, wound up, and slammed the side of the pan into the wall. A spray of plaster flew off into the room. After several swings, larger pieces fell away and onto the floor, stirring up more dust into the air. The slats of wooden lath behind the plaster appeared. Frieda stopped to shake out her hands.

"Keep going," Keller said.

Bernadette watched Frieda twist her body like a golfer cocking a swing. She unwound rapidly, the edge of the pan rattling the exposed lath and breaking away a good-sized flat sheet of plaster. The more she chipped away, the faster the rest fell free of the slats.

Frieda stopped, pressed her face close to the wall.

"There's something in there." She turned to look at Bernadette, who felt like she was watching her own soul being invaded, all her stories crumbling. Her truth had been hiding in the wall for so long.

For almost half a century.

"It's okay, dear. There's a bag back there." She looked at Keller who appeared mesmerized by the slow reveal of the wall's secrets. "Carry on."

The outline of the bag behind the lath slats became visible, as Frieda cleared the plaster.

"Break the wood," Keller told Frieda. The thirteen-year-old girl took a great swing at the slats in front of the dark shape and succeeded only in dropping the pan from her hands.

Frieda wrung her hands and shook her head. "I don't think I can."

Keller walked over to Frieda, gave her a great shove and said, "Move."

Frieda backed up to where Bernadette stood. Keller leaned back on his right foot and shot it forward, putting his body into the kick. His foot connected with the slats between the vertical studs of the wall. Wooden pieces broke loose, and he knocked them to the floor. He wound up and kicked again. This time, his kick was so hard that Bernadette heard the oven move on the other side of the wall. He hit the wall like this twice more, each time stopping to knock away the jagged ribs that blocked him from the dark shape. With every blow, the oven creaked and groaned in the kitchen. Finally, the hole was large enough for Keller to reach in and pull out the bag.

The blue canvas duffel bag caught on the wood and snapped more slats as he forced it out of where it had lain for almost half a century.

Had she really expected to never see it again?

As Keller pulled it from the wall, Bernadette recalled the weight of the bag in her arms so many years ago.

Just over twenty pounds. It hasn't changed at all.

CHAPTER FIFTY-SIX

Henry sprinted across the grass. He was certain that Tess would follow, but as he scaled the Adirondack chairs to the window, he looked back anyhow. Sure enough, she was right below him.

"Do you hear anything?" she asked.

He listened for a moment at the window. "No." He lifted the blinds. The room was bare, and through the open door, it looked to Henry as though the next room was empty as well. He climbed in and stopped to listen again. Hearing nothing, he leaned back out the window.

"Wait here," he said.

Tess showed him her middle finger and scampered up the chairs like a mountain goat. Before he could protest, she already had one leg swung over the windowsill. That was that.

"Have you been in here before?" she asked.

It was an inverted layout to Henry's apartment but covered in dust and devoid of signs of occupancy. The bare apartment felt to Henry like a haunted version of his own, and he shivered.

"First time."

"Well, we can add this to the growing list of weird things."

They walked in quiet, measured steps through the apartment to the front door. Torn pieces of newsprint littered the floor. Henry looked at them as they stepped past, half-expecting these to be his missing crosswords.

"Wait," he said. "Here's the plan. If we assume Bernadette's door is locked, there's no barging in. I'm going to go upstairs. I'm going to let Keller know that I want to exchange myself for Frieda. You wait at the bottom of the stairs and help her get out, okay?"

Tess thumped his chest with her fist. "No. She needs you. You get Frieda out. I'll stay there with Bernadette."

Henry felt the stalemate in her strength. She stood with her feet planted shoulder width apart, as though she were physically preparing not to budge.

She started to speak, but he held up his hand. Tess slapped it away. "Don't shush me," she said. "We can't both go in there."

"Stop it! No. Be quiet. There's a noise." He dropped his voice to a whisper.

They listened. A scratching sound came from across the apartment. Tess darted into the kitchen and they froze again. The scratching repeated itself, from the pantry. Henry cautiously opened the door, ready to swing a punch.

Shima shot out of the pantry as though he were on fire. His claws scrabbled on the hardwood as he cornered and ran into the bedroom, without so much as a hello.

"That was not what I expected," Henry said.

Tess tapped Henry on the shoulder. She pointed wordlessly at the spiral staircase.

Keller turned to face the room and knelt next to the bag on the floor, setting down his knife to open it with his good hand.

Bernadette backed up and pushed Frieda behind her,

toward the bathroom. Keller's head snapped up in their direction.

"What's this?" He pulled a wad of US twenty-dollar bills from the bag. The elastic band holding them together fell off, dried from age, as he waved the stack at Bernadette.

"That's your money, Jack."

"There should be millions. It should be worth millions now."

"Jack," she repeated, "That's your money. That's the money I found. It's nothing less than what you asked for."

He looked askance at the bag, as though it were going to offer him some greater understanding of the situation.

"You mean, this is DB Cooper's actual two hundred thousand dollars from 1971?"

Keller stared at the bundle of cash in his hand. He placed it back into the bag and took out another. It was exactly like the first.

His voice rose as he spoke. "All these bloody bills are traceable. They recorded the serial numbers." He threw the bundle into the bag. "I can't use this. It is worthless." His face reddened and he made to rise. "You lying bitch."

"That's not all, Jack," she said, stabbing her finger in the air at the bag. "Keep looking."

Keller pulled out bundle after bundle of cash, placing them all on the floor. He pulled out something else: small, black, leather, the size of a pack of cards.

"What is this?" he asked, unfolding it.

"It's his. It's DB Cooper's wallet," Bernadette said. "You see the name, Jack? It's Wayne Fullarton. It's not your dad."

Keller pulled cards from the wallet and inspected them.

"I found his family, his brother. He told me about Wayne. They were supposed to be in business together, but Wayne wanted to be an engineer. So he went down south to work for Boeing, and he must have fallen on hard times. Kevin told me a lot of things about Wayne, Jack, but he never once said anything about Wayne having kids."

Keller threw the wallet into the bag. He stood, his chest swelling with deep breaths. "You're lying. My mother told me."

Frieda spoke. "It's your medicine. You're not taking your pills, so you're remembering things that aren't real."

Keller blinked at the mention of his pills.

"You don't know what's real," he said. "Stop lying. Stop trying to confuse me."

He reached into his back pocket and pulled out the stun gun, stepping over the bag and scattered cash, heading for Bernadette.

She turned her back to Keller and pushed Frieda hard into the bathroom. "Lock the door."

Henry and Tess listened from the kitchen. Bernadette talking, about someone called Wayne. Everything went quiet. A tiny voice. Frieda? Then Keller spoke, his voice escalating to a roar.

Henry couldn't make sense of the scene. Even the air in the apartment smelled odd.

Tess whispered something about the stove, but a glimpse of Frieda from around Keller's wide figure hooked Henry's attention. Bernadette shouted as Henry ran into the living room, gathering what momentum he could across the short distance.

His shoulder hit Keller right in the middle of his spine. Both men rolled to the floor. Henry got up first. From his knees, Keller pointed both arms at Henry. In one, the stun gun's tiny metal teeth grinned; the other ended in a crooked, broken hand.

Keller rose. "You hit me." His expression wavered between rage and confusion.

"This stops now, Jack," Henry said holding his empty palms

up in a pacifying gesture. "The police are outside and they're going to get you help."

"Wait." Keller looked from the stun gun in his hand to Henry. "Am I the bad guy?"

Henry stepped forward and reached for the weapon. "It's okay."

Keller backed away, cautious, doubtful. Afraid, even.

His heel kicked the duffel, still heavy with cash. Keller looked at the bag of lies with disgust. He stood taller and his wide jaw bared its teeth. He pointed at Henry with the stun gun, its two electrical prongs a foot from Henry's chest.

"You're the bad guys," he growled.

Tess dove between the two men.

Time stopped, and Henry had the briefest moment to wonder whether she had simply popped into existence right there. Her nearly horizontal body defied gravity as she reached for Keller's arm, which held the stun gun. Her mouth opened as she drifted in the air. Keller's head recoiled as she entered his space. Both of Tess's hands, wrists ringed with bloody scrapes, locked onto Keller's hand.

Henry didn't register the sound of the stun gun. But he caught the flash of its small, blue lightning firing back and forth in thin strings before an explosion slammed Keller and Tess into him.

He lay on his back beneath them. Tess extricated herself from Keller's dead weight. Something in the room had changed.

Did I die and go to hell?

Tess helped him onto his knees, and he saw the stream of fire spewing from the wall to the kitchen. The sound of the roar from the hole in the wall was as intimidating as the pounding heat. The stun gun had ignited a gas leak. He looked down at Keller's blackened torso, which had taken the brunt of the initial explosion. Keller's arms stretched over his head, and his body lay still.

Tess looked at Henry and he read her lips. "Are you alright?" He nodded.

Fire cut across the room, blocking them from the main door and the kitchen.

Henry felt someone tackle him around his shoulders. He recognized the small arms as Frieda's and kissed one of her hands. "We have to get out of here."

Bernadette pointed at the bedroom "There's a window over here." They ran over, and Henry looked down. It was right above the once-stacked Adirondack chairs. He looked at the group in front of him: a woman in her sixties, a teenager, and a ninja comic book artist.

Broken limbs or fire. Nice choices.

"I have an idea," he said. "Fred, where's your cloak? Quick."

She ran into the living room, steering clear of the side with the flames, and took her cloak from the couch. Henry followed, grabbing the two wool blankets that he could reach. Frieda tossed her cloak to Henry and he motioned for them to follow him into the bathroom. He knocked the back off the toilet and dunked Frieda's cloak in. It came out soaking wet and he handed it to her.

"Put this on. We're going out the front door."

Henry soaked the two blankets in the same manner and handed one each to Bernadette and Tess.

"Share mine," Tess said.

Henry didn't think twice; he just nodded.

They crawled into the living room, which was filling with smoke. Henry wondered which was worse: sending Frieda into the flames first or going through without her, unable to make sure she followed?

"Fred, you're going first. Keep yourself covered." The fire didn't appear to have spread to the door itself, but she would have to run the edge of the jet of flames to get there. He gave her a kiss on the forehead and pulled up her hood.

Something shot up between them, narrowly missing their faces. Frieda screamed. Keller's boot slammed down from its kick.

Henry looked up and saw Keller standing over them wearing a scowl full of rage and grinding teeth. Before Henry could rise, Keller leaped onto him, a mess of limbs. Henry's hands squeezed Keller's thick wrists as he scrabbled at Henry's throat. Unable to grip Henry's windpipe with his broken fingers, Keller used his bodyweight to crush it closed.

Lightheadedness crept in. Only the sharp scrape of jagged, uneven bone held him conscious. He couldn't spare any strength from wrestling the meaty hand holding the knife. Henry tried with his elbow to support some of Keller's massive weight.

He wanted to shout, *"Run! Run!"* But his airway pressed shut, and his vision closed in, like the twisting iris of a camera lens.

He hoped the others were gone.

CHAPTER FIFTY-SEVEN

H enry's cheek burned.
    Fire?
    He opened his eyes to see Tess, surrounded by smoke, tears cutting clean streaks down her face. "Get up!" she shouted. She held her arm out, palm open, ready to slap him again. He rolled to his hands and knees for the second time that day.

"Frieda."

"Already out," Tess said. She draped a warm, water-soaked blanket over him. The skin of her arms beneath the cover felt just as wet. They were both drenched in sweat from the heat of the room.

Henry looked behind him and saw Bernadette kneeling over Keller. He lay on his back, his arms over his head. Bernadette wiped something with the wet blanket she wore across her shoulders. She handled and squeezed it in her right hand, with deliberate motions, before dropping it next to Keller's side. The blade of a kitchen knife flashed orange and red from the flames.

Before he could process what he had seen, Bernadette shouted and waved them away.

Tess put her arms around Henry, and they ran in a crouch

through the jet of flame to the open door. The hallway was full of smoke, but the sudden drop in temperature made Henry aware of how close they had been to the fire itself. Henry let go of the blanket and they went down the stairs one after the other.

As they passed Unit 1, Henry pushed his key into the lock and opened the door. "Shima!" The little cat flew past them, and out the front door, with a speed belying his age. They raced after him onto the front lawn.

Frieda was already there, crying in her hood, attended to by a firefighter. Henry inserted himself between them and wrapped his arms around her. He kissed her on top of her head, and she squeezed him back and said, "Shima."

Henry spoke. "He got out." But she wasn't asking. She had seen the old cat hiding under the hedge dividing their lawn from the next, and she set off after him.

The firefighter put a dry blanket around Henry's shoulders. Henry pulled it tight, a chill setting in to his damp and sweaty clothes. "We've just shut off the gas. Is there anyone else inside?"

Henry looked back at the house. He hadn't seen Bernadette leave.

She was supposed to be right behind us.

"Tess, where's Bernadette?"

The look of horror on Tess's face was answer enough. She turned to look back at the house.

"There are two people in there," Henry said. "A senior woman and a middle-aged man. He's dangerous and . . ." Henry looked at Tess. He didn't know whether she had seen the knife. He didn't even know what had happened with the knife. "He's injured," Henry said.

Firefighters poured into the house. Almost immediately, Bernadette emerged, wrapped in her blanket, leaning with her elbows into the supporting arms of the men on either side.

Coughing, she made her way to a gurney on the sidewalk, where she managed to shout a hoarse, *"Frieda."*

Frieda, with Shima swaddled safely in her wet cloak, walked over to Bernadette. Shima howled his displeasure. Bernadette took an oxygen mask from one of the firefighters and waved him away. Henry and Tess started to approach, but Bernadette gave them an open palm to stay away.

Henry and Tess sat on their own gurney, their wet blanket traded for two dry ones, as the firefighters sprayed hoses into Bernadette's suite. Henry watched Bernadette speaking to Frieda, who began to cry, and Bernadette brought her in for a hug. He caught the older woman's eye; she nodded, and Henry and Tess came closer.

The foursome sat together and watched the firefighters extinguish the fire. Bernadette sat on the gurney, with Tess, Henry, and Frieda huddled together on the sidewalk. Firefighters brought Keller out and another gurney met them at the front door. As though in one swift motion, they got Keller on oxygen, into an ambulance, and off to the hospital.

I guess he's alive.

A paramedic approached the group. "The fire teams think they have it all out. Sounds like it was contained to just the one apartment. As for you, you're all clear. No burns, some minor smoke inhalation. All in all, you folks are very lucky. There are still some police who would like to speak with you. We've kept them at bay for as long as we could, but we're going to head back to the hospital at this point."

Over the paramedic's shoulder, Henry could see Sergeant Khatri watching them, arms crossed, waiting.

"Would any of you like to come in to be looked at further?" This last question was directed at Bernadette.

Bernadette gave the young man a grin and a bicep flex. "No. We're fine."

After checking in with Frieda and Tess, Henry said, "I think it's time to face the music."

The sergeant exchanged words with the paramedic before approaching the group.

"Quite a night," he said. And, to Henry, "you don't listen very well, Mr. Lysyk."

"You're not the first person to notice," Henry said. "But you know that you now have the man responsible for everything. The break-ins, Julian's murder, this . . . whatever this was. All him. But, please, dig into his medical records, will you?"

"We will."

"So," Henry said, "do I get that ride to the station now?"

"No," Khatri said, unsmiling.

"Tomorrow?"

"I'm not here to arrest you, Henry. Not that it's your lucky day either," Khatri said, motioning at the house. "I'm letting you know you used your get-out-of-jail-free card today." His stiff index finger signaled to Henry that there would be no second pass.

Henry struggled to follow what had just happened.

"And to tell you to stay out of trouble and keep out of police business."

"Of course. Thank you."

The sergeant nodded. "Don't thank me. I told you I knew who you were. That's not from the papers. My mother has told me more than once what you did for her, and other businesses like her restaurant."

"Natali?" Henry was stunned. "That was... What I did for her... It was just the right thing to do."

"Well, thank you," Khatri said, holding out his hand.

Henry stood and shook the sergeant's hand, a long-absent calm coming over him.

Serious now, Sergeant Khatri said, "That's your one.

Constable Tipton still has questions for you, but you can wait until tomorrow. Do you need a ride anywhere?"

Henry looked back at the motley group sitting on the curb. His cat, his niece, and his friends and neighbors.

"No, we're just going to stay with our home, for the time being. We'll sleep at a friend's tonight."

Khatri left, the paramedics checked in once more before departing, and the firefighters walked in and out of the building like ants.

The streetlights came on.

As they answered Constable Tipton's questions, the odd person would interrupt them. The café across the street brought coffee and sandwiches, someone produced sweaters, and yet another neighbor brought a cat carrier.

CHAPTER FIFTY-EIGHT

T he early afternoon sun poured in through the window as Henry, Frieda, and Tess stood around Mr. Benham's hospital bed. It was a different room than yesterday, although everything looked similar: the bed, the curtains, the brightly painted walls, and the hard, hard floor.

Henry had planned to call Benham the night before, after returning to Luba's but he had passed out on the couch after a long, hot shower.

Henry rubbed the bruise on his forehead as he recounted yesterday's events.

"That explains why there were no more police outside my door when I woke up," Mr. Benham said.

"Keller's alive," Henry said, "but he's in rough shape. It might be years before he's back on his feet again."

Mr. Benham shook his head in disbelief. "And he's not related to DB Cooper?"

"Not at all, it seems. Keller's just a guy who fell on hard times and couldn't get the help he needed. He found a community online, and his mind had its own way of trying to make sense of everything. The good news is that he'll get help now."

The mood in the room was feeling down and sad. Henry

wanted no more of it. He clapped his hands. "The better news is that the fire department has already said that we can go home. We're heading there after this to check things out."

There was a knock on the door. Everyone turned. Henry expected to see Bernadette, so much so that he looked over the shoulder of the person walking in. After a moment, he recognized the man standing in front of him in a suit.

Henry blinked twice.

"Alex? What are you doing here?"

Mr. Benham spoke. "Bernadette's not coming. She and I spoke last night, and I called Alex to join us this morning."

Henry's hand returned to the bandage. His head turned back and forth between the two men. "How do you know each other?"

Am I the only one that's not getting this?

"Hi, Henry," Alex said, ignoring the question. "You must be Tess. And, Fred, I'm glad to see you're taking care of your uncle." He shook hands with each and addressed them with recognition and inexplicable admiration.

Mr. Benham gave a weak smile and said, "Close the door. Alex will explain."

"Mr. Benham and Ms. Pruner are beneficiaries of the Windfall Trust. Lawyers from my firm have operated as trustees since it started in the seventies. One stipulation of the trust is that, should Ms. Pruner cease to be a beneficiary, the list of beneficiaries changes. The new beneficiaries are the current residents of 1584 Richardson Street."

He looked Henry squarely in the eyes and added, "even if you move to Toronto."

Tess turned to Henry. "What is he talking about?"

"Back up a second, Alex," Henry said. "You're saying that something has happened to Bernadette?"

"Correct."

"Bernadette was fine," Tess said, looking at Mr. Benham. One of her palms rose to her chest.

Henry felt Frieda's hand slip into his.

"Ms. Pruner," Alex continued, "has decided to move to the States. I spoke to her this morning, and she told me that last night she reached out to her sister in Amboy, Washington. Ms. Pruner has been having some health issues. From what I understand, her sister will take care of her."

"Mr. Benham, did you know anything about this?" Henry asked.

"I knew Bernie was ill. She can't get medical care here in Canada. That's a long story. She has always loved our home, but I think Bernie had some unfinished business with her family down there, too."

"Under the terms of the trust," explained Alex, "since Ms. Pruner is ceasing to be a Canadian resident, she is no longer a beneficiary. This triggers a change-in-beneficiaries clause."

Frieda sniffed back tears. "She didn't say goodbye." Henry put his arm around her, and she leaned against him. Tess placed her hand on the young girl's shoulder.

"She gave me some notes for you," Alex said, almost as an afterthought. He handed envelopes to each of Henry, Tess, and Frieda.

Henry just held his, wanting to open it in private; Tess did the same.

"Yours," Alex said to Frieda, "feels like it has something else inside."

Frieda made a mess of tearing open her envelope and shook the contents into her hand. A folded note slid part-way out, and she caught the brass ring of her brooch. She couldn't have appeared more surprised if Alex had just turned around and passed through the wall. "I thought this was gone."

"Is that yours?" Tess asked.

"It sure is," Frieda said, holding the brooch close to her face. She squinted at Henry through the odd metal circle and swirl.

The last few days flashed through Henry's mind. From the anger and frustration of the crossword to Frieda's arrival, to lying on the couch with Tess's hair tickling his nose, to the danger and violence of Keller and the fire. Despite the chaos, Henry felt alive. He felt calm. He felt himself again. Words wouldn't form in his mouth.

Frieda read the note, sharing pieces with the group. "She says that she told me her story, and now it's mine to write about if I want." Frieda looked at Tess, "Would you want to work with me on Bernadette's story? It's a good one."

"If you think it would make a good graphic novel, then I would love to work with you, Fred. I can't wait to hear you tell it."

Henry watched Frieda read on, her lips moving slightly as she neared the end of the letter. He knew she was trembling, not mouthing the words. The note in Henry's hand felt much larger than what they were learning now. Still, the accountant inside of him kicked in, continuing the line of questions.

"What's in the trust?"

Alex grinned. "Well, the trust itself will be wound up, and its assets will be distributed to its ultimate beneficiaries. That's you guys as residents of 1584 Richardson Street and a Linda Fullarton." Alex paused.

Always with the dramatic effect.

"The Windfall Trust owns all the shares of 121702 BC Ltd., a private company that owns—"

"Our home," Tess interrupted softly.

Alex looked at her as though he understood what those words meant to her. "Yes, the Richardson Street house."

Tess threw her arms around Henry and made a squeezing noise. Then she turned and tried to do the same to Mr.

Benham, who sat up inches to oblige. "We have our own home."

Frieda got in on the excitement and gave Henry a hug. Henry lifted her up and swung her feet back and forth in the air.

Alex held up his hands. "There's more."

Henry put Frieda down. Tess straightened up.

"Over the years, the trust has only distributed capital funds to its beneficiaries as needed. Well, it turns out that income earned in the trust was reinvested in the company for additional real estate. In the seventies, it purchased a piece of commercial real estate downtown. East Hastings, though. Not the nicest neighborhood. And, in the early nineties, it purchased several condos in Yaletown on presale."

"Presale?" Tess asked.

"They got in early," Henry said. "Cheap."

Alex continued. "These are currently rentals. So you guys will have to agree whether you want to be landlords, or whether you want the trust to sell the properties and just give you the cash."

Numbers flew through Henry's head.

An approximate value of a Yaletown condo, estimate the capital gain, less the taxes . . .

"That's what? Three or four million dollars?"

"Closer to five," Mr. Benham said.

Henry spun and looked at him. "You knew about this, too?"

Mr. Benham nodded. "Son, I helped set this up nearly fifty years ago. I didn't think I'd see the day it would all come to fruition. Bernie understood what she was doing when we put this into play, and we all sure as heck knew just how much everything was worth."

"The Windfall Trust. *WFT*," Henry said, recalling the pawn-shop ticket. "There was no fifty thousand, was there?" he asked Benham, his voice tinged with admiration. "The Silver and

Gold loans money to the trust on the security of the insurance money. The trust loans the funds to the company to purchase Richardson Street. And the company borrows against Richardson to lend money back to the Silver and Gold. A bit of rent and income from the pawnshop, and eventually things get paid down."

Just marks on paper. A grand, simple plan.

Benham smiled proudly. "We did okay."

"Actually," Alex said, "a woman named 'Paulette Johnston' apparently settled the Windfall Trust. Then she just vanished. She's something of a mythical figure around my office. Could you tell me anything about her, Mr. Benham?"

"She was real," Frieda said, looking down at the refolded note from Bernadette.

Benham nodded his agreement. "That's about as much as I can tell you."

Alex patted Henry on the back. "I'm going to miss you when you move, you know that?"

"Are you kidding?" Henry said. He looked at Frieda and at Tess. "I can't leave. My life's here."

They both slammed into him at once, pinning his arms with their own.

"Then, I will see you at Natali's," Alex said, tucking his leather folder under his arm. "But before I go, did you hear Stewart's been cleared?"

"Great news," Henry said from between Frieda and Tess. "Good for him."

"That's not all, Henry. Read the newspaper."

———

Henry, Frieda, and Tess stood on the sidewalk, looking up at 1584 Richardson Street. An enormous blue tarp covered the top right corner of the building. What poked out from the edges looked blackened from smoke. In stark contrast, the left side of the home was pristine and welcoming.

Shima moaned his impatience from the carrier in Frieda's arms.

"Where do we start?" Henry asked.

Tess pointed her thumb at the cat and said, "Let's start with your suite, then work our way up."

Henry led the way into the house. As he walked through the front glass door the first thing he saw—before he smelled the residue of smoke, before he saw the stains of water on the walls and the stairs—was a newspaper. Someone had delivered the Saturday Globe and Mail. He collected it, and, without looking up from the paper, walked through the still-unlocked door of his suite.

The headline read, *Business Owners Defend Robin Hood Accountant*. It was there in its entirety: Natali, Mr. Munroe, Dr. Well, and all the others. The newspaper had gotten a hold of his emails and the businesses. The article expounded on corporate greed and social responsibility.

Stewart?

"This is good, right?" Tess asked.

"It sure looks that way," he said with a smile.

Henry strode straight to the couch and sat down. As though in a trance, he unfolded the sections: British Columbia, Business, Focus, Arts. He opened the Arts section and, there on page four, exactly where it should be, was the crossword. Henry settled back onto his Ikea hide-a-bed couch and felt his entire body relaxing as he sighed.

He closed his eyes and listened to Frieda, in the kitchen, coaxing Shima from the borrowed carrier. Tess took a seat next to him, closer than necessary given the size of the couch. She leaned her weight against him, settling her head on his shoulder. Tess's hand found his, and their fingers interlaced.

They sat like that for a long time, with only the sound of a young girl, cooing at an old cat, floating in the air. The fire-fighters had left all the windows open, but there was still a lingering smell of charcoal in the suite.

Something welled in Henry. A sense of belonging that had been missing perhaps for years.

Frieda walked into the living room, saying something about Kilimanjaro. She held Shima, purring, draped over one arm. She stopped in mid-sentence, stiffened, and pointed, her free arm as straight as an arrow.

"What's that?" she asked, her tone flat and serious.

An old, blue canvas duffel bag leaned against the wall behind the front door.

AFTERWORD

Unlike every other character in this novel, DB Cooper is a real person/event.

That is to say, on the evening of November 24, 1971, a man purchased a ticket on Northwest Orient Airlines flight 305 from Portland to Seattle, under the name Dan Cooper. News reports and lore have also referred to him as DA Cooper and DB Cooper. The name itself has not been linked to an actual person, only to a European comic book series about a Canadian military flying ace.

Once the plane was off the ground, the man calling himself Cooper revealed to a flight attendant that he had what appeared to be a briefcase bomb. He allowed the thirty-six passengers to leave the plane in Seattle but demanded two hundred thousand dollars in "negotiable American currency" and four parachutes. The remaining flight crew was to take him to Mexico. In mid-flight, near the border between Washington and Oregon States, Cooper jumped from the plane with two parachutes, the money, and his briefcase.

One of the many things that attracted me to Cooper's crime is how it seems to say so much about the point in time at which it took place. In 1971, America was withdrawing troops from

Vietnam, but public sentiment was still divided. Canada's Prime Minister in 1971, Pierre Elliott Trudeau, is credited by some with having said at the time that "Canada should be a refuge from militarism," although I've been unable to find the exact context of this quote.

The many media reports from that era also include protests by Canadians against their own government, suggesting that this country, too, was divided. Nevertheless, in March 1969, Trudeau explained to the National Press Club in Washington DC that Canada's immigration policy was "blind" on the question of draft dodging and desertion. A good number of US citizens crossed the border to settle in Canada, and many are still there today.

Also, in the United States in 1971, leaked documents revealed the government had not been forthright about the extent of loss of life overseas. The North American economy was slumping; the Boeing Company, based in Everett, Washington, laid off an incredible thirty-five thousand workers in 1970 and another fifteen thousand the following year.

There are reams of resources online, which will provide the curious reader with as much detail and evidence as they would like about Cooper's incredible crime as well as theories involving the circumstances (e.g., Cooper was a disillusioned Vietnam veteran, or a disgruntled Boeing engineer). References to Vietnam, Boeing, riots, *et cetera* in this story are not intended as political statement; rather, they are included to provide a broad cultural context of the Pacific Northwest in 1971 and as a nod to these theories.

Amateur and professional sleuths alike have taken advantage of the fact that the FBI openly released many of their records in a plea for public assistance in finding Cooper. Some dedicated individuals have gone so far as to undertake microscopic analysis on particles found on a tie suspected to have belonged to Cooper. Despite all these efforts, the identity of the hijacker and the fate of the ransom money remain mysteries.

There has been an enormous amount of investigation and speculation in the Cooper case, and I don't intend to revisit it all here. Indeed, because there are so many internet sites, articles, documentaries, and podcasts that re-iterate the same information, and it would be impossible to compile a complete citation of sources for those who wish to find out more. I include this addendum simply to provide some background on a few of the pieces of Cooper's tale that I've chosen to weave into Bernadette and Keller's narratives, and to offer you some good places from where to start your own research.

From there, every person will follow their own, unique path down the rabbit hole that is the disappearance of DB Cooper.

The money – serial numbers

The FBI purports to have recorded the serial numbers of all ten thousand twenty-dollar bills that made up the ransom payment. There are websites that still contain this list of serial numbers, including at least one search engine, to confirm whether a serial number that you type in is part of the ransom.

The money – found bills

In 1980, a young boy named Brian Ingram found five thousand eight hundred dollars buried in a sand bar on the Columbia River. These bills were confirmed to have been part of the Cooper cash. Speculations on how the cash got there include an intentional burial, drifting on the Columbia River, or dredging. This find plays a major role in most theories about where Cooper may have landed.

In our story, Bernadette discovers Cooper's body at the mouth of the Washougal River. She notices that some of the money carried in the spare parachute had already spilled out before she arrived. As she points out, when she talks about disposing of Cooper's body, the Washougal flows into the Columbia River, upstream from Ingram's find in 1980.

The parachute – choice and survival

A skydiver named David Robinson offers some unique insight into the parachuting component of the story on a podcast called *Generation Why* (Episode 111). Robinson explains the differences between the chutes available to Cooper and the sort of person who may have chosen one over another. He provides what I feel is compelling logic that Cooper likely would have died on his descent. Cooper wore only a business suit, and he faced the wind shear of jumping from a jet airplane in a thunderstorm.

In our story, Bernadette erroneously believes that certain red parachute cords were deliberately cut as sabotage. This is again a reference to comments made in Robinson's interview. The parachute that Cooper is believed to have chosen would have red cords which were to snap apart and provide for some limited steering ability.

At the very least, without gloves, it would have been virtually impossible for Cooper to control his chute by pulling on wet, icy cords with his near-frozen bare hands.

The parachute – Amboy

Bernadette leaves us in the end to reunite with her sister in Amboy, Washington. In 1971, as she heads north to the Canadian border, Bernadette stops in Amboy *"just to wash up ... and get rid of the parachute equipment and some of Jim's things from the trunk."*

In 2008, a group of young boys found a buried parachute near Amboy, Washington. Although the FBI has said that this is not Cooper's canopy, many theories contend that it still could be. Much of this turns on statements of the FBI's expert, who said that the Amboy canopy was made of silk and not nylon like the Cooper canopy. However, online sleuths point out that photographs of the Amboy canopy do not show the amount of rotting that would be expected of buried silk material. Other local stories exist to explain the existence of the Amboy chute.

Flight crew - Brenda

At first blush, the victims of Cooper's stunt appear limited to the insurance company, the inconvenienced passengers, and the reputation of the airline. The truth is more complicated.

Many people who were there that day have chosen to enjoy, even capitalize on, their association with Cooper. However, there are also those who have tried to distance themselves from this experience.

For this reason, I have deliberately not portrayed any specific member of the crew of Flight 305. While interwoven with facts, "Brenda" is not intended to represent any real person or the actions of any single individual.

Also, readers may note that I have retained the disused term "stewardess" for scenes taking place in 1971, while present day references are to "flight attendants." This is merely an artistic decision.

Cooper – the continued hunt

In 2016, the FBI declared that they were ceasing all investigations into the Cooper hijacking. Forty-five years had passed, so who could blame them?

The general public, though, appears unwilling to let the story end there. As I mentioned, there is a vast amount of discussion and research online, with a wide number of podcasts discussing Cooper's crime and the available evidence, and the internet community known broadly as web sleuths continue to carry the torch. There are just as many groups online engaged in serious, disciplined research as there are those enjoying speculative theories (e.g., Cooper was a government distraction from the Vietnam War).

Of particular note, a small group named The Cooper Research Team or Citizen Sleuths have approached the evidence from a scientific and objective perspective. With the cooperation of an FBI agent formerly assigned to the case, Special Agent Larry Carr, they have compiled one of the most comprehensive resources on the Cooper evidence.

Some resources

FBI Files online
https://vault.fbi.gov/D-B-Cooper%20/

Cooper Research Team/Citizen Sleuths
https://citizensleuths.com/

Archive of Cooper-related documents
https://website.thedbcooperforum.com/

Historical newspapers: Statesman Journal (Salem, Oregon) and The Capital Journal (Salem, Oregon)
www.newspapers.com

Dropzone (discussion forum for parachutists)
http://www.dropzone.com/
Forums:Skydiving:Skydiving History & Trivia:DB Cooper

Boeing layoffs 1969-1971
Stein, Alan J. "Boeing Bust (1969-1971)." *HistoryLink.org* Essay 20923, posted December 16, 2019.
www.historylink.org/File/20923

Boeing 727 details (comprehensive article, with incredible centerfold of technical drawings)

Gunston, W.T. (Technical Editor). "Boeing 727: A Carefully Optimized Short-Haul Jet." *FLIGHT International*, Number 2826 Volume 83, 9 May 1963, pp. 675-688. Iliffe Transport Publications Ltd., London, 1963.

Pierre Elliott Trudeau on draft dodgers

http://www.cbc.ca/archives/entry/trudeau-opens-the-door-to-draft-dodgers

ACKNOWLEDGMENTS

I've wondered to what extent authors are playing at being modest when they thank these great lists of people involved in the creation of their novel. They aren't playing. I get it now.

Windfall would not be the same without the insightful editing and generous time of Andrew Lowe; and the tremendous talent and patience of Jamie Keenan.

Windfall would not be *at all*, were it not for the unrelenting curiosity, enthusiasm, love, and support of family and friends.

I am deeply grateful to nieces and nephews Mya, Nolan, Liv, Henry, Deacon, and Spencer for providing immeasurable inspiration—especially to Henry, for his trust.

A nod of humble appreciation to those writers and authors who share their experience and knowledge, without ego and without competitiveness. It is an incredible community.

And to Tiffany, with whom countless weekends and walks were consumed by talk of characters and clues; thank you so much. We can recycle those old drafts now.

-*Byron TD Smith*
November 20, 2020

WINDFALL BOOKMARK & READERS GROUP

Thank you for spending time with Henry, Fred, and the cast of *Windfall: A Henry Lysyk Mystery.*

Jamie Keenan, who designed our cover, has also prepared an amazingly cool **Windfall bookmark in the form of a 1971 luggage tag for flight 305!** I can email you your own to print and use when you sign up to join my Readers Group.

I promise not to email often - only to notify you of give-aways, new releases, and maybe some personal updates from behind the scenes of my next books. I may even ask if you would like to be part of an exclusive Advance Readers Group for my next novel, before it is published!

Just head to my website: btdsmith.com/bookmark

Enjoy!

-Byron TD Smith

BOOKCLUBS

For reading guide and discussion questions, please visit
www.btdsmith.com